*Other books by Laurie Salzler . . .*

Positive Lightning
A Kiss Before Dawn
In the Stillness of Dawn
Right Out of Nowhere

Eye of the Beholder

After a Time

The Day Cagney Lost Her Wag
Cagney and the Missing Rooster

*Other books by Laurie, under pen name Laurie Eichler*

To Be Determined
Precipice of Doubt

# Them
# Three

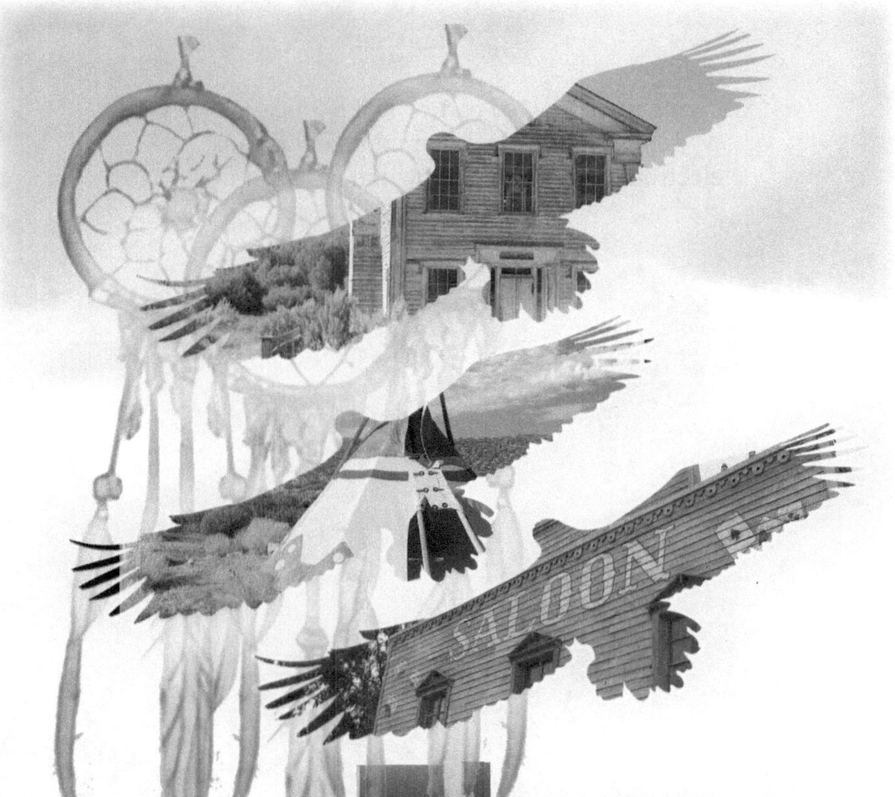
SALOON
LAURIE
SALZLER
Them
Three

*Bink Books*
Bedazzled Ink Publishing Company • Fairfield, California

978-1-960373-72-4 paperback

Cover Design
by

Sapling
Studio

Bink Books
Bedazzled Ink Publishing Company
Fairfield, California
http://www.bedazzledink.com

Them Three *is dedicated to all members of the Shoshoni tribe, past and present, as well as all the brave women who lived during the 1800s when the west was in turmoil, not unlike the world today. I hope I did them justice in the writing of this book.*

# Chapter One

BETTY COATE ROLLED onto her back and coughed. Her broken nose streamed blood into her throat and threatened to trickle into her lungs. She was barely conscious, having come to only moments before. She coughed and gagged again, trying to dislodge the metallic clot clinging to the back of her tongue. Her head pounded in time with the throbbing of her nose. She lay very still, trying to figure which parts of her hurt and which didn't.

A soft breeze crept in from the open window and played with a strand of her errant red hair, halting, when it became stuck in the blood at the corner of her puffy and bruised lips. She groaned and dared open her eyes. Her right one refused. It was swollen shut.

She took a deep breath and forced back a cry. A single tear rolled out the corner of her eye and dribbled down into her ear. As near as she could tell, he'd only assaulted her face. Although he'd been rough down there, it wasn't anything she hadn't already experienced before with so many others. At any rate, she was numb between her legs. She could deal with that later.

The room was quiet and empty. Thankfully, he had gone. The dull roar from downstairs told her the saloon was in full swing with patrons buying drinks and playing cards. The piano offered a musical backdrop to the mingled low voices. Light steps on the stairs, followed by heavier ones were indicative of how busy the girls were too.

Betty wondered how long she'd been unconscious. Deep shadows crept across her room, but she could still make out the outline of the dresser and the washbasin that sat on top. A couple of hours. Maybe. She was actually surprised no one had come looking for her. But then again, they usually respected her privacy and didn't look for her unless she asked them to. She doubted anybody even noticed him leaving. There was always a steady stream of customers going up and down the stairs as they visited the girls to satisfy their needs. Needs their wives couldn't or wouldn't, or ones that arose from long hours in the gold fields, or atop a horse tending cattle.

She ventured a deep breath. Her chest and ribs were a little sore, probably from when he had all his weight on her, but thankfully nothing seemed broken. Encouraged, she rolled over onto an elbow and pushed herself up into a sitting position with her free hand. She closed her good eye against the rebelling dizziness and throbbing in her head and took several deep breaths to will the pain away. She carefully swiped the bottom of her nose. Her finger came away clean, no more blood flowed from her nostrils.

"Damn you," she muttered and winced as she felt her lip split open. She dabbed it with the back of her hand, not surprised when it came back bloody.

It wasn't the first time she'd been slapped around or beaten. The time in Chicago had been pretty bad. That customer had hurt her so bad, she'd never be able to bear children. No, this wasn't the first time. But it sure as hell would be the last.

For six years now, she'd owned and oversaw Big Nosed Kitty's, the only saloon in Oro Fino, Idaho. Everyone knew her as Kitty here. There was only one person who knew her by her real name, but she hadn't seen Nathan in a few years. If she were to ever move on, she'd more than likely take on a new name, as was common practice of painted ladies. She loved mingling with the men, listening to their stories, and even sometimes giving them advice. But as the years had gone by, she grew very tired and less tolerant of the groping, petting, and the bedding. She'd put up with a lot over the years. She'd spread her legs for men with rotten teeth, unwashed bodies, beards with who knows what crawling inside, and some very handsome ones as well. But, it was time to stop.

She was coming thirty-one years old and had been told she was considered a respectful citizen despite the notoriety of her forte. Unlike the majority of women engaged in her profession who had poor education and were largely illiterate, she managed to complete her schooling through the eighth grade. Daddy and Mother had pushed her to further her learning but that idea had gone by the wayside when Mother had fallen ill and eventually died of consumption. Betty had taken care of Daddy until he joined Mother a few years later.

With balled hands, she pushed down on the mattress, leaned forward, and tentatively rose to her feet. She once again closed her eye against the dizziness, but thankfully it didn't last as long. She took two wobbly steps before she had to reach out and steady herself against the wardrobe. She leaned heavily on it, making it thump against the wall, rattling the gold-plated mirror that hung above it.

"Well, Madam, let's see how bad he messed you up." She grasped both sides of the wardrobe and drew her gaze from her manicured fingers to her reflection.

Her hair remained stylishly curled on top of her head with the exception of a few loose strands. A few ringlets hung carelessly over her forehead and in front of her ears. Her lips were devoid of the red she'd applied earlier, now swollen and bruised. She skimmed the cut in her lip with a finger and hissed. "That's going to need a stitch. Bastard."

The small mole that decorated her right cheek was surrounded by black and blue. It matched her puffy eye. "Aren't you a colourful mess?" She ran a finger over her perfectly plucked eyebrows and sighed. "Could've been worse I s'pect."

Using a kerchief from the top drawer, she dampened it in the basin and cleaned herself up the best she could. After a few minutes, she stared back at a more presentable reflection. It would be clear to those who saw her that she had been roughed up. The girls would be horrified and fuss over her. But for the most part, her bruises would be ignored. She would act as if nothing happened and depend on makeup to cover up what she could. But it would be hard to disguise the swelling. Maybe she could blame it on a food reaction. She chuckled and regretted it when she smiled. "Oh." She gently licked her lip and then applied bright red lipstick to them, carefully avoiding the wound. If it bled a little between here and Doc's, hopefully people would assume she smudged her lip paint. She'd try to sneak out the back, but she still needed to go downstairs and out the door behind the bar undetected.

Betty changed into one of the plain dresses she kept for when she had to venture outside the saloon. The one she chose this time was blue. Although she was still recognized when on the streets, she found if she dressed less flamboyantly, folks tended not to belittle or feel as threatened.

During the day, the streets were often very crowded with men arriving into town to seek their fortune, as well as the families of those already out in the gold fields. Sometimes she was lucky to converge into a crowd of strangers. Other times, not so much.

She checked her appearance one more time in the mirror before stuffing a wad of money and the room key in her bodice and opened her door.

It was quiet in the hall as she stepped out. The voices from the first floor mingled together to create a dull roar that rose and lowered in tempo. She looked both ways and closed the door behind her. In her nonchalant normal way, started down the foyer toward the stairs. So far, so good. The room she occupied was at the very end of a long hallway after going through a door that led into a different section of the building. This allotted her and the other girls the privacy they needed to conduct business as well as affording space of their own.

Betty had four doors on either side to pass and was nearly to the dividing door when a man she didn't recognize stomped out of Clara's room without looking her way. He slammed the divider door behind him and disappeared.

Clara was one of her favorites. They were nearly the same age and she enjoyed Clara's wonderful sense of humor. Betty considered Clara the sister she never had. Knowing Clara would throw a fit if she didn't duck in, Betty took a deep breath and walked through the doorway.

Clara's room was decorated very similarly to her own. Plain. Other than dresses and makeup, their possessions were few. Betty made sure all the girls maintained a healthy diet. That, and a roof over their head kept them content.

"Kitty!" Clara stopped touching up her lipstick, rushed over, and led her by the arm to the bed. "What horse's ass did this to you? You must tell Miles."

"No." Betty shook her head. "You musn't tell him. We'll lose business."

In addition to the bar keep, Miles had appointed himself as protector of Betty and the girls. Hugely well-muscled, the spectacles and his long moustache made him appear that much more ominous.

"Oh, Kitty. You coulda been badly hurt, or worse."

Betty patted Clara's knee. "It's okay. I promise you it will be the last time something like this ever happens to me."

"That's why you need to tell Miles. So that man never steps foot in here again."

"Sweetie, if it wasn't him, it might be another man. What I'm trying to say is that I'm through. No man will ever touch me again."

Clara gasped. "But, but, don't you . . . like it?"

Betty fixed her with a stare. "No. I never have. As a matter of fact, aside from my daddy, I've held an intense hatred for men for as long as I can remember."

"Then why—?"

Betty shrugged. "Because I was damned good at it."

Tears formed in Clara's eyes. "Does this mean that you'll close the saloon?"

"I haven't thought that far ahead yet." Betty leaned into Clara. "We'll talk later. Right now I have to go see if Doc will put a stitch in my lip. But don't worry. Whatever I decide, you and the girls will be taken care of. I promise."

"You should have him look at your eye too."

Betty left Clara and managed to slip outside into an alleyway. Fortunately, there wasn't a soul around. Beyond the shadows of the buildings, enough light remained to see clearly and navigate her way three streets over to Jake Brown's house.

Doctor Jake Brown operated a practice out of his two-story home. The ground floor was dedicated to treating patients and the second story was his personal dwelling. The house was set on the tiniest of a rise, white-washed with a chimney at each end. Well-worn paths from every direction led straight to the house's entry.

A black horse harnessed to a buckboard stood quietly by the front door. A second horse, a buckskin, was tied haphazardly to the wagon by the reins. Both horses were streaked with white, dried sweat. There was no doubt they'd traveled hard and arrived in a hurry.

Betty climbed the two steps onto the wide wooden porch. She barely glanced at the slate hanging between the door and shaded window. The door sat slightly ajar. She pushed it open enough to walk through and closed it behind her.

To the right, in a small room, sat a dark maple desk, behind which stood a floor to ceiling bookcase filled with medicine bottles of all sizes and colors. A human skeleton stared bleakly from its glass case in the corner. Two paintings depicting English fox hunting decorated the wall beside the desk. She turned to the left and entered a parlor that was the waiting room. A blackened fireplace, framed with stone, occupied the far wall. She knew from earlier visits that the adjoining pocket doors led into Doc's surgery. Low, imperceptible voices dribbled through.

The waiting room was empty but for two children. The boy had ebony black hair, and she didn't doubt for a second that he had a lot of Indian blood in his heritage. The girl whose hand the boy held had brown hair. There was a slight similarity in their facial structure, which led Betty to think they might be related in some way. They both wore layers of dust from the prairies outside of town, broken only by the streaks of dried tears running down their cheeks. They both looked sad, scared, and hopeful. Something bad had happened, and Betty's heart went out to them.

She took a seat at the end of the room so as to not make the children feel uncomfortable. She folded her hands together in her lap and stared straight ahead. She was probably in for a long wait. But she had nothing else to do.

# Chapter Two

A FLASH OF white streaked through Emma Kauffman's brain like a lightning bolt. It nearly brought her to her knees as she stood at the wooden bench in the kitchen, chopping vegetables. She dropped the knife, stepped back, closed her eyes, and hung on. Her chin dropped to her chest and her long black braids dangled freely. The pounding of galloping hooves only just preceded a vision of a downed horse and a gunshot. Something was wrong. Terribly wrong.

She blinked hard and took a deep breath before turning toward the door. The other side of which, she knew her nine-year old son, Henry, would be galloping toward on Jake, his buckskin horse. She felt the sensation of her hair lifting on her arms and nape of her neck.

"Ma?" Her daughter, Grace, ran to her side as Emma swung the door open. "You saw something. What's wrong?"

Grace, although only seven years old, was astute and very familiar with her mother's visions.

They both looked on as a distant figure slapped a horse's side with the end of the reins. A cloud of prairie dust exploded beneath the horse's hooves as it galloped closer. Waves of heat distorted the identity of the person headed toward them, but Emma knew. It was Henry. She also knew with growing dread that something had happened to her husband.

John and Henry had left at sunrise to gather and herd the mares and foals back to the farm to sort for sale. The sun blazed high overhead without any hint of clouds to impede its intensity. Emma knew from previous roundups that the herd would normally be arriving in a few hours. Barring any trouble, that is.

"Grace, bring Coal up from the back corral." Emma shaded her eyes with her hand as Grace ran to catch the black gelding.

"Yah!" Henry's voice could be heard now, urging his horse to run harder. Emma ran out to meet him.

Henry pulled back hard on the reins. Jake tucked his hind legs under him and hopped to a stop next to Emma. Henry's dark brown eyes were wide with fear and anguish.

"Ma! You have to come. Pa's hurt real bad."

Emma took a hold of Jake's reins with one hand and grasped Henry's leg with the other to steady him. "Tell me."

"Uri. He broke his leg in a prairie dog hole and rolled on top of Pa when he fell." Tears tracked through the dust on Henry's ashen face, and he swiped them with the back of his hand. "Uri kept trying to get up and it was hurtin' Pa real bad. I had to shoot Uri to make him stop. I couldn't . . . I couldn't get Pa out. You have to come."

"Stay right here and let Jake catch his breath. I'll go hitch the wagon." Despite the shakiness in her legs, she pushed herself into a stiff-legged jog. Her stomach felt rock hard with fear.

"Hurry, Ma. Please."

The desperation in Henry's voice spurred Emma to run toward the barn.

Grace held Coal while Emma harnessed him up. "Grace, get in the wagon." Emma backed the horse between the wagon shafts and quickly hooked him up. She handed the long reins to Grace to hold while she climbed in. Once seated, she slapped the gelding's back with them. "Hup, hup." Coal leaned into the harness and trotted forward.

Emma steered the wagon toward Henry. She nodded at her son, who reined Jake around.

"Hold on tight, Grace."

As if sensing the urgency, Coal lengthened his stride and finally broke into a canter to keep up with Jake's pace. The wagon creaked and complained as it jostled over the uneven ground at the unfamiliar speed.

Emma braced her feet against the footrest and pushed back into the seat. She clenched her jaw to keep her teeth from clacking together. She glanced at Grace, who had taken an identical position and stared straight ahead. Her eyes were damp and overly bright. Emma read worry on her face, with tears at the ready to spill from her eyes. She moved the reins to her left hand and patted Grace's leg. "It's going to be all right."

She split the reins, held them in both hands, and urged Coal to go faster.

"Ma, I'm scared."

"I know, little one. Me too. But your Pa is a strong man. He's gone off horses before and come out with near a scratch." Emma hoped her words rang true. But she'd already "seen" John. He was hurt bad.

Henry waited for them at the river crossing. He lifted his hat and swept the back of his hand across his forehead, leaving a streak of dirt.

The bank was steep, but there was no other way across. Fortunately, the water was running low because of the lack of rain over the past several weeks.

Emma helped Coal navigate the rocky slope by braking the wagon every few steps. Once in the water, she gave him his head to quench his thirst. Henry followed suit with Jake. They all knew a life depended on keeping the horses watered. It was a long way into Oro Fino, where the doctor was.

She knew they were close as several of the horses wearing their brand were quietly grazing on the short grasses that grew along the riverbank. The foals, suspicious by nature, watched their approach. They peeked their little heads from around, and beneath the safety of their dams.

"He's just over the hill." Henry pointed at the short ridge that led onto miles and miles of open high-grassed prairie.

"You go. We'll catch up. Tell your Pa we're coming."

Henry dug his heels into Jake's sides and was gone in a clatter of hooves and flying sod.

Emma slapped the reins on Coal's back and got him moving again. Water splashed up from his hooves and the wagon wheels. Once across the river, she reined him to a stop.

"Grace, hop on down and fill the canteen."

Grace held the leather flask under water with one hand and took mouthfuls of water in the other. It took all of two minutes. Emma prayed to the spirits it wasn't too long.

"Good girl." Emma hoped her smile was reassuring. "Come on, Coal." She clucked once, which sent the horse into a fast walk. She had to trust Coal to avoid any holes.

Henry waved his hat above the tall grasses. His arm and hat were all Emma could see. She drove the wagon to the other side of where Jake grazed.

"Stay here," she said to Grace and handed her the reins. "If something spooks these horses, we're in a world of hurt. Can you do that?"

Grace wordlessly nodded and took the leathers from Emma.

Emma hopped down and rushed to where Henry stood.

"John, are you trying to get out of selling those foals again?" Emma tried to mask her fear with frustration. Her breath caught in her chest as she looked into his eyes. Terror, uncertainty, and pain radiated from him. Beads of sweat rolled down his face and disappeared into his beard.

The stream of blood from the gunshot to Uri's head had already dried. His kind eyes stared sightlessly skyward as if to avoid looking at his broken leg. Vultures had already started circling overhead. Several brazenly swooped lower.

"Never mind that, woman. Those birds are looking for an easy meal and I'm kind of stuck here," John said between forced breaths.

Emma knelt at his side. His pelvis and legs were trapped beneath the horse. "Are you in much pain?"

"Just my backside. I think I landed on a rock." John blew out a breath and licked his lips. "I sure am thirsty though."

"Henry, give your Pa a drink." Henry raced to Jake to retrieve his canteen.

Emma took the opportunity to talk to John in private. "How bad?"

"It's bad, darlin.' I can't feel my legs anymore. I'm sure they're both broke."

She drew back the hair from his forehead and smiled bravely. "Doc will surely fix you up."

Henry arrived with the water, dropped to his knees, and gave it to John who drank thankfully.

"We're going to need both horses to get your Pa free," Emma said to Henry. "Unhitch Coal from the wagon and bring him and Jake over."

Henry jumped to his feet, ran off, and in short order, returned with Jake and Coal. Both horses showed the whites of their eyes and snorted when they smelled the blood and saw their dead herd mate.

Emma kissed John's head and got to her feet. She helped Henry turn the horses around and back them to within a few feet of Uri's body. "Can you keep them steady while I tie them to Uri?"

Henry nodded.

She took Henry's rope from his saddle and John's from his and fashioned a series of knots to form a noose around the dead horse's legs. An ache formed in the back of her throat as dread set in at having to cause John more pain to free him. There was no way to lift Uri off him. The only way would be to drag the horse off.

Emma went to John's side and said in a quiet voice, "This is likely to hurt bad, my love. I'll do my best to make it as quick as possible."

John blinked in understanding. He placed his palm against her cheek. "I don't want the kids to hear me scream. Can you get my stock whip off the saddle?"

Emma handed him the crop and waited as he wedged the handle between his teeth and clenched his jaw. She bit her lip as their eyes met. It was time. She rose to her feet and walked to Coal. She took the reins from the surcingle and moved behind him. She held the leathers in her left hand and the remaining length in her right. She slapped Coal's back and Jake's rump in one motion. "Hup, hup. Come on, get up!"

Henry pulled on Jake's reins from the front to encourage him. The horses pranced in place, then leaned forward. Uri's body slid an inch. Coal and Jake stopped and backed up a step.

John's moan tore at her heart. Emma choked back a sob and yelled at the horses. "Haw! Haw! Get up, come on!" She swatted them over and over again to get them moving. Slowly, inch-by-inch, the horses dragged Uri off of John. Emma focused on keeping the horses going, trying her best to ignore John's screams despite the whip in his mouth. Then no sound but the stomping of hooves and jangling of harness.

"Whoa, now. Back up a step. Easy there." Emma looped the reins onto the surcingle and untied the ropes from Uri's legs. "Henry, get Coal hitched back up to the wagon."

Emma didn't wait for a reply and returned to John's side. Thankfully, he lay unconscious, the pain too much for him to bear. She took the whip from his now slack mouth, put her head on his chest and listened for a heartbeat. He was still alive. She looked down at his legs. Tears streamed down her cheeks. Both legs were twisted in unnatural angles and one side of his hip was lower than the other. He'd be lucky to ever ride again. She shook her head. That was the least of their worries. They needed to get him to the doctor. And fast.

The creaking of the wagon made her look up. Henry sat in the seat next to Grace. He carefully navigated Coal so that the back of the wagon was close to John.

"Is he—?" Grace's lower lip trembled.

"He's still alive. I'll need both of you to help me lift him into the wagon. We have to hurry and do it while he's still unawares. It'll be easier on him."

Henry and Grace scrambled off the wagon and came to Emma's side.

"I need each of you to gently lift a leg while I carry him, okay?"

Both nodded.

"Put one hand above his knee and the other below."

Emma grasped John under his arms and waited for the children to lift his legs.

"Ma, I can feel his bones move," Henry exclaimed.

"Me too. Ma, I can't." Grace carefully placed John's leg down and tucked her hands into her armpits.

"You have to. I can't do this myself and your Pa needs us more than ever." Emma had a thought. "Henry, get your bedroll off your saddle. We'll roll him onto it and then lift him. You won't have to hold his legs then. Hurry."

Emma carefully wrapped a lariat around his legs, to hold them together. She then laid the makeshift blanket alongside John. "Henry, push him up onto his shoulder. I'll take care of his legs. Grace, when we have him on his side, push the bedroll as far under him as you can. Ready?"

Henry braced himself and Emma slid her hands under John's legs. She swallowed the bile that rose when she felt the broken bones shifting. Both grunted as they pushed John onto his side and held him steady while Grace shoved the bedroll as close as she could.

They gently laid him back down. Emma adjusted John so that he lay more in the center of the bedroll.

"Okay, both of you hold onto a corner and lift."

They painstakingly and very slowly managed to get John onto the wagon. He groaned every once in a while, but didn't regain consciousness.

"Both of you are going to have to ride in the back. Grace, put your Pa's head on your lap and keep him still." Emma boosted Grace up and helped her rest John's head on her leg. Henry, tie Jake to the back of the wagon and get in. You have to keep Pa from sliding around. I'm going to go as fast as I can, and until we get onto the road into town, it's going to be rough."

Emma climbed aboard the wagon and urged Coal forward. Although every part of her urged for speed, she knew deep down that it was safest to keep the wagon moving at a steady pace. She sympathized with every bump and jolt, knowing that if John were awake, he'd be feeling the pain magnified a thousand times over.

John groaned from behind her.

"Ma, Pa's coming to," Grace said excitedly.

Emma pulled Coal to a halt, set the brake, and climbed over the seat. She crouched next to John and pulled the blanket over him.

"natainnappettsi," Emma said in her native Shoshone language and touched his shoulder. "You're safe now. I'm sorry about the rough ride. Please try to hold on until we get to the doctor."

"Thirsty." John's voice was raspy, but seemed strong. His face was drawn and pale.

Henry looked at Emma for approval before lifting his canteen to John's lips. He swallowed twice before coughing.

"That's enough for now." Emma stood up. "We have to go."

John nodded and closed his eyes.

Emma met Henry and Grace's eyes before climbing back into the driver's seat. She gathered the reins, released the brake, and clucked to Coal.

Henry refilled the canteens while she let the horses drink again at the river. Once over the steep bank, Emma was able to push the horse into a ground-covering trot. Her gaze settled over the top of Coal's ears and let her mind wander.

When John had brought her as his new wife, to his farm years ago, they'd worked hard to eradicate the colonies of prairie dogs that had probably lived on their land since the beginning of time. Bison and pronghorns had been the only residents of the prairie at that time. They seemed to instinctively know where the holes were and avoided them. It was slow work, as the prairie dogs disappeared into their holes at the slightest hint of danger. But eventually all were gone and over the course of a few months, they had filled in all the holes.

Back then farming or raising stock was the last thing on either of their minds. John had run a trap line in the Clearwater Mountains. He'd come to know the resident Shoshone tribe while on the trail. Eventually they'd invited him to their village, became acquainted with their chief and her father, Bear Hunter, and began trading with them. Over the course of a few years, her tribe was pleased to see him learning their language and could effectively communicate.

A blizzard blew in one winter while John was in the village and dumped four feet of snow on the ground. Bear Hunter insisted he stay with the tribe and quickly ordered a tepee erected next to his own. Despite the storm lasting only three days, John ended up living with the Shoshone tribe for four months until the spring thaw. During his stay, he and Aka, meaning sunflower, became more acquainted and they eventually fell in love.

Aka had gone back to live with Bear Hunter after losing her husband in a tangle with a rattlesnake. Her time of mourning was ended and Bear Hunter arranged for her and John to marry. Along with Aka's hand in marriage, Bear Hunter presented John with three Spanish mustangs and a permanent tepee within the tribe. However, John felt he couldn't sufficiently support a family in the mountains. Despite Bear Hunter's offer, John and Aka took the horses to his land on the lowlands and tried to scrape out a living there.

Living on the flat lands and not within the safety of the mountains had been quite a change for Emma. For years, the lack of trees made her feel exposed. There were so many more white people in this part of the world and their stares added to her unease. Her name seemed to point to the fact that she was Indian even though her skin color made it obvious. She and John decided she might fit in better if she had a more conventional name. Hence, with John's help, she adopted the name of Emma.

Henry was born shortly thereafter, and two years later Grace came into the world. Their family was complete, and she'd never been happier. John was well respected in Oro Fino, and his horses were much sought after for their endurance, steadiness, and intelligence. Coal was one of the horses Bear Hunter had given to John. He was like another member of the family. Although up in years now with a grey flecks covering his face, he was as energetic and steadfast as a four year old.

Emma's back and shoulders ached from tension. Relief was like a cool breeze when they reached the road. Coal alternated trotting and cantering the rest of the ten miles into town.

When they finally arrived at Doc's house, John groaned, clearly in a lot of pain. She rushed into the house and thanked the spirits Doc was home and wasn't attending to anyone else.

With Doc's help, they carried John inside and laid him on the surgery table. Emma thought it best that Henry and Grace remain in the waiting room. She knew it was hard on them to not be with their Pa, but she didn't want them to see what John was going to have to go through.

"This will help with the pain," Doc said as he plunged a needle attached to a glass tube, into a small bottle filled with yellow liquid.

"What is that?" Emma had never seen such a thing.

"It's a drug called morphine," he said in a kind tone. He tied a tourniquet around John's arm, pulled his eyebrows down in concentration and felt for a vein near John's elbow. A large one popped up and Doc swiftly inserted the needle and depressed the plunger. "He'll require more than a piece of wood to bite on to tolerate the pain when I set his bones." Doc wetted a white cloth with liquid from a bottle and placed it over John's nose and mouth. "This chloroform will put him out and he won't feel anything until he wakes up."

John's eyes fluttered closed. Doc listened to his heart and nodded to himself. "It's best I get busy. You may stay if you have a hard stomach."

There was no way Emma was leaving her husband's side.

# Chapter Three

"I'M SORRY, MISS Vela, there must have been some kind of mix up. Our school teacher, Mrs. Johnson, began her position a month ago." The man patted his already slicked-back greasy hair and smiled condescendingly. He looked the typical bank manager. Apparently, he also doubled as the mayor of Oro Fino.

Anna opened her mouth and then closed it, not sure of what to say. Suspicion rose in her chest. "May I ask one question?"

"Of course." He folded his hands on the desk. His eyes wandered up and down her body with obvious disdain.

"Why did I have to send a picture of me with the application?" Anna folded her arms over her very amble bosom.

The man broke eye contact and looked everywhere but at Anna. He shuffled some papers in front of him. "Oh. Ah. Well. You would know that it's very important to find a teacher who the children will be comfortable with and of course who has an air of discipline that they won't challenge or question." He finally looked at her and a false smile split his face.

Anna narrowed her eyes. Anger replaced suspicion. "One more question?"

The man sighed and rolled his eyes.

"Is this Mrs. Johnson skinny?" She pursed her lips and raised her shoulders, daring him to lie to her face.

"I can't see what difference that would make. Now, Miss Vela, if you would excuse me, I have work to do. Good day."

"Fine. I already know the answer. You didn't think a fat woman like me could do the job. If you had read my credentials more carefully, you'd see I graduated at the top of my class and have been very sought after back East."

"Then may I suggest you seek a job back East?"

Anna slammed her fist on his desk, making him jump backward in his chair. "No. You. May. Not. It's men like you who make women like me hate self-serving, egotistical idiots such as yourself." She smiled sweetly and brushed her hands down the front of her dress, accentuating her very curvaceous figure. "Good day." Anna spun on her heels, nearly losing her balance, and stomped out of the bank.

She marched unseeingly past people and shop entrances. When she came to the end of the boardwalk, in front of Big Nosed Kitty's, she stopped. What was she to do now? On a whim she pushed through the swing doors of the saloon, went in and approached the bar. A large, bespeckled man approached her while wiping a glass with a grey towel that she imagined had been white at some point ages ago.

"Help you, ma'am?" He tucked the glass under the bar and flipped the towel over his shoulder.

"Yes. I'll have a gill of whiskey, if you please." Anna hadn't indulged in spirits since graduation. But given the circumstances, she thought she'd celebrate the fact she hadn't wrung the mayor's neck in front of everyone.

The bartender raised his bushy eyebrows but didn't question her. He set a short glass on the bar in front of her. He turned and selected a bottle from a group of others behind him that sat on a counter above which a grey wolf hide hung.

Anna watched the four ounces of gold liquid swirl in the glass as he poured. "Anything else?"

Anna shook her head. "No, thank you."

"That'll be two bits."

Anna dug around in her purse for the twenty-five cents and put it on the counter in front of her. When the bartender took the money and turned his back to put it in the register, Anna took a sip of the whiskey. The taste was powerful and like fire in her mouth. Her eyes watered as it burned its way down her throat. She blew out a breath, licked her lips, and enjoyed the warm, cozy feeling that enveloped her. The fumes seemed to sit in her nasal passages, and it made her heady. She downed the remainder in one gulp and set the glass down with a thump. Blinking back the tears, she rummaged around in her purse and slid another two bits toward the bartender. Without a word, he retrieved the bottle and refilled her glass with one hand and pulled the coins toward him with the other.

Up until now, she had held onto the anger of being passed over for the teaching position because she was fat. Well, he hadn't come right out and said that, but the implication had been pretty clear.

She sipped her drink and sighed. What was she going to do now? She'd spent nearly all her money to get here, not hesitating in the least because of the expected income when she would have begun teaching. She watched a young girl, dolled up to the nines in makeup greet a man, take his hand, and lead him up a set of stairs.

Anna covered her mouth and giggled as she imagined herself working as a painted lady. Just as quickly, she damned her parents and the propensity they had for producing overweight children. Her brother managed to stay a tad skinnier only because of the work he did on a pig farm. Her time at school, sitting at a desk hadn't helped a bit. She'd focused so much time on her studies, wanting to do well to make her family proud. And what did it get her? Not a heck of a lot. A very long trip which ended in her still being unemployed, out of money for the most part, and no place to go. And she was still fat.

"Refill?" The bartender had reappeared with the bottle of whiskey at the ready.

She put her hand over the top of her glass and shook her head. "I'm afraid two is all I can afford."

The bartender glanced from side to side and said in a low voice, "You sort of look like you're down on your luck. This one's on the house."

Anna wordlessly uncovered her glass and watched as he poured.

"Hope things look up for you soon, ma'am."

Anna smiled thinly. "Me too. And thank you for your kindness."

When he left to serve another patron at the end of the bar, she ventured a look around. The interior of the saloon was a crude affair with minimal furniture. Four vacant tables and chairs stood on either side of the doorway. Seven stools were tucked under the overhang of the bar. A single wood-burning stove sat at the base of the stairs.

Movement from above got her attention. A door opened and a woman with red hair piled on top of her head slowly descended. She wore a pale blue dress. The neckline squared off, fashioned an empire waist, which was two to three inches above her natural waistline and fell just below her bust. The front skirt hung in straight folds, nearly to the floor. She seemed to avert her eyes and hide her face. In a moment, she was gone without a sound or having gained the attention of the barkeep. Anna thought she might have even imagined it.

She blinked hard and decided it was time to go. If she was lucky, she might even be able to arrange for transportation back East within the day. If not, she wasn't sure what she would do. At this point, she decided she didn't give a damn.

Anna slid off the stool and made sure her feet were solidly under her. She waited until the room stopped its slow spin around her. Despite the little bit of dizziness, she felt good. Deep down, she now knew things would be fine and that she would somehow come out on top. There would be other teaching positions, and she was sure any one of them would be in a nicer location.

She twisted at the waist and took her purse off the bar. She made the mistake of trying to take a step forward while still half turned. One foot got tangled around her leg and threw her off balance. She tried to steady herself by making a grab at the counter, but her weight won the battle, and she started to fall. Her head came into contact with the side of the stool before her bottom hit the floor and she flopped flat on her back. Everything went black. She lay there dazed. She blinked, but the black didn't recede. "Oh my god, I've been struck blind."

"Ma'am. Are you okay?" The barkeeper's voice seemed very far away.

Anna felt something drag over her head and suddenly she could see. Just as quickly, she realized that she wasn't blind. Her layers of dress had flipped up over her head when she fell and completely obliterated any light. Sputtering with embarrassment, she struggled to get up, straightening her dress over her pudgy legs at the same time. When she brushed away a tickle on the side of her head, her fingertips came away red.

"Just hold on one second. You banged your head pretty hard, and you're bleeding."

Anna sat patiently while he dabbed the cloth against her wound. She grimaced from the sting of the wet fabric, yet felt relief against the heat of her reddened face.

"I think you might better see Doc to have a look at that."

Pain sobered her up quickly. In addition to the pounding in her head, she thought she might have twisted her knee on the way down. "I don't know where."

The barkeeper helped get her to her feet and guided her to a chair. "Sit here for a minute and get your wits about you." He lifted her hand to replace his that held the rag against her head. He then went to behind the bar and returned with a glass of water.

Anna dragged her pasty tongue from the roof of her mouth and drained the glass. She was surprised at how thirsty she was. "Thank you for your assistance. I believe I can take care of myself from here." She averted her eyes, looking anywhere but at faces who were no doubt covered in amusement.

"Ma'am, I have to insist you see Doc about your cut. That thing's going to keep bleeding unless you have a stitch, or at the very least, a bandage."

Anna nodded and instantly regretted it. Her head pounded with the beat of her heart. "Very well. He might possibly give me something for my headache."

The barkeeper smiled sympathetically. "His place ain't far. Just up a street on the other side. You can't miss it. Seems all roads lead to Doc's."

"If you would help me up." Anna extended her hand to him, which he gently grasped. She braced her legs beneath her, swearing lightly from the pain, but with his help, rose to a standing position.

"You right?" The concern in his kind eyes was unmistakable.

"Yes, I think so. I'll be on my way." Anna took her purse when he handed it to her and shuffled slowly out the door.

She blinked against the low sun. Her head pounded harder and her knee was stiffening quickly. Once she made it across the rutted street, her feet met shaded grass. The path to the doctor's was well worn, but smooth, and tree lined the entire way.

As she approached, she noted the two horses, one hitched to a wagon, the other tied to the back of it. Their heads drooped low as if they were exhausted. A fact accentuated by the streaks of dried sweat clinging to their hides.

A shingle stating the house was indeed where the doctor resided, hung between two windows. The door creaked when she took hold of the handle and pulled it toward her.

Anna recognized the sweet smell of chloroform when she entered the house. Her brother, Charles, had needed an infected tooth extracted years ago and she'd had to help hold him down until the doctor knocked him out with the chloroform. Charles was normally a very brave man. She'd seen him stare down a rogue bull in a pasture one time while she and a friend ran to safety. But whenever it involved mouth pain, as in anything to do with his teeth, he was a big baby.

She frowned when she discovered she'd more than likely have a wait on her hands. Two Indian children, a boy and a girl, sat across from a door she suspected led to an examination room. They both stared expectantly in that direction. It was obvious someone they cared for was being tended to. Surprisingly, both wore trousers and long-sleeved cotton shirts, the only difference being the boy's were deer skin and his sister's were linen.

The red-haired woman she'd seen in the saloon sat diagonally across from the children. At first glance, it became obvious to Anna why the woman had hidden her face. She'd been battered, and her face showed the effects of it. Given where the poor woman had come from, Anna suspected a man she had bedded was the culprit. She met the woman's eyes, offered a slight smile, and took a seat on the same side, but closer to the children.

Anna took the cloth from her head and examined it to see if she was still bleeding. Although it had slowed, there was still fresh blood on it. She sighed and put it back against her head and closed her eyes. Several silent moments passed.

"What happened to you?"

At first Anna thought she was dreaming when she heard the voice. She looked up in surprise when she found the young girl standing a mere foot from her. Anna met dark round eyes full of kind curiosity. "Oh, hello. My clumsiness got the better of me and I hit my head when I fell over."

The girl cocked her head. Her eyes roamed from the top of Anna's head to her feet. "You skinned your knee." She pointed to Anna's right knee.

"I did?" Anna stretched her leg out. It was the only way she could see over her belly. Sure enough, her knee was red and abraded, though not bleeding. "You're right. Thank you for noticing. I'll have to have the doctor clean that too."

The girl shrugged, but remained where she was.

The teacher in Anna found its way forward and her voice took on a more soothing tone. "Are you not well? Is that why you're here?"

The girl looked over her shoulder at the boy. He sat unmoving with his hands folded in his lap and stared at the door in front of him.

"My brother and I ain't sick. Ma ain't either. But Pa got hurt."

"I'm sorry to hear that. I hope not too bad." Anna ignored the bad grammar and tapped the seat beside her, silently inviting the girl to sit.

After a brief hesitation, the girl sat down. She shrugged again. "My brother and him were bringing in the horses. Pa's horse fell in a hole and landed on top of him. His legs are broke."

"Oh my. Well, I'm sure the doctor will fix him right up." Anna patted the girl's leg in reassurance.

The girl leaned forward, peered at the other woman, and then focused her attention back on Anna. "My Ma is in there with Pa. Didn't anybody come with you?"

"Uh, no. I'm new in town. Actually, I'll be leaving as soon as I can make the proper arrangements." Anna smiled gently.

"How come? Don't you like it here?" The girl's eyes grew big as if Anna had insulted her by wanting to leave.

"There doesn't appear to be a job for me here. Aside from teaching, I'm not trained in anything else."

"Oh." The girl picked at her fingernails before speaking again. "What's your name?"

Anna smiled brightly. "Anna Vela."

"Annavela? What kinda name is that?"

Anna chuckled. "Tell you what. You just call me Anna, all right?"

"Okay, Anna. My name is Grace and that's my brother, Henry."

Anna looked over at Henry. He maintained the same position. His face told of the emotional turmoil he'd been through. She could only imagine how helpless he would've felt seeing his father injured. Anna wished she could take the children's pain away.

"Did you come here to teach?"

Anna raised her eyebrows. With all that was going on, Grace had remembered what she had told her. The fact that Grace was interested in her showed a tremendous amount of intelligence, or she inadvertently was trying to forget about her Pa for a while.

"As a matter of fact, I did. But I got here too late and someone else took over the position."

"We don't go to school. Ma and Pa say it's too far for them to haul us every day. They say it's not safe for us to go alone." Grace sighed and scrubbed her hands over her face.

"They're probably right. I don't think this territory is completely settled yet."

Grace sat up straight and smiled brightly. "You could do it. You could be our teacher."

Anna chuckled. "Oh, sweetheart. That's so very kind of you. But—"

"You could. Ma said once that someone would come. You see, sometimes she has these visions." Grace nodded as she spoke. "She said she saw a wanderer who would make a big difference in our lifes."

"Lives," Anna corrected.

"See? Henry and I kin learn so much from you." Grace raised her eyebrows and offered a questioning gaze.

Anna frowned and shook her head. "I'm sorry, but I don't think that it would be appropriate right now, what with your Pa hurt and all. Your Ma will have enough to do without an extra person in her way."

Grace broke eye contact and lowered her head. Dejectedly, she slowly got up and resumed her place next to her brother.

Anna's heart nearly broke for the young girl. She touched the bump with her fingertips and was pleased to see there was no fresh blood. Maybe she should just get up and leave.

There was movement in the doorway, catching the attention of both children whose faces had turned from worried to hopeful. Anna turned her head to look and met the eyes of one of the most beautiful Indian women she'd ever seen. Her high cheekbones and almond shaped, almost oriental-looking deep brown eyes were framed by black, braided hair. Full lips and dark skin complimented everything about her. It was quite clear whom Henry favored in looks, although Grace had a few similar attributes.

Anna stared back, unable to look away.

The woman looked on for several moments before focusing on the children who'd gotten up and run to her. She squatted and wrapped her arms around both of them. She spoke quietly, too quiet for Anna to hear, before standing up and guiding Grace and Henry into the room from where she came. Before the woman followed her children she met Anna's eyes again and nodded.

Something passed between the two of them, but Anna couldn't put her finger on it. Had the woman overheard Grace talking to her? At any rate, it didn't matter.

She stretched her legs out in front of her and grimaced at the stiffness and pain. She sighed and frowned. She'd been here this long she may as well stay and see if the doctor could prescribe something to make her more comfortable.

# Chapter Four

IT HAD TAKEN a while, but thankfully the doctor, with her help, had been able to successfully align the bones in John's legs. The size and strength of John's leg muscles made the setting extremely difficult because they had contracted and resisted relaxing. They'd had to pull and stretch his legs before the bones could be moved into place. During the entire ordeal, Emma had been thankful John couldn't feel the tugging or hear the gross readjustment of his broken legs. She'd had a hard enough time trying to block the sound out herself, and only managed to overcome it by humming a song her grandmother used to sing to her as a child. Her children had listened to it ever since birth and it had a calming effect.

Doc had splinted John's legs by placing a flat piece of wood on either side of each leg. He'd then wrapped wide straps of leather around both before stabilizing the hide with small blocks of ice to stiffen it.

"That should do it." Doc wiped his hands on a towel. He placed fingertips on John's neck and checked his pulse. "Nice and steady, like it should be." He looked up at Emma and smiled briefly. "Thank you for your help. I surely wouldn't have been able to do that alone."

Emma nodded and glanced at John when he moaned.

"The chloroform will wear off quickly. He'll be conscious in a few minutes, but very groggy." Doc covered John with a blanket.

"How long before he's awake enough so I can take him home?" Emma stroked John's hand.

"I want to keep him here for a few days so I can keep an eye on him. I want to make sure he isn't bleeding internally or have an infection before I send him home."

"Emma," John croaked.

"I'm right here, natainappettsi." Emma kissed his forehead.

John breathed deeply and seemed to fall asleep again.

"What does that mean? What you said to him." Doc leaned against a counter and crossed his arms.

"It means dear husband."

"Shoshone?"

Emma narrowed her eyes. Whenever anyone asked about her tribe, she became suspicious. "Yes. Why is it you need to know?"

Doc raised his hands in surrender. "Just curious is all. I treated a few Lakota in Wild Bill Cody's show when they traveled to Buffalo, New York." He frowned. "Shame that Jack McCall got let off for shooting him in the back of the head."

"I don't know who that man is." Emma turned to John and combed his hair back with her fingers.

Doc flipped his hands toward her. "Doesn't matter."

"May I bring the children in to see their father?"

"Absolutely. I'm sure they've been very worried. I forgot they were even out there."

"I'll be right back, natainnappettsi." She squeezed John's hand and set it down.

Emma had heard Grace talking to someone earlier while the doctor had splinted John's first leg. The voice had seemed so familiar, but she was sure she'd never heard it before. When she walked out the door and glanced to the left, she knew. The woman had entered into one of her dreams long ago, sat down at their table, and opened a book. The children had stood around her. Emma had dismissed it because although she hadn't been able to differentiate any facial features during her vision, she knew the woman was white. How absurd, she'd thought at the time.

She stared at the large middle-aged woman. She was rather plain looking with hazel eyes. Her brown hair was matted with what looked like blood on one side. Emma's breath caught and a fluttery feeling came alive in her belly. She would've continued to stare and probably approached the woman had the children not brought her back to the present.

Emma squatted down and wrapped her arms around Grace and Henry. Their earthy scent was welcomed after the hours spent in the surgery that smelled of antiseptic. She stood up and guided Grace and Henry into the room.

"Pa?" Henry went to John's side and peered at him.

"Boy," John said huskily. "You done good." He coughed and tried to clear his throat.

"I'm here too, Pa." Grace rushed to the other side of John and touched his hand.

"Hi, Pumpkin." John blinked and smiled at Grace.

Grace beamed back at him. Somehow the use of her nickname seemed to make her feel less anxious.

"natainnappettsi, the doctor wants to keep you here for a few days to start your healing."

John nodded and closed his eyes.

"I think that's all you're going to get out of him today. It's good if he sleeps now." Doc pulled the blanket up over John's shoulders. "You can see him tomorrow if you like."

Emma nodded and ushered the children out the door.

"Ma, that's Anna," Grace said, pointing. "She's a teacher."

"Yes, I know." Emma nodded politely. She glanced briefly at the other woman sitting at the far end of the room. Her chest fluttered, but she paid no attention this time. She approached Anna and sat down next to her. "We will wait while you're tended to."

"Oh, there's no need. Grace has told me you live a fair ways away. You should be going." Anna spread her fingers out in a fan against her breastbone.

"We will wait." Emma leaned back in the chair and crossed her arms to end the discussion.

Grace sat on the other side of Anna and took a hand in hers. "That's settled."

Anna shook her head with seeming disbelief. "Indeed."


EMMA KNEW ANNA had come into their lives to teach Grace and Henry. But there was something else niggling at the back of her mind. Anna's presence would also serve another purpose, but as of yet, Emma could not recall what else the dream had told her. At any rate, Anna would need a place to sleep. There was no room in the house for an extra person. Ah, the barn. Of course.

When John had settled on his property, he'd built the barn before the sod house. He'd needed a place to shelter the horses as well as store his traps. He'd also built a secure room for his stacks of hides. It was here he would store the dried pelts until he sold them. The room was obscure and not readily noticed by those unfamiliar with the barn. Back when he'd spend weeks and sometimes months away, he could do so knowing his hard work was hidden safely away.


THE RIDE BACK to the farm was much slower than the ride in. Although both horses had been able to rest for several hours, Emma was sure Jake and Coal were hungry and very tired.

Grace sat in the back with Anna, who was nursing a headache and two stitches in her head. Emma smiled at the excitement in Grace's voice as she talked to Anna.

"You're very quiet," Emma said to Henry as he rode Jake up beside the wagon. Henry shrugged.

"Your Pa will be as good as new in a few months after his legs knit."

"Yes, but there is so much for me to do."

"Ah. You worry that you won't be able to live up to your father's expectations."

"He's been teaching me, sure. But I don't know half of what he does." Henry turned a pained gaze her way.

Emma smiled affectionately. "It'll all be right. We'll manage. I think I can hold up a good portion of your Pa's end."

Henry glanced behind him at Anna and Grace. "Is that why you're bringing her home with us?"

"Anna will be your teacher instead of having to go into town every day."

Henry shook his head. "I won't have time for learning. There's too much work to do. We have to sort the horses and then move them back up to—"

"We will have time to do both. I will make sure of that." Emma looked at the sun lowering itself on top of the mountain.

"Henry, ride ahead and open up the pelt room in the barn. Sweep it out best you can and let it air out. That's where Anna will stay. Make sure mice haven't gotten in and chewed the old cot. If you finish before I get back, light a lantern in the house."

"Okay."

"Be careful."

"I will." Henry clucked Jake into a trot and in a few minutes, they'd disappeared over the grass covered ridge.

Emma held Coal to a walk. As soon as Jake had passed him, he'd tossed his head and tried to move into a trot to keep up with him. "Easy there, black boy. We'll be home soon enough."

She sat back against the seat and let her mind wander. Henry was right to be worried. There was a lot to do. John had amassed nearly a hundred horses to support the family. The yearlings had to be sorted from the main herd and halter trained. The foals had to be branded. Most importantly, the sale of three- and four-year-olds had to be confirmed with the livery owner and then driven to the stockyards. Although the list was small, the work involved was huge. Emma sighed. Could she do it? Even with Henry's help? She didn't have a choice, did she?

"Ma," Grace said, breaking into Emma's thoughts.

Emma half turned in her seat. "Everything okay back there?"

"Yes. Anna is going to teach us how to count and do maff."

"Math," Anna corrected.

"Yeah. That." Grace smiled adoringly at Anna.

Emma met Anna's eyes. "You'll have your hands full with my daughter. She loves to learn. How are you feeling?"

Anna touched the bandage on her head. "Just a tiny headache, that's all."

"Probably from Grace pestering you with her nonstop chattering."

"I never discourage a child in their pursuit of learning. She's been good company. I'm quite looking forward to working with your lovely children."

"You may find my son is a little resistant. He has it in his head that he alone has to do all the work while John is laid up. But don't worry. He'll be sitting right alongside Grace."

"Grace tells me you have quite a large herd of horses."

Emma nodded. "After you get settled and are feeling better, we'll match you up with a horse."

"Oh. Um. Thank you, for your generosity, but I don't know how to ride."

"We'll teach you." Grace bounced excitedly.

"Oh, sweetheart. Even if I wanted to learn, I'm afraid I'm just too large of a woman to put a horse through holding my weight."

"Grace, let it be for now." Emma frowned. If Anna was going to live with them for the present, she was going to have to learn how to ride. But, she wouldn't push it until she got to know Anna a little bit better.

A pinpoint of light came into view. A few brave stars hung in the darkening sky. Coal neighed and was answered by several other horses. Emma wanted nothing other than to be still and let relief sink in. It had been an arduous and very taxing day. She was bone tired and was sure Grace and Henry, especially Henry, were as well. Supper would have to be bread and slices of cold meat, and then off to bed for all of them.


"CAN I CALL Anna in for breakfast?" Grace rose halfway out of her chair.

"No, you may not. She had just as long a day as we did yesterday. Let the woman sleep until she wakes up on her own." Emma nursed a cup of steaming coffee. She was pleasantly pleased with herself for getting up before dawn, and the children, to feed the stock. There'd been no sound from the hide room where Anna slept. Even Coal had seemed to sense the need to be quiet. Instead of prancing next to her like he usually did in the morning, he walked quietly while he was led out of the barn.

Grace slid back onto her chair and put another forkful of egg in her mouth.

Emma ruffled Henry's hair. "I'm going to go back into town today."

"To see Pa?" Henry looked up with hopeful eyes. "Can I come?"

"Yes, I'm going to stop in to see your father. But I also have other business to tend to. So no, you have to stay here. If it's all right with Anna, you can start your learning today."

"But—"

"No buts. If we're going to get through having to run this farm by ourselves, you'll have to do as I say. Understood?" Emma looked at Henry and then at Grace to make sure they both had heard her. The two of them nodded in agreement, Grace more vigorously than Henry. Emma wasn't surprised.

There was a knock at the door. Grace jumped up and let Anna in. "You don't gotta knock. You live here."

"Have to knock," Anna corrected gently. She looked up. "Good morning. I'm sorry to have risen so late. I'm usually up with the chickens."

Emma stood up and poured a fresh cup of coffee. "Please don't worry about it. Everybody needs a late day now and again." She set the coffee where she'd been sitting. "Have a seat. Eggs and bread suit you?"

"Oh my, yes." Ann sat down and took a long sip from her cup. "Oh, that's heavenly."

Emma took the eggs and now warm bread out of the pan hanging above the fire. She quickly dished the meal out and served Anna.

"I was just telling Grace and Henry that I have to go into town again today."

"Of course you do. Your husband will be happy to see you." Anna shoved some egg onto the warmed bread and took a bite.

"Do you feel well enough to mind the children?"

"Aside from a little stiffness in my knee, I'm good. We can take this opportunity to get to know each other a bit more and maybe even begin a lesson."

"Goodie," Grace said and clapped her hands.

Henry rolled his eyes.

"Henry? Do you think that's a good idea as well?"

"Yes, ma'am." He took his plate to the sink and drained the milk from his glass. "Miss Anna, I have some chores to do."

Anna raised an eyebrow. "Do you need help?"

Henry looked shocked that Anna would even suggest such a thing. "No, ma'am. I'm quite able to do them by myself." He grabbed his hat from where it hung from an antler on the wall and walked out the door.

Emma bit her lip to keep from laughing. She poured water from a bucket into a blackened pot and hung it over the fire. "Grace, when the water is hot, you can clean the dishes. I'm going to get ready to leave."

Anna winked at Grace. "I'll give you a hand."

# Chapter Five

BETTY CAUGHT HERSELF in mid yawn and stopped before her lip stretched and reopened. By the time Doc had looked at it, he deemed it too late for a stitch. But he thought her split lip was already starting to heal despite the swelling. After some choice words about the man who'd harmed her, he gave her some salicylic acid to reduce the puffiness and pain relief for her contusions.

A very groggy man had lain in a bed in the surgery where Doc had brought her. Both of his legs were heavily splinted. Betty didn't have to guess that it'd been his family that had sat in the waiting room for so long. What had confused her was the willingness of them to take the woman, Anna, or so she'd said her name was, under their wings and off to their farm. It seemed the instant the Indian woman had laid eyes on Anna, she'd made a decision. Betty was sure they'd never met. Hadn't Anna said she was from out of town? Back East? She doubted the Indian family had ever stepped foot out of the west.

Betty got out of bed and looked in the mirror. Her swollen lip had indeed gone down some. Her eye however had darkened considerably and already, yellowish green splotches had formed below it and over her cheek. Makeup wouldn't cover enough of her blackened eye to look normal, but well enough to allow her to venture out of her room now and again. She'd already decided to take her meals upstairs. Clara had promised to deliver three meals and tell Miles that Betty had fallen ill and needed as little disturbance as possible.

The door swung open after a quick, light knock.

"Oh, my. You're getting quite colorful." Clara walked in and set the tray with two cups of coffee and a plate with four slices of buttered toast on the wardrobe. "How do you feel?"

"Better than yesterday. Doc gave me some powder and it seems to have helped overnight." Betty took the steaming mug of coffee from the tray and sipped gratefully. "Miles still makes the best coffee. Even for a man."

Clara took the second cup and sampled it. "Mmm. Yes, he sure 'nuff does." She sat down on Betty's bed and rested the cup on her lap.

Betty noticed the worried look on Clara's face. "Is something troubling you?"

Clara shrugged. "I know you haven't had much time to think about what you're going to do."

"Actually, I have."

"Did you change your mind?" Clara's eyes gleamed with hopefulness.

"No. That is most definitely something I will not do."

"Oh." Clara's demeanor quickly sagged, and she stared off at nothing. Her eyes looked glassy.

Betty tilted Clara's chin up with a finger and met her eyes. "I think you'll like what I've come up with. I had a lot of time to think when I was waiting at Doc's." She sat down beside Clara and nudged her with a shoulder. "I'm not going to sell Big Nosed Kitty's. At least, not yet. I'm going to speak with all of you, but I thought you should know first."

Clara smiled. "Really? Honest?"

Betty nodded. "You know how I always take a portion of your earnings? I'm no longer going to do that. All you girls will in fact be getting a raise. The more clients you care for, the bigger the raise."

"But you said you're not going to work anymore. How will you live?"

Betty patted Clara's leg. "I have a bit stashed away and the saloon earns enough from drinks and meals that I can take a portion of that income."

"But isn't that how you pay Miles?"

"Just leave it with me. Miles will be well taken care of. Don't you fret. I'll be fine."


LATER, AFTER DONNING more makeup than she'd ever done in her life, she met with Miles and the other girls and told them of her plans. Her news was met with much excitement. Of course, only Clara knew the entire story and Betty's reasoning behind it.

It was no surprise that Miles had remained silent throughout the meeting. He had waited for everybody to leave so he could speak with her alone. Betty knew Miles, of all people, would be suspicious of her motives.

"Kitty, I know you'll do what you want, but I think I deserve to hear the real story." Miles crossed his arms over his big chest. His eyes, through the glasses he wore, made it feel like she was beneath a spyglass.

Betty rubbed his muscular forearm in reassurance. "Honestly, I need some time off. I've been doing this for a lot of years, and truth be told, I'm tired of always giving. What did it give me the last time? A black eye and a split lip for my troubles."

"If I ever find out who did that, they'll get more than that for their troubles." Miles punched the palm of his other hand.

"Miles, I need a change and a rest. You and the girls will be well taken care of."

"What will you do?"

Betty chuckled. "I'll be around. Don't worry. But now I'll have some time to spoil myself."

"If it don't work out, then promise me you'll go back to way things was."

"I know you hate change, dear man. But my absence will make it one less lady you have to keep your eyes on when the saloon fills with those hungry men."

"That may be true, but—"

"Don't you need to open up the bar?"

"Yes, ma'am." Miles took a breath as if to say something else, but quickly exhaled and disappeared to the front of the saloon.

Betty returned to her room, changed into a plain dress and freshened her makeup. While she had a pretty good idea of how much money the bank was holding for her, she decided to pay a certain Clarence Hopwood a visit and get an accurate account.

She squinted against the bright sun when she walked out. The sky was clear, above the cloud of dust hanging in the air from the horse and foot traffic going back and forth through town. The dry heat warmed her, but not so much that the air couldn't cool her skin. Betty briefly recalled growing up in the humid east and living in a constant state of sweat during the warm months.

The stockyard behind the livery was empty. But probably the next herd of cattle or horses to be sold off weren't far off. Often, they were combined, so it could be driven over the mountains to Eagle Rock, where they'd be shipped out by railway. The cattle would supply butcher shops at other gold camps, and there were always uses for a good horse.

Betty smiled to herself and then breathed a pensive sigh. She'd met and become friends with a young girl on that train once. Mayme Watson had been forced to board it from Chicago by her father, and for all intents and purposes, abandoned. She'd lost touch with Mayme when the girl had gotten off the train while she'd continued on to San Francisco. Somehow fate and circumstances had brought them together again in, of all places, Oro Fino. Much to her disbelief, Mayme had disguised herself as a boy to deliver mail as a Post Rider. She'd disappeared a few years back. There were rumors that she'd gone to live with the Indians and still others claimed she was dead. A fate not uncommon in that line of work. In any case, Betty missed her friend, as they'd become quite close. Mayme used to stay at Big Nosed Kitty's whenever she rode into town on her big, blue roan horse. She'd be in town for a couple days to give Duster a rest, and sometimes new shoes, collect the mail from the postmaster, and then ride out again for a month or two.

Betty crossed the road and climbed the two steps to the bank's heavy oak door. She flicked off the dust that had gathered on her, straightened her dress, and went in. Two people stood in line in front of her, so she sat down on the single chair, a rickety thing worth more for firewood than for someone to rest their bum on.

The only sounds in the room were low murmurs and clinks against metal. Betty assumed the man being waited on was a gold miner having his find weighed. The man behind him stood up on his tiptoes several times to look over his shoulder. But the man in front seemed to want to block his view.

Finally, it was her turn. She stood and walked confidently to the banker's counter.

"Can I help you?" Clarence said, not bothering to look up as he scribbled some notes in a logbook.

When Betty didn't answer, he looked up in seeming surprise and then drew his face into a scowl. "What do you want?"

"An apology would be nice, but since I know that won't be forthcoming, some respect as a bank customer would be more than appropriate."

Clarence snorted. "I don't owe you nothing."

"Look Clarence—"

"That would be Mr. Hopwood to you."

"That's not what you asked me to call you the other night when you visited my bed."

Clarence looked around in alarm. "Will you be quiet, woman? Someone might hear you."

Betty smiled. Humiliating him would be just as satisfying as an apology. She placed her palm over her chest and feigned innocence. "What's the matter? Afraid someone might tell your sickly wife? Or overhear me say that you were the cause of my black eye and split lip?"

Clarence banged his hand down on the counter. Papers fluttered, the scales rattled, and his pencil rolled off onto the floor. "Enough. Just tell me what you want and then get out."

"Your bank holds my money. I merely want an accurate accounting."

He forcefully opened a drawer on his right and withdrew another logbook, which he slammed onto the counter with a resounding thump. After quickly flipping through a number of pages, he stopped and ran his finger down one of the columns.

"One hundred forty-nine dollars and twenty-five cents."

Betty felt a flush of anger. "There must be some mistake. Are you sure that you're not looking at somebody else's?"

"Your name is Kitty Reynolds, correct?"

"Yes, that's me." Her pseudo name sounded dirty coming from him.

"That's the total."

"No. I refuse to believe that. There should be close to a thousand dollars in my account."

Clarence snickered and closed the book. "Well, maybe you shouldn't have made all those withdrawals."

"Clarence, I never made a one and you know that." A painful lump grew in her throat, and she felt the burn of tears behind her eyes. She wouldn't let this pig see her cry.

He merely shrugged and looked behind her at the man who'd just come in. "Now if you'll excuse me, I have other respectable clients."

"Damn you." Betty recognized his dismissal. Not wanting to create a scene in front of other people, she glared at him. "Give me what I have then."

"I'll have to take ten percent because of your prompt withdrawal." Clarence stood up and walked to the wall safe. He swung the door open, grabbed some paper bills, held them like a card deck while he counted, and tossed them toward her.

Betty grabbed her money off the counter and stuffed it into her bodice. "I won't forget this." She spun on her heel and marched out. Only when she turned the corner and out of sight of anybody, did she release her tears. "You bastard," she muttered between sobs.

"Git outta here, you danged Injun!"

Betty looked up in time to see the liveryman brandishing a stock whip and threatening a woman.

"We don't do business with the likes of you. Now git."

The woman ran to her horse and untied the reins from the hitching post.

The commotion had gained the attention of two cowboys who'd just ridden in. "What are you doing in here, squaw?"

Betty widened her eyes in surprise when she recognized the Indian woman from the doctor's office.

The cowboys rode toward the woman, loosened their lariats, and swung them over their heads, threatening to rope her like a cow.

The woman leapt onto her horse and tried to break through but was blocked by the cowboys.

"Where you going, Injun? Gonna bring the tribe down?" He snickered as he mocked her.

"Leave me alone!" The woman yanked on the reins and tried to change direction.

"Well, I've had enough of that." Betty stormed over to them. "Leave her the hell alone."

The men glanced her way and smiled.

"Hello, Kitty," said the one who seemed to be leading the assault. "Don't you worry, we're just protecting the town from garbage like this."

"I said, leave her alone." Betty marched into the middle.

The leader nodded to the other, who kicked his horse into a gallop toward the saloon.

Betty knew he was going to get reinforcements. She brazenly grabbed the end of his rope and quickly wrapped it around his horse's legs. The horse panicked and reared.

"Hey!"

"Get out of here," Betty said to the woman. "It's going to get worse."

The woman rode up to Betty and extended her hand. "Come with me."

The cowboy turned his horse in circles, trying to untangle the rope. A crowd of men flowed out of the saloon.

"This is crazy."

"Come. Hurry."

Betty reached up and grasped the woman's hand. The horse moved forward and with that inertia, she was flung up behind the woman.

"Hold on."

Betty wrapped her arms around the woman and hung on for dear life. Wind whipped through her hair, her heart pounded in time with hooves as the horse galloped between the livery and the stockyards, and out onto the prairie. She heard the boom of a gunshot, and moments later a bullet whizzed by. Her insides twisted. Betty ducked her head behind the woman's shoulder and tightened her grip.

# Chapter Six

EMMA HAD NO idea why she insisted the woman go with her. She only knew that when she had the woman's hand firmly within her grasp, the dark shadow within the recesses of her mind disappeared. She'd woken with it that morning and was worried it had something to do with John. She didn't let on to the children about what she feared was a sense of foreboding. That was also the reason she'd insisted they stay back at the ranch with Anna.

The woman's grip tightened around her waist an instant after she heard the distant boom of a gunshot. Emma dug her heels into the horse's sides, silently thankful of her decision to saddle the bay mare, Sihu, rather than harness one and drive the wagon into town.

Emma directed Sihu over the ridge and turned east into the grove of cottonwood trees that lined the river. She followed the steep bank until it was low enough to enter the moving water. Once in, she rode upstream to where the river panned out into a shallow basin. It was there she finally reined the blowing mare to a stop, let her catch her breath, and have a well-deserved drink.

When Emma felt the woman loosen her arms and lean away from her, she half turned in the saddle. "Are you all right?"

"Uh, yes. I . . . I think so. Can you help me off?"

Emma slid her left foot out of the stirrup and pushed it backward with her heel. When the woman had her foot securely in it, she grabbed Emma's forearm and swung off. But as soon as her feet hit the ground, her knees buckled and she crumpled onto her rear.

Without hesitation, Emma flung her right leg over the neck of the horse, unstrapped the canteen from the saddle horn, and jumped off. She knelt down and peered into the pale face.

"You're not all right. Here," she said, uncapping the canteen and lifting it to the woman's lips. "Drink."

The woman grasped it and drank long, ignoring the water escaping the corners of her mouth. She dabbed at her lips and handed the canteen back. She took a deep breath and blinked hard. "You were at the doctor's yesterday with your children."

"Yes. My husband needed tending to."

"I overheard your daughter say he had broken his legs. I'm so sorry. Will he mend properly?"

"The doctor seems to think so, but not soon enough." Emma got to her feet and walked away from the noise of the water. She didn't think they'd been followed, but she couldn't take any chances. She narrowed her eyes and scanned the breaks through the trees. A pronghorn family trotted toward the direction they'd come. She breathed a sigh of relief when they didn't reverse their direction. That would've been an indication the men had taken chase.

"Would you mind telling me what happened back there? And why you insisted I come with you?"

Emma returned to the woman's side and stared into her eyes, one of which was blackened and colorful. She saw the honesty she somehow knew she would. "What is your name?"

"Kit—um, Betty. My name is Betty Coate."

"And I am Emma Kauffman." She glanced through the trees again. "We should go. I will tell you everything when we get to the farm."

"When will you take me back to town?"

"You can't go back now."

"What?" Betty pushed herself up and put her hands on her hips. She snorted. "What do you mean I can't go back? Are you holding me hostage or something?"

"No. Nothing like that. When you defended me, you were instantly labeled an Indian lover. You will have nothing but trouble and harassment if you go back now."

Betty knew she was right, but shook her head. "Then what do you suggest I do?"

What would she do? Emma had no idea. Suddenly a hummingbird buzzed around her head, seemingly to get her attention. At times it stopped mere inches from her face, and hovered miraculously, almost motionless in front of her. Its wings hummed. Its iridescent plumage changed color in a pearlescent blur. It was a sign. One she could not ignore.

She glanced at Betty who stood mesmerized by the bird's actions.

"I don't know the reasoning behind what the spirits want. But for now, you will stay at my home with my family and the woman called Anna."

"But I don't understand." Betty looked like a nervous filly, ready to flee at any moment.

"I don't either. But you can trust me. I'll take you to the farm, explain everything, and if you want to go back, I will take you tomorrow at first light."

Emma didn't wait for an answer. She led Sihu into the river, cupped her hands, and splashed water onto the mare's sweaty hide. Streams of dirty white sweat trickled down her legs and were moved away in slow swirls by the river. The mare stood quietly with her eyes closed, clearly enjoying the makeshift bath. Emma finished by scraping the excess water off her hide with the edge of her hand.

When she brought the mare back to where Betty stood, she stepped into the saddle and waited. She'd given Betty a few minutes to think. It was up to her to make a decision. Finally, Betty reached up for Emma to grasp her hand. She put her foot in the stirrup and let Emma pull her up.

Emma guided the mare back into the water and followed the river to make doubly sure they hadn't been followed. The undercurrent would quickly carry away any trace of their passage.

The sun sent the tops of the mountaintops aglow as they approached the farm. The house and barn were awash in shades of gold, interrupted only by the creeping shadows of the approaching evening. Jake and Coal paced in the corral. Emma knew they were eager to be let out to graze for the night.

As if on cue, the wiry form she knew could only be Henry, came out of the house, paused, and when he caught sight of her, waved enthusiastically. Grace and Anna soon joined Henry and stood by him to welcome her home.

Their smiles quickly turned to looks of confusion when Emma stopped in front of them.

Grace cocked her head and stepped forward. "Ma, is that the other lady from the doctor's place?"

"Yes. Her name is Betty." Emma gave Betty the stirrup and helped her to the ground. She quickly dismounted and handed the reins to Henry. "You can let Sihu out with the others. She's earned it."

"Did something happen?" Henry looked at her with concerned eyes.

"I'll explain everything when you come back. In the meantime, I have to get supper started."

"Oh, we already did that, Ma." Grace took Anna's hand in hers.

"I hope you don't mind," Anna said. "I felt like I should do something to haul my weight around here."

Grace sniggered, and Emma glowered at her.

"How's Pa?" Henry bit his lip and stared, unblinking at her as if he might miss something.

Emma put her hand on his shoulder and squeezed. "He had a tough night, but Doc stayed downstairs and helped him through his pain. Pa will be there for a few more days though."

"When can we go see him?"

Emma flitted her eyes at Betty. "We'll talk about that later. Right now, you have some stock to take care of." She patted Sihu's neck. "Give her a good brushing and some oats before you turn her out."

Henry looked at Betty suspiciously, but nodded and led the horse off.

"Anna, will you please take Betty inside and let her freshen up? I'll be back in a minute."

"Absolutely." Anna smiled at Betty. "You look a little haggard. Let's get you inside. While you wash up, I'll make you a cup of coffee."

"That would be very nice. Thank you."

Emma watched the three of them walk into the house. When she'd met John all those years ago, a feeling of completeness had settled over her. The painful hole in her heart she'd harbored when her first husband died had scabbed and healed. New hope had sprung from her chest, like the flowers of a tulip tree. That feeling seemed to have germinated again. Only this felt different. There was something unique about the two women inside her home. She couldn't quite put her finger on it.

Kikikiki-ki-ki-kuk . . . kuk . . . kuk . . . kuh.

Emma looked toward the sky. Three golden eagles soared above her on long, broad wings with their distinct fingerlike feathers at the tips. A tingling formed in her chest and spread throughout her body. Three eagles. Coincidence? Or another sign? The last of the afternoon thermals pulled the eagles eastward, toward the mountains, and soon they were tiny specks in the darkening sky. Those birds should be perched on their evening roosts by now. The sensation diminished as quickly as it came. She looked down at her palms for answers but found none. Her grandfather once told her when she saw such signs, to continue on the path intended. But what was the intended path? What roles would Anna and Betty play? Were they to join her on the trail the spirits seemed to point her?

When she entered the barn, she heard Henry's soft voice coming from the stall he'd taken Sihu into. She stood in the doorway and watched as he lovingly scrubbed her hide with a brush in one hand and rubbed her with the other. Henry had always been kind to animals. And the beasts all seemed to have a soft spot for him as well.

She remembered losing Henry as a toddler. She and John had raced around for an hour in search of him. They'd feared the worst that he'd been taken by a coyote or a brazen wolf that had come down from the mountains looking for easy prey. On a whim, John had checked the small paddock. He'd run back and led her to where Henry lay asleep, next to a resting mare who had recently foaled. Although the mare was lying down, she was keeping careful watch over Henry and her newborn colt, on which Henry had his head. Emma and John knew right then and there, that Henry would forever share special bonds with all creatures.

When Henry came out of the stall with Sihu at the end of a lead rope, Emma made her presence known. "She looks beautiful, Henry. Thank you."

"She ate her oats right down, that's for sure." Henry stopped and stroked Sihu's neck. "Do you need my help for something?"

Emma smiled at his intuition. "As a matter of fact I do. Come back here after you've let her out to graze."

Henry nodded and hurried past her. Sihu broke into a trot to keep up with him.

Although the barn was full of shadows, Emma knew right where to go. Fifteen tepee poles leaned high in the back corner. It was the frame for the tepee that her father had given John. He'd further insisted they take it with them when they left the tribe. Every tepee in the Shoshone tribe was distinctive. Not only were the bison hides painted with unique symbols, every pole had a special meaning. Emma mentally ticked their names off: respect, humility, happiness, love, faith, kinship, cleanliness, thankfulness, sharing, strength, good child rearing, hope, protection, control flaps, and obedience. She smiled to herself. Grandmother had spent a long time teaching her the names, ingraining them into her heart so she'd never forget.

By the time Henry returned, Emma had four of the poles lying on the ground outside the barn.

"What are you doing?" Henry followed her back into the barn.

"Raising the tepee. Anna and Betty will be more comfortable in this than the hide room." Emma carefully lowered another pole.

"That other lady is staying too?"

"Her name is Betty. And yes, she is staying. She may not feel it yet, but the spirits have something in mind for her."

With Henry's help, all fifteen poles were soon outside. Emma went back into the barn and returned with a large bundle made of tanned bison hides that were sewn together. She opened it up and removed a long tether made of elk hide, which she used to bind four pole tops together. Henry helped her stand them up and slant them outward from the center tie. This formed the outline of a cone. They leaned the remaining poles against the framework to strengthen it.

Using wooden lodge pins, Emma joined the covering at the top, leaving an opening for the smoke hole. The entrance had closable flaps and was located right below the seam. Emma left the flaps open to allow for air circulation, but she'd positioned the opening to face east because of the prevailing west winds. She tugged on the poles so that the entire shelter tilted slightly toward the east to lessen the pressure of the wind on it.

Emma stood in front of the tepee with her hands on her hips. A smile tugged on her lips.

"Why are you smiling, Ma?" Henry pushed his hat back and looked up at her.

She put her arm around his shoulders and pulled him close. "This tepee brings back a lot of memories. Your great grandmother and grandfather made it for your Pa and I."

Henry squinted his eyes and frowned. "Is that where you and Pa made me?"

Emma burst out laughing. "No, dear son. You came later after we moved here to the flatlands." She tipped his hat over his eyes. "Help me move buffalo hides in for them? Then we'll be ready for supper."

THE SWEET AROMA of cooked meat made Emma's mouth water before she walked into the house. She found Betty sitting at the table while Anna and Grace busied themselves setting bowls of vegetables and potatoes amongst the plates and silverware.

"My, my. You two are a force to be reckoned with." Emma quickly washed her hands at the sink. "This all looks delicious."

Grace beamed. "Anna said she's gonna teach me how to cook."

"Going to," Anna softly corrected.

Emma watched as Grace looked at Anna with adoring eyes. A tinge of jealousy passed through her, but the screams of the eagles in her mind quickly dissipated it. The spirits always have a reason. If Grace, and for that matter, all of them, were proceeding down the path intended, then she would accept that.

When the food had been placed on the table, they all sat down and began eating. Emma's stomach had been hard with worry all day and hadn't at all insisted on food. But now, it seemed to loosen and sent a ravenous signal.

"When can we go see Pa?" Henry said through a mouthful of meat.

Emma sighed. "I don't know." She glanced at Betty and then to Henry. She set her knife and fork down. "After I saw your Pa, I went to the livery to arrange sale of the horses. Unfortunately, because I'd never been there before, I was run out."

"What? Why?" Anna exclaimed.

"Because she's Indian," Betty muttered and clenched her knife and fork so hard her knuckles paled.

"But how will we sell the horses?" Henry drew his eyebrows together with worry.

"We'll just have to wait until your Pa gets better, is all." Emma suddenly lost her appetite again when the weight of her words settled in. The horses were their only source of money.

"How will we have money to eat?" Grace surprised Emma by making the connection first.

"Don't you worry. We'll manage." Emma did her best to put up a false front as if everything was going to be okay. But deep down, despite the eagle's assurances, she knew they were in for some hard times.

LATER, AFTER SHE'D tucked Henry and Grace into their respective beds, she returned to the table where Anna and Betty sat. All the food had been eaten and clean up was shared by all, except Henry, who'd agreed to check on the horses, unroll the buffalo hides, and add a few blankets in the tepee for Anna and Betty.

Anna slid a cup of hot tea toward Emma when she sat down.

"Thank you." Emma stared into the hot tannin colored liquid.

"I don't mean to pry, Emma," Anna scooted her chair closer to the table. "If you can't sell your horses, how *will* your family survive?"

Emma shook her head. "I'm not sure yet. John will be laid up for a long time. And when he comes home, there'll be another mouth to feed besides the five of us."

Betty put her cup on the table. "I would loan you some money, but I seem to have unexpectedly come up short." She growled in irritation and mumbled, "damned banker," under her breath.

"Wait, did you just mention the banker?" Anna fixed Betty with a stare.

"Yes. The bastard stole most of my money. He's also the one who banged me up."

"He hit you while in the bank?" Anna's eyes grew wide.

Betty sighed and shook her head. "No." She paused. "I hope neither of you think ill of me. I run Big Nosed Kitty's."

"The saloon?"

Betty chuckled. "You ask a lot of questions, but yes."

Anna opened and closed her mouth like she wanted to say something. Apparently, she gave up on politeness. "You're Kitty? And you're a—?"

"A prostitute, or as I prefer, madam. Yes, to both questions."

"And that banker stole your money?" Anna shook her head. "I had to interview with him for the teacher position. But I was told I was too late, that it had already been filled."

"You must be joking." Betty leaned back into her chair and lifted a single eyebrow.

"I'll have you know, I'm very suited to be a teacher. I may be a large woman, but . . . " Anna hesitated for a moment to take a breath.

Betty held her hand up. "What I was trying to say is that I heard that the position is still open. One of my girl's, er, clients, told me that no one suitable has been found yet."

"When did you hear this?"

"Just this morning as a matter of fact."

Anna slammed her hand down on the table. "That bastard." She glanced around and then at Emma. "Oh. Sorry. I hope I didn't wake the children."

Emma snorted. "No need to worry. They can both sleep through the viciousness of a blizzard."

"I just remembered something." Betty set her tea on the table. "Our esteemed banker also owns the livery. So, I'm sure he delegates everything that happens there as well."

"I can't believe this." Anna stood up and paced. "All three of us have had run-ins with that horse's behind."

"Apparently so." Betty sighed. "But there isn't a dang thing we can do about it."

"That man should pay for what he's done." Anna's face had turned red in response to her anger. "But we're just women. There's nothing we can do."

"Oro Fino doesn't have a sheriff, so even if we proved his wrongdoing, it wouldn't matter." Betty patted her injured lip and glowered.

"Emma, you've been very quiet. It would seem you'd have something to say as well." Anna placed both hands on the table in front of her.

Emma blinked quickly and looked up at Anna. "I do have something to say. But I think you should sit down for this."

Anna glanced at Betty who nodded.

"You could begin by telling me why it was so important to bring me here." Betty frowned. "You did promise to explain."

"That I did," Emma said and smiled reassuringly. "The Shoshoni, the tribe of my People, believe in spirits with supernatural power. They are called *puha*. They are the guardian spirits of the Shoshoni visionaries."

"What's that have to do with all the tea in China?" Anna folded her arms over her amble bosom.

Emma looked directly at Betty. "Do you remember when the hummingbird visited me at the river?"

Betty's eyes widened. "Yes. I've never seen anything like that. Anna, it flew in and hovered in front of Emma like it was trying to tell her something."

Anna rolled her eyes and shook her head in disbelief.

"I've heard of Indians having visions, but I thought it only happened to young boys."

"That is usually the case. But it happened to me as an adult. When my first husband died, I wandered deep into the trees to mourn his passing. I didn't care about my pain, only his loss. I had no food or water with me and eventually I lay down in a hollow, wanting to die, my grief was so deep. Deep into the night, the Bear spirit came to me in a dream."

Anna loosened her arms and clutched her throat. "Weren't you frightened?"

"Terribly so. But even though Bear spirit looks like a bear, he is different from the bear in that he suddenly appears and disappears. He is like a shadow, a *hïgiɛxn*. He has a bear's form, but is a spirit. But he has nothing to do with the animal bear."

"Can he be other animals?" Betty's voice held no disbelief.

"Yes. Although he is conceived as a spirit, he can appear as a bear, a wolf, an eagle—"

"Or a hummingbird," Betty said.

"Yes."

"I don't understand."

"Anna," Betty said. "Emma was visited today by her guardian spirit."

"Twice."

Betty and Anna looked at Emma in amazement.

"Your hummingbird followed us here?"

"No. *Puha* showed himself in the form of an eagle this time." Emma was secretly pleased she now had Betty's full attention and hopefully support.

"I find that hard to believe. I didn't see any eagles land here. And I was watching you earlier." Betty narrowed her eyes.

Emma smiled. "You wouldn't have. He talked to me from the sky."

"Okay, this is getting weird. And what exactly did this eagle say?" Anna raised her eyebrows.

"There is one thing you must know. Eagles are very solitary. Unless they are mating in the sky, you only ever see one."

"So?"

"*Puha* came to me as three eagles."

There was silence in the room as Emma gave the two women a minute for it to sink in.

Betty was the first to speak. "Are the three of us supposed to be together?"

"Wait a minute," Anna said. "Your *Puha* brought us together. For what reason?"

"I believe it is to make things right." Emma leaned in toward Anna and Betty and set her elbows on the table.

"With whom? Your spirit?" Betty tilted her head and pursed her lips.

"No. *Puha* wants us to make things right . . . for us." Emma suddenly felt a sense of calm worm its way through her chest. But what did the guardian want? She closed her eyes and behind her eyelids she saw the eagles again. But this time, instead of their black coloring against the sky, they morphed into bright gold, which radiated every which way from their bodies.

"How?" Anna stared at her blankly.

Emma stood up and took her cup to the sink. "Oro Fino doesn't have a sheriff you say?"

"Not yet. There's been talk, but so far nobody has stepped up."

"I'm surprised," Anna said. "Especially with all the gold the miners are bringing in."

"There's not a lot you can do with raw gold here. So, they turn it in at the bank and collect their bills and coin."

"Is your friend the only employee in the bank?"

"He's not my friend," Anna and Betty declared at the same time. They looked at each other, giggled, and shook their heads.

"Well, I'm glad we have that sorted now. Given what happened at the livery today, he's not my friend either. But you haven't answered my question."

Anna looked at Betty and shrugged. "I've no idea."

"I've never seen anyone in the bank with Clarence, other than patrons. No doubt the fool doesn't trust anyone with him behind the counter." Betty frowned. "What are you getting at, Emma? You're asking some very odd questions."

Emma felt her heart rate rise in anticipation of the solution she was going to propose. She bit her lower lip, sat down, and clasped her hands on the table in front of her. "The way I see it, all three of us have a vendetta against the banker."

Anna covered her mouth with her hand and looked at her with widened eyes. She shook her head. "No. I will not be a part of a conspiracy to commit murder."

"Don't be ridiculous. We're not going to kill him, silly."

"You can't be serious." Betty shook her head and placed her hand against her breastbone. "You want to rob the bank?" Her shoulders shook as she laughed. "I've never heard of anything so preposterous in my life."

Emma opened her hands and spread them wide. "Exactly."

"We can't rob a bank, Emma. We're women." Anna waved her off.

Betty met Emma's eyes and a slow smile grew on her face. They both turned their heads and stared at Anna.

"No, no, no, no. Are you crazy? Obviously, you both are. Who ever heard of a woman, let alone three, robbing a bank?" Anna glared at Betty. "You can't mean it. You agree with her? You would actually do this? Rob a bank."

"He did steal from me. All I want is what's mine." Betty chuckled. "And maybe a bit more."

Anna stared at Betty with her mouth hanging open.

"Anna, look at me." Anna slowly tore her eyes away from Betty. "I can't do this unless we're all in."

"Why? Why can't you leave me out of this?"

"Because *Puha* said three. Me, Betty . . . and you."

"He did rob you of a job. That has to be worth something, doesn't it?" Betty got up, put her hands on Anna's shoulders, and looked at Emma. "Do you really think this could work?"

Emma shrugged. "Three bandits. They'd only expect men. Not women. And certainly not us."

# Chapter Seven

"DO YOU REALLY think we can get away with it?" Anna pressed her lips together and shared a look with Betty.

"Yes. I do. Nobody will ever recognize us."

"Emma," Betty said. "I hate to put a damper on this. But aren't all your horses branded?"

"Mhmm. Good point. The ones we use regularly are, but we have stock that aren't. Those are in with the herd that John and Henry were trying to bring in."

Anna sighed. "Too bad they weren't able to get them here before all this happened."

"Anna, if John hadn't broken his legs, you and Betty would still be in the same predicament."

"Oh. Yeah." Anna rolled her eyes and giggled. "I'm such a dunce sometimes."

"Coming from a teacher, that's a little scary." Betty refilled their cups with coffee. She turned to Emma. "Do you have a plan?"

"No."

Anna tucked her hands behind her elbows. "We obviously can't just waltz into the bank and demand he hand over all his money. We'll need disguises and maybe a gun. But I'm not holding any gun. You can do that." Her knee bounced up and down with nervousness.

"That's fine. You can get the money out of the safe then."

"You make it sound so easy, Emma. What if someone comes in while you're holding Clarence at gunpoint? What if one of us slips up and talks? He'll know we're women then. Hell, he'd know my voice." Betty tapped the table with her fingernails to seemingly drive her point home.

Anna looked at Emma expectantly. "So many questions. Oh! And what is your husband going to say when he finds out?"

"I haven't figured that out yet either. Look, it's late. I think we should all go to bed, and we can discuss this again tomorrow. We have a lot of work to do before any of us actually walks through those bank doors."

Betty stretched her arms over her head and yawned. "That sounds like a brilliant idea. Where would you like me to sleep?"

"Henry and I raised a tepee near the barn. I think you'll both be very comfortable in it. Betty, you'll need something to sleep in. I'll be right back."

Emma disappeared into her bedroom and returned with a nightgown. "You and I are about the same size. This should fit nicely."

Betty accepted the long flannel gown. "Thank you. Are you planning on visiting your husband tomorrow?"

"I was hoping to sneak in unnoticed, yes."

"May I accompany you so that I can retrieve some of my own clothing?"

Emma grinned brightly. "So, you'll stay?"

Betty snorted. "If we can pull off what you're planning, then it gives me hope that horse's ass will get what he deserves."

"Just one more thing. John can't know about any of this. It's going to be hard enough not raising questions with the children."

"Mums the word," Anna said, making a zipping gesture across her lips with two pinched fingers.

Emma pulled Betty into a hug and then raised an arm to include Anna. "People will be talking about us three for a long time."

"Only they'll be referring to 'them three, whoever they are.'" Anna giggled. "I'll admit to being scared shitless. But this might be the most excitement I've had in my entire life."


ANNA HELD THE oil lantern in front of her that Emma had given them as they made their way to the tepee. Betty walked right beside her. When the light cast against the white hides of the tepee, Anna stopped.

"I've read about these things, but I've never seen one in real life. They're a lot bigger than I would've ever thought. I certainly never imagined I'd be staying in one." Anna lifted the lantern higher. "Interesting."

Betty nudged her. "May I suggest you wait until it's light out to examine it further? I'm exhausted."

"Oh. Sure. Sorry." Anna pushed aside the drop, stooped over, and walked in.

Two huge bison hides lay spread with the fur up next to each other with rolled up woolen blankets on each end.

"Oh. We have to sleep on the ground then?" Anna noticed her suitcase had been brought in. She'd packed it again before she left for breakfast to keep any mice out and to keep the musty old hide smell from permeating her clothes. She sniffed the air. It smelled fresh, unlike the dusty barn or the stagnant water scent of the hide room.

"Looks like it. But I'm betting these are more comfortable than a lot of beds I've slept on." Betty pried her shoes off and placed them next to the hide on the left.

Anna raised an eyebrow and decided not to remark. She set the oil lamp down and rummaged in her suitcase for her nightgown. Once she had it, she and Betty turned their backs to each other for privacy while they changed.

"Are you dressed?" Anna dared not look.

Betty answered a few seconds later. "Yes, you can turn around now."

Anna watched as Betty laid down on the buffalo hide and pulled a blanket up over her.

"How is it?" Anna grunted as she knelt down and rubbed her hands through the thick pelt.

"It's actually quite nice and warm," Betty replied sleepily.

Anna relented and sprawled out on the other hide. The pelt seemed to instantly radiate warmth and the long fur felt like it was hugging her. She used one of the blankets as a pillow and pulled the other up over her. She pushed herself up on an elbow and extinguished the lamp, plunging the tepee into complete darkness.

It wasn't long before her eyes adjusted to the complete lack of light. And then she noticed the opening at the top of the tepee, giving view to a million stars. She stared, enthralled, until sleep claimed her.


THE NEXT MORNING broke sunny and cool. Anna snuggled under the blanket and relished the comfort and warmth. Betty snored softly beside her and showed no signs of waking. Unlike the morning before, when she woke in the barn, stiff from the cot and her nose full of dirty mucous, Anna felt refreshed, revived, and without any residual discomfort. Of course, she hadn't moved yet to test the lack of pain. She knew well that her joints were very likely just waiting for a first move to make their presence known in the form of cold aches and inflexibility.

Anna heard scratching on the drop flap.

"Anna," Grace whispered. "Are you awake yet?"

Anna sighed, knowing she couldn't ignore Grace, nor put off waking her joints. She extruded herself from beneath the blanket and heaved to her feet. Her knees crackled noisily but didn't complain like they usually did. Before she pushed aside the drop, she blew out a big breath. Her heart beat fast against her chest from the exertion, the result of being overweight.

She looked back to make sure Betty was still sleeping, finger combed her hair, and sported a smile before opening the flap. "Good morning."

"Hi." Grace bounced on the balls of her feet. "Wanna help me milk the cow?"

"Want to," Anna gently corrected.

"Yeah. So do you?"

"I didn't even know you owned a cow."

"Well, we don't really own it, own it."

Anna cocked her head and raised her eyebrows. "Is this a make believe cow we're supposedly milking?"

"No, silly." Grace put her hands on her hips. "Make believe is for kids."

"Grace, I just don't understand what you're saying then. Do you or don't you have a cow?" Anna felt the beginnings of a headache. Or maybe it was her body calling out for a strong cup of coffee.

"There's one behind the barn." Grace shrugged quickly.

Anna moaned. She obviously was going to have to play Grace's little game in order to get any answers . . . and coffee and breakfast. Her stomach growled at the thought, competing with the ache in her head calling for caffeine.

"All right. Yes, I will help you milk your imaginary cow. Just give me a minute to get dressed."

Determination flashed over Grace's face a moment before Anna turned back into the tepee. She quickly pulled a clean, light blue dress out of her suitcase, stripped out of the nightgown, and slid it over her head. The big bulk of material slid down her body easily and she buttoned up the neckline.

After sliding into her shoes, she walked outside, and squinted against the bright sun. Grace had pushed up her sleeves and picked up a bucket that Anna hadn't noticed until now.

"Lead on, McDuff."

Grace gave her a quizzical look, but didn't comment.

Anna shaded her eyes with her hand and looked at the ground to get some relief. She followed Grace around to the back of the barn and ran into her with her big belly when Grace came to a sudden halt. "Oh! I'm sorry."

Grace stood with her legs apart and hands on her hips. "See?" She pointed in front of her.

Anna raised her focus and looked in the direction Grace indicated. She squeezed her eyes shut in disbelief. She opened them, and the cow was still there. But it wasn't any ordinary cow. Aside from her rangy and spotted hide, her huge belly pulled her skin taut over her back and hips. The cow had horns that looked as long as Anna was tall. The cow's udder was swollen with milk, and as they stood there, she dipped her head low and bawled at them.

"She wants to be milked," Grace stated bluntly.

"So, I've gathered. What is it you want me to do?" Anna swallowed hard.

"Have you ever milked a cow before?" Grace frowned.

"Uh. No. I can't say as I have had that experience." Anna looked at the cow's sharp hooves. There was no way she was going near them. Or that huge, swollen udder. And if she were honest, she wasn't even sure if she'd be able to bend down that far, let alone see what she was doing with her own belly in the way.

"Okay. You can be in charge of the front then. I'll do the milking."

"In charge of the front? What does that entail?"

Grace shrugged. "Not much. You just have to keep her attention so she doesn't run off while I'm milking her."

Anna bit her lip and looked at the cow, whose long tongue slid out and dipped into each of her nostrils before disappearing into her mouth again. Anna swallowed her revulsion and squished her eyebrows together. *How the heck does one keep a cow occupied?*

Obviously, Grace read her confusion and giggled. "It's really easy. She likes to be scritched under her jaw. Sometimes she likes to be rubbed between her eyes, but it depends on her mood."

Anna nodded and poked her tongue into her cheek. "Right." She took a deep breath and blew it out slowly. She could do this, despite her intense desire to flee. She pasted on a smile, curled and uncurled her fingers, and said, "Well, let's get on with it then."

The cow whipped her tail around as Grace carried the pail toward her backend. She flung her head back toward her shoulder at an errant fly. Long strings of saliva flew everywhere and reflected in the sunlight.

Anna moved forward quietly and approached the cow with an outstretched hand. Her mouth was dry, and her head took up a heavier pounding.

"Hello, cow. We're going to take this nice and easy, aren't we?" Anna tentatively patted the wet nose.

The cow extended her neck and bawled in Anna's face. A malodorous smell, somewhat sweet, somewhat gaseous, insulted her nose. Anna coughed and covered her face with her forearm.

The cow moved her hind end to the side.

"Come on cow," Grace complained from the back. "Anna, are you scritching her?"

"Uh." Anna stepped to the side of the cow's head and rubbed under the huge jaw. The hair was thick and coarse. Oily dirt coated Anna's fingertips and wedged grossly under her fingernails. Anna curled her lip and continued a methodical stroke, which oddly kept time with the soft splash as the milk hit the bottom of the bucket.

*This isn't too bad once you get used to the smell.*

A sudden wet plopping noise sounded from the back.

"Aw, cow. You couldn't wait to do that until after I was done?" Grace sighed loudly.

Anna chuckled. She decided she would much rather be subjected to the cow's smelly burp than get pooped on. From the tone of Grace's voice, Anna guessed it wasn't the first time the cow decided to defecate while being milked.

By the time Anna accompanied Grace to the cabin, her stomach had set up a chorus of growls and gurgles. This apparently amused Grace to no end because she giggled every time she heard it.

"Don't worry Anna's stomach," Grace said between titters. "It won't be long now."

"Ha. Ha." Anna retorted. "Very funny." But to be honest, she really did hope breakfast would be soon. She couldn't remember the last time when she'd been so hungry.


BETTY AND EMMA were already sitting at the table sipping coffee when Anna and Grace strolled in.

Emma smiled at them as she rose and poured another cup and set it on the table.

"Which end did Grace put you in charge of?"

Anna rolled her eyes. "If it had been up to her, I would've been the one in back while she made nice-nice with that beast. Fortunately, though, I don't know how to milk a cow."

"That's tomorrow's lesson," Grace said from the sink where she set the bucket.

Betty giggled. "Lucky you."

"It's only fair, I think." Grace moved to Emma's side. "Anna teaches me, and I get to teach her something."

Emma chuckled. "Are you up for this?"

"Hmm." Anna closed her eyes as she swallowed her first sip of coffee. "As long as I have coffee, I can do anything."

"Well, that's good to know," Grace said, and looked at Anna with the devil in her eye.

# Chapter Eight

"I'M GOING BACK into town today." Emma rose from her chair and took her cup to the sink.

"Do you think that's wise?" Anna said from the table.

Emma turned around and crossed her arms over her chest. "I need to see my husband."

"And I'm going with her so I can pick up some things from my room." Betty rose as well. "Don't worry. I doubt anyone will see Emma. It's usually deserted around Doc's place in the morning. And I'm a master at being discrete."

"Okay. Just promise me you'll both be careful."

Emma gave Anna a reassuring smile as Grace put her arms around her waist and squeezed. She hugged her back. "You and Henry listen to Anna, okay?"

"Yes, Mum."

"Speaking of Henry, where is he?" Anna craned her neck toward where the children slept.

"He got up early to check on the herd. He should be back by the time the sun is high. Betty and I shouldn't be long afterward." Emma rubbed Grace's back with affection. "You listen to Anna, all right?"

"Yes, Mum. Don't worry. We'll be fine. Tell Pa I miss him and to come home soon."

"I will, *Teai*."

Grace craned her neck toward Anna and smiled. "That means 'little one' in Shoshone."

Anna chuckled. "Well then. Thank you. Maybe you can teach me some new words after our lesson."

Emma pried Grace's arms off her and gently pushed her toward Anna. She watched as her daughter leaned against Anna's ample belly as opposed to trying to wriggle herself onto her small lap.

"I'll be outside hitching up the wagon." Emma took a coat from an antler peg nailed to the wall and slid her arms into it. As an afterthought, she hefted the small .22 rifle into the crook of her arm.

"I'll be there in a few minutes." Betty followed Emma outside and left her to go into the tepee.

Emma pulled the light cart out of the barn and draped the harness over one of the shafts. She whistled once and within moments the pounding of hooves signaled Coal racing to greet her at the gate. He nickered affectionately as she approached him.

"Ready to go again, big guy?"

Coal tossed his head in seeming agreement. His long mane and forelock accentuated his movements. He put his muzzle to her cheek and inhaled. Emma opened the gate, stood in front of him, and gently blew into his nostrils.

Emma's father had taught her the language of horses when she was little. Eventually when she was older, she was allowed to help with the training. While the boys tended the herd, she'd taught horses to allow someone on their backs. Coal was the last horse she'd trained for the tribe before she'd met John, and she'd always shared a special bond with the horse.

She stood to his side, grabbed a handful of mane, and vaulted onto his back. With her legs as guides, she rode him to where Betty waited by the cart and then maneuvered him between the wagon shafts. She put her hands on Coal's withers, pushed herself back onto his rump, and slid off behind him.

"That was impressive." Betty smiled broadly.

Emma winked at her mischievously. "Most Injuns can do that."

They shared a laugh while Emma put the harness over Coal's back and hooked him to the cart. When he opened his mouth for the bit, she slipped the bridle over his ears and attached the long lines.

She climbed into the seat and offered Betty a hand up. But Betty waved her off.

"If we're going to be convincing as men folk, I'd best be doing men folk things." She hiked her dress up over her knee. As she put her foot onto the back step, she simultaneously grabbed the tailboard and pulled herself up. When she finally plopped onto the seat next to Emma, she was a tad out of breath. "There. That wasn't so bad, right?"

Emma bit back a smile. "With a little practice and a fitting pair of trousers, you'll get the hang of it."

Betty nodded. "I think so."

Emma gathered the reins and jiggled them over Coal's back. "Come on, black boy, let's get a move on."

Coal leaned into the harness and gathered enough momentum to move into a ground-covering jog. He tossed his head and grunted. Emma knew it took a lot for the horse to refrain from breaking into a gallop. He'd been trained to do so as soon as his rider was settled onto his back. Sometimes it could be a matter of life or death depending on the horse's ability to do that . . . for horse and rider.

They drove in silence for a while, the jingling of the harness and the creak of the wagon were the only sounds. Emma loved the beauty of the prairie that was wild and full of color, alternating between the blues of fescue and wheatgrass. The bunch grasses grew in clumps and shared the space with wildflowers such as lupine, hawkweed, and paintbrush. Shadows on the rolling hills where the sun hadn't yet reached, changed the hues of colors to quieter shades.

Emma smiled when she saw Betty close her eyes for a moment and offer her face up to the sun's warmth.

"It is very difficult to travel quickly through here. Everywhere you look is *baaru gwahavit*."

Betty squinted against the bright sunlight. "What is that?"

Emma pursed her lips and shook her head. "Sometimes I have a hard time with the English words. John helps me most times. It means, hmm, many colors, like what you see in the sky after rain."

"Ah, rainbow."

"Yes! That's it. My people live mainly in the *yoyapitta*. You call them mountains. But when John brought me here, I had never seen so many colors I don't have names for."

"I realized something today. I've spent the better part of the last ten years cooped up between four solid walls under a dark roof. I had the best sleep last night and woke up with not much of a worry." Betty looked at Emma and put her hand on her arm. "I want to thank you for that. If you hadn't whisked me off yesterday, I'm not sure what would've happened to me."

"We help each other. You and Anna are meant to be here. The spirits have spoken."

"We'd best listen then."

Emma slowed Coal to a walk to forge the shallow but rocky creek bed.

"You said you had a worry."

Betty sighed and frowned. "I didn't want to say anything in front of Anna, for fear of insulting her. But," she said and briefly bit her bottom lip. "What we're planning, this bank robbery—Well, do you think Anna will be able to help pull it off without giving away the fact that we're women? I mean—her weight I guess is what I'm most concerned about. And the poor dear doesn't even know how to ride."

"Do you? Know how to ride, I mean?"

"It's been a number of years, other than yesterday's wild adventure behind you, that is. But yes, I think I can still stay on top of a horse. I might need a bit of practice."

Emma stayed silent until she'd safely guided Coal onto solid ground. She lightly slapped the reins on the horse's back, sending him into a slow jog. "It will take time before we can carry it out. I need to get my husband back home. We will teach Anna how to ride. Things will work out. You'll see."

When they reached the rise that looked out over the town, Emma maneuvered Coal and the wagon out of the blazing sun and into the shadows of a thick stand of white pine trees. The soft needles silenced their passage and made it easy for them to stay hidden while taking advantage of the comings and goings of town traffic. The mixed scent of cinnamon and yeast made their hiding place that much more lovely.

Betty stood up in the wagon and shaded her eyes with a cupped hand. "I don't think anyone is watching for us, do you?"

"Probably not. But I don't want to be surprised if there is." Emma watched as teams of horses pulled heavily laden wagons in the direction of the gold fields. In front of them rose the giant green and brown walls of the Bitterroots, the range stretching away on either hand in violet and deep blue masses. "I'm going to back track a little so that I come into town right behind Doc's house. Will you be all right to go from there?"

"Yes. Of course." Betty sat back down and put her hand on Emma's arm. "I understand your need to be guarded. But you can't be overly cautious as to raise suspicion."

Emma nodded. Betty was right. To a point. She'd overheard too many stories as a child. When her mother and father thought she was asleep, she'd actually been alert and listening from the buffalo hide that covered her, to the horrors inflicted upon hers and neighboring tribes. The white man had a lot to answer for. To this day it still amazed her that she'd fallen in love and bore two children with a man whose face was as pale as the driven snow.

It took a bit of time and skill to navigate Coal and the wagon through the trees. She'd overestimated the gap a couple of times and had to ask Coal to painstakingly push the wagon backward. Betty was quite helpful in lifting low hanging branches up and over their heads as they went.

Finally, the way became clear, and Emma could make out the roof of the doctor's house peeking just over the top of the hill. She once again pulled the wagon to a stop and surveyed the surrounding area. "See anything?"

Betty shook her head. "I'd say it's all clear."

Emma nodded and took a deep breath. She was anxious to see John, but she didn't want that to override caution. Her shoulders hurt from the tension of expectation. She watched Coal's ears closely. He had an inert ability to let her know when danger was ahead. But so far, his ears remained relaxed and perked.

A soft breeze announced their arrival as Emma brought the horse and wagon to a stop in the same place as when they'd brought John just two days prior. Other than that, all was quiet.

"I'll meet you back here," Betty said as she hopped down. "I'll be quick. But you spend as much time as you need with your husband."

Emma nodded. She set the brake and wrapped the reins around it. After a cautious glance around, she jumped to the ground and strode into the doctor's house.

"Oh, hello." Jake set his glasses on the desk and rose from the chair. "I was hoping you'd come in today."

Emma narrowed her eyes. "Is my husband all right?" She studied Doc, mentally daring him to lie to her.

He clasped his hands in front of him, dipped his chin, and stared at the floor for a moment, seemingly to collect his thoughts. Or come up with excuses. She wasn't sure which.

Growing increasingly suspicious, Emma spun on her heel and marched to the surgery where she'd last seen John.

"Mrs. Kauffman, wait."

She ignored the doctor and despite his hurried footsteps behind her, she pushed through the door and gasped. "John!"

John lay beneath a pile of blankets. His teeth chattered. He moaned in pain every time his body shook as apparent fever wracked his body. His face was drawn and pale. He looked at her with dull weepy eyes. "a'ni ki."

Despite Emma's concern, she smiled at his pet name for her. One time when John was courting her, a flock of mountain chickadees flew into the trees around them. One took a particular liking to her and sat on her shoulder for several minutes before rejoining its flock.

"natainnappettsi. You're sick." She looked at Jake with accusing eyes. "What have you done to him?"

He raised his hands in surrender. "He took fever in the middle of the night. Unfortunately, your husband isn't responding to any of the medicine I have here."

Emma brushed the sweaty hair back from John's brow and stood up. "I will take him to my People."

Doc shook his head. "I'm sorry but I think he would do better here so I can monitor him."

"Like you've done so far? No. He needs my People's medicine." Emma stared hard into Doc's eyes. "He will only die here with your white man medicine."

Doc shook his head in resignation. "I don't like it. But I'll admit there's a lot of medicine that your People know and I don't. Let's say I do let you take him."

Emma raised an eyebrow, not sure what to expect.

"When he gets well, will you come back and tell me what your medicine man did?"

She stood unflinchingly and considered his request. Finally, she nodded. "I will need your help to load him into my wagon."

"I will give you some morphine pills for him. It's best if he sleeps as much as possible. Then you'll know he is without pain. Give him plenty of water while he still has this fever. If you do that, he should survive the trip up the mountains." Doc turned toward the shelves of pills, took a bottle down, and shook a large handful into another smaller bottle. With Emma's help, John managed to swallow four of the white pills with several sips of water.

They used nearly all of Doc's blankets to pad the back of the wagon to make John as comfortable as possible. They gently slid John onto a board.

Betty arrived just as they were about to lift him and begin the slow walk to the wagon. "Let me help." She quickly moved to Emma's end and grabbed one side.

Between the three of them, they managed to carefully shuffle their way to the wagon and position John in the least painful way possible, which was difficult given the wooden splints on his legs.

With John safely stowed in the back, Emma and Betty climbed onto the wagon seat. Emma unwrapped the reins from the break lever and released it.

Doc stepped back. "Good luck to you. I hope your People can help your husband."

"They will," Emma said confidently. She slapped the reins on Coal's back. The horse leaned into his harness and picked up a trot as if he instinctively knew there was a need for urgency. He tossed his head, black mane flowing freely as he surged forward.

Emma glanced down, seeing for the first time, the small bag at Betty's feet. "You didn't bring much."

"Didn't see the need to bring any frocks with me. I left them for the girls. Just brought the important stuff." Betty looked over her shoulder. "He's in a bad way, isn't he?"

Emma took a deep breath. Butterflies born of nerves rose and fought to escape through her chest. Up until now, she'd been acting on impulse. With Betty now at her side, she allowed her fear to show, and a silent tear rolled down her cheek. "I have to take him to Crow Old Man so he can drive the sickness from him."

"Back to your village? But won't that be a dangerous trip for him?"

"It is the only choice I have."

"I'll go with you."

"We'll all go." Emma glanced at Betty. "I will need yours and Anna's help. When we get to the village, the children can stay with their father. They'll be safe and well taken care of. And we can carry out our plan."

"You've thought this out." Betty frowned.

"It's what I must do."

"Then we will do it."

John groaned in the back. Without a word, Betty crawled over the back of the seat, put John's head in her lap, and offered him some water.

Emma got lost in her own thoughts as Coal took them home. She'd never seen John so sick. Her village was a strong three days' ride once they got into the mountains. The wagon could only take them so far into the foothills. She'd have to fashion a travois to move John over the rocky terrain from there. She shook her head in doubt. Was she doing the right thing in taking him to Crow Old Man? She only hoped her decision wasn't one that the spirits disproved of. If they did, they would take him from her, and she couldn't live with that.

# Chapter Nine

"I'LL STAY AND take care of the farm." Henry's hardened eyes reflected his determination to be granted the responsibility.

"No, my son. We all must make the trip." Emma rested her hands on Henry's shoulders.

He shook his head. "Think about it, Mother. If we all go, it'll just slow you down." He pointed his chin at Anna. "I overheard her say she doesn't ride. You can't take a wagon into the mountains and walking that far would be impossible."

Emma sighed. She knew her son was right. It would cost precious time. Time that John didn't have. "You can't stay here alone. Grace and Anna will stay with you." Anna nodded agreement. "Betty, can you come with me? I don't think I can handle the trip alone."

Betty pushed away from the table where they were filling packs with food and other items required for the trip. "Of course. I'll collect some things from the tepee."

Aware that they'd need to leave immediately, Emma opted to leave John sleeping in the back of the wagon instead of moving him unnecessarily. Now that the decision had been made for only the three of them to make the trip, there were fewer things to gather.

"Henry, go catch and saddle Snowdrift for Betty. Make sure you tie on a bedroll and scabbard. We'll be taking the Winchester."

"I'll get a couple bags of oats too," he said and hurried out the door. Emma heard his whistle for the grey mare as she shoved the last of the dried meat into an empty flour bag.

In an uncanny organized fashion, the five met at the wagon with parcels filled with food, cooking items, and extra padding for John. At the last minute, Henry fetched a buffalo hide and with his help Emma tucked it closely around John to keep him as immobile as possible.

She brushed hair back from his face and whispered, "natainnappettsi, Crow Old Man will mend you."

Emma appraised the wagon approvingly, and nodded to Betty, who had changed into a pair of grey wool trousers and a long sleeved, pale cotton shirt. She herself had donned her full deerskin outfit. It was customary for Indian women to wear a dress, but Emma had found trousers to be more useful when traveling or working with stock. Fringe fell from the sleeves and sides of her leggings. The shirt was decorated with beadwork, shells, elk teeth, and porcupine quills. The red, yellow, blue, and black colors readily identified her as a member of the tribe of which she was always welcome.

A vast silence reigned over the land. The prairie grasses were still, and shadows of clouds sat immobile on the ground. It was if something were waiting. The sky suddenly came alive with the calls of two eagles all mingling but with a final clear rapid sequence of descending notes. They floated in the thermals above them, then one by one floated off towards the mountains, where Emma's people lived.

No one was lost on the irony of the eagle's message. Emma gathered the reins of the wagon and Betty mounted the white horse. "Let's go. We need to make the foothills before nightfall." She jiggled the reins over Coal's back. He leaned into the harness and slowly the wagon wheels turned.

Emma looked back twice as the distance grew between her and her children. Finally, they were but three muddled figures, distorted by the heat waves rising like a mirage.

"They'll be fine, you know, Emma." Betty rode alongside the wagon.

Emma breathed a big sigh, knowing she was right. Henry was a miniature version of his father and more than capable. She worried he would try to take on more than he needed. Grace clearly idolized Anna. She looked over to her left and gave Betty a wry smile. "You're sitting that horse well. Let up on the reins a little and she'll lower her head and be less on her toes."

"It's coming back to me. Feels good to be on a horse after all these years." Betty let a few inches of the leather slip through her hand and then settled the borrowed straw hat deeper on her head.

"Give it a few hours, and you'll be wanting to sit on the wagon next to me."

"You do remember what I used to do for a living." Betty raised the back of a hand to her chin and batted her eyes in a come hither fashion.

It took Emma a few seconds to comprehend before chuckling. She relaxed a bit and pondered the miraculousness of this woman coming into her life. Anna as well. The spirits had guided her for as long as she could remember. The difference was, the visions had always been related to those close to her, or an animal. They'd never reached out to bring strangers into her life. She studied the back of Betty as Snowdrift's long strides put her alongside Coal. When was the last time she'd had a woman friend? It had been more moons than she could remember. As a youngster, she ran amok with the tribe's children. Then as she matured, she focused on learning the duties of young adult, both in the tepee and with the horses. She'd spent equal time with mother and father.

The river was just beyond the next rise. They would water the horses and fill canteens there. The ground was dry on these prairies. In between storms there was oftentimes long periods with no rain. But sometimes the storms were nothing more than lightning and noise. The air tasted as dry as ash. Or maybe it was the stress she felt in regards to what she was attempting. At any rate, the cold glacial water from the mountains would be a welcome relief, albeit temporary, until they reached the foothills.

The sound of the river rose to meet them as they approached. Fortunately, the water was slow where Emma planned to cross. Large boulders were spattered downstream just before white capped rapids began their voyage down a steep drop and around sharp bends. The bank was flatter on the far side and a good place to stop. The sloshing and dull thuds of hooves and wagon wheels meeting the rocks beneath the surface mixed with the cool breeze generated by the water's flow. Coal had to pull hard against the current and rocks, causing the wagon to jostle. John moaned in his sleep. Aside from a few stumbles, both horses made it across with relative ease.

Once across, both women dismounted. While the horses drank, Betty filled canteens, and after wetting a bandanna, Emma climbed onto the wagon to check on John. She wiped the dust from his face and neck, relieved to find his fever had subsided a bit. He slowly licked his lips, so she squeezed a few drops of water from the cloth into his mouth. She watched as he worked the moisture around with his tongue. John's eyes fluttered open. "More, please."

Betty, who was now standing next to the wagon, took the bandanna to the river, rinsed it, and returned without wringing it out. She mutely handed it up to Emma.

"natainappettsi, suck on this slowly." Emma placed the tip of the cloth between his lips and held the bandanna up so he didn't have to work too hard for the moisture to flow towards his eager mouth. "Are you in pain?"

"Not. Too. Bad." His voice was raspy, yet it sounded stronger. Or maybe Emma was just being hopeful.

"It will be a little bumpier from here on. I will give you some medicine to help you sleep."

John blinked twice, then met Emma's eyes. "You wanted to see your family again." His lips quivered with the effort of a smile.

"An old buffalo doesn't hurt himself for attention." Emma fought back tears. "Crow Old Man will mend you. All will be well then." She leaned over and reached into her bag. She easily laid her hands on the bottle the doctor had given her. She removed the wooden plug and tipped one pill into her hand which she gently placed on John's tongue. "Sleep now, my love." She tucked the buffalo hide under him as deeply as she could to secure his broken body. The terrain ahead would only get rougher.

They traveled through tall poplars and cottonwoods for a while after the river crossing, which eventually gave way to great stands of oak, maple, beech, and chestnut. The sunlight was muted because of the tall, thick canopies. Patches of mountain laurel provided some color, but mostly the sound of their passing was absorbed by the various mosses and short grasses that were brave enough to attempt growth in the shadows of the tall trees.

By the time the sun touched the tips of the mountains in its slow decent into night, *Qui-am-i Winton Poot-see*, the north star, was emerging from its daytime nap. They had reached the foothills. The tall leaf canopies had given in to the statuesque pines. Emma pulled Coal to a stop when she found the familiar slab of rock.

It was tall and worn smooth by the years of weathering on the mountaintop. Many years ago, when the mountain was barren of trees, it had let loose from higher up and slid down to form a protective wall. When it had finally reached the bottom, it imbedded itself in the ground and formed a natural overhang as it tipped menacingly forward. Two large red cedar trees had grown on either side, and stood like sentries, keeping the rock from ever falling over. The trunks were massive, easily ten feet through. The natural enclosure was a perfect place to make camp.

"Someone has been here before." Betty nodded to the circle of rocks as she dismounted.

"John used this when he was building his trapline into the hills. We have been here together as well." Emma expertly navigated Coal to back the wagon nearer to the rock. She'd placed it so the heat of the fire would reflect back onto John, thereby avoiding the need to move him, but yet keep him warm.

While Betty collected larger firewood, Emma gathered dry kindling, snapping dead branches from the pines and soon had a sufficient pile in the fire circle. She removed a piece of flint from the small bag around her neck and slid a knife from a special pocket between her tall moccasin and calf. She struck the steel against the edge of the flint with quick downward motions. Using deliberate, powerful strokes, she directed the sparks toward the tinder bundle. The sparks quickly took hold, and soon small flames licked the wood. She added more from what Betty had piled nearby, and soon heat and light were reflecting off the rock and onto John, enabling Emma to easily see him. Satisfied of the wagon's positioning with regards to the fire, she unhitched Coal from the wagon and systematically removed the harness.

"Should we tie them up?" Betty loosened the girth and pulled the saddle off Snowdrift.

"They won't go too far. If they wander off, it'll just be just to graze or find some water. They'll be back before we wake in the morning." Emma gave Coal a pat on the neck. "Thank you, my friend," she murmured to him. Coal blew softly against her ear before wandering off to find some grass. After Betty removed the bridle, Snowdrift approached Emma and laid her muzzle in her hand. "My good girl." Emma placed her forehead against the horse's and rested a moment with closed eyes before releasing her as well. Soon both horses were eagerly snatching at the sparse clumps of tussock.

"You have an amazing way with them," Betty said, as she removed the various bags of food from the saddlebag.

"I spent much time with them when I was living among my People. They are friends who we share a common destiny with." Seeing that John was sleeping peacefully, she turned to help Betty prepare a meal.

Emma sat cross-legged next to the food bags. The fatigue of the last few days had settled heavily in her shoulders. She methodically massaged them before noticing Betty's appraising look.

"You just sit and let me make us some food. You've had enough to do and worry about." Betty stood up with her hands on her hips. "And to be honest, it's been years since I've had the opportunity to cook."

"How did you survive?" Emma couldn't for the life of her, remember an instance where she hadn't prepared a meal. It was her duty as wife and mother."

"My barkeep, Miles, is a very good cook." Betty mixed flour and water together and stirred. "He's also the girls' protector. He'd behave like a raging bull if anyone got rough with one of us. He would've killed Harwood if he'd known it was him."

"You didn't tell him?"

"No. That man would've caused too much trouble for too many people if Miles had confronted him. One of the girls, and Doc knew that I'd ended up at the wrong end of a fist. Clara knew who, but I swore her to secrecy. Doc was too polite to ask, I reckon."

Emma shook her head. "I have never heard of a man hurting a woman until John brought me into the white man's world. The Shoshone are so very connected with the earth and life around them that much of our sense of self comes from this bond."

"Please tell me more about your People." Betty poured the mixture into a pan and settled it on the fire to cook.

"We unite humans, animals, and plants, the physical with the spiritual, and the living with the non-living to create a sense of self which sees the wholes rather than individuals. Physical separation from the land causes my people to be disoriented and have a decreased sense of purpose."

"Us whites could learn so much from you. But they're mostly stubborn men stuck in their own ways." Betty frowned. "The women are made to believe what the men make us learn."

"But you are different."

"I've had a lot of life experiences that helped me figure out my own way without anyone's help. Well, my parents had their ideas for me when I was a little older than Henry. Things changed when my mother passed from consumption. I took care of Daddy until he died a few years later." Betty shrugged. "Couldn't live without her I guess." She moved the pan of now cooked pancake off the fire to let it cool.

"You've never been married or had children?"

"Nope. I'd been tied down long enough taking care of family, I sure didn't want to add more to it. I wanted my own life. So, I up and left Boston and headed west."

Emma wanted to ask more, but she didn't want to seem too familiar. Anyway, there were many more nights on the trail to come, and more opportunities to get to know each other better.

The night was beginning to come alive. Emma watched the slow rise of the new full moon. "Hello, daa'za-mea.'"

"Does that mean 'moon' in your language?" Betty rose to sit next to Emma.

"It means 'summer starting' moon. Each of the full moons has a name to keep track of the passing year. The next moon is called 'daza-mea' which means summer."

A barred owl called from above them, it's signature "who-cooks-for-you" interrupting their quiet conversation. It was soon answered by another in the distance. The women listened to the exchange between the birds.

A soft breeze moved the treetops as the silent cold crept in on the ground. Emma rose and added wood to the fire. "I will check on John, but you should sleep. Tomorrow will be long."

Betty took a sip from her canteen and nodded.

"Use my bedroll. I will sleep next to my husband." Emma handed it to Betty who had followed her to the wagon. She glanced at Betty as she walked toward the fire. She is a good person, she thought to herself.

From her saddle bag, she took a small piece of venison jerky, broke it in half and placed a piece in her mouth to soften it up before sliding it between John's teeth and cheek. He opened his eyes and offered her a crooked smile. "I'm glad I'm not so far gone that you thought you had to chew it for me."

Emma kissed his forehead. "You still have teeth, my kamangande. How is your pain?"

"It's there." John looked at the stars that had slowly emerged into the black sky. "We are at our special place."

"Yes. Both of our children's spirits entered me here."

"We should come here more often." John winked.

"When you are well, we'll talk about it." Emma lifted the buffalo hide and slipped underneath next to him. She adjusted the hide to cover both of them and then slid an arm over his chest. His body was still hot with fever. "Now you must sleep. The rest of our journey will be hard on you. The wagon can only go a little further before I have to move you to a travois. It scares me that you will be hurting."

"Put me to sleep with the medicine and I'll be fine."

"oos."

"How are Grace and Henry?"

"They are safe at the farm. A teacher named Anna is staying with them."

"Where did you find her? And who is the woman with us?"

Emma stroked his unshaven cheek. "It is too long of a story for tonight. We must both rest now." She doubted John had heard her last words. His breathing had slowed as he drifted into sleep. She closed her eyes and let the day's worries slip away.

# Chapter Ten

ANNA AND GRACE watched for a while until the wagon and horse and figure were swallowed by the heat shimmer.

"Why can't we see them anymore? They're not that far away." Grace shaded her eyes with her hand.

"Well, you know how the sun heats the ground?" Grace nodded and Anna continued. "It also heats the air just above it. When the sun light comes down, the hot air bends it and from a distance it acts like a mirror."

Grace looked at the ground, scuffed a foot, and then up at Anna. "It's cold in the mountains. So, it doesn't happen there."

Anna smiled at her pupil. "You are one smart young lady." She looked around for Henry, but he had silently disappeared.

"Henry is checking the horses. He used to go with Pa, but . . ." Grace shrugged.

"Your pa will be right as rain when he gets back." Anna hoped she sounded more convincing than she felt. John had sustained some horrific injuries. She wondered if he'd ever ride again, let alone walk. If he couldn't provide for his family, then it made it even more imperative to follow through with Emma's proposition. But there was a lot of work and planning to do beforehand. Foremost, the women had to come home safely.

" . . . one for you too."

Anna blinked, broken out of her thoughts by Grace's sudden enthusiasm. "I beg your pardon?"

Grace rolled her eyes and put her hands on her hips. "I said, Henry is bringing a horse back for you."

"Don't be silly. I don't know how to ride."

"I know."

"So what's the sense in . . ."

"I'm going to teach you."

"You're going to . . ."

"Teach you how to ride." Grace stared at her with determination and then smiled brightly. "I reckon it's only fair. You're teachin' me, so I'm gonna teach you somethin'. Besides, Momma said." She took Anna's hand and pulled. "Can we do some book learning for a little while today? Tomorrow you can start your learning."

Anna was too stunned to correct Grace's vocabulary. She let Grace lead her back to the house. She knew she'd eventually have to learn to ride if the plan was to go through. But she never expected to be taught by a little girl, let alone, Grace of all people. And, the biggest drawback was her weight. How could she ever, in good conscience, expect a horse to carry her fat self on its back. She already felt sick with guilt, thinking of putting a horse through that abuse. Her imagination started on track with her getting on the poor animal, its back quickly collapsing from her bulk and forever giving way to a swayback. Her feet would drag on the ground. The horse would be absolutely miserable. And she would never forgive herself, let alone ever recover from the embarrassment.

As Anna closed the door behind her, she heard the cadence of hooves, signaling Henry's return. She couldn't bring herself to glance at the poor creature whose destiny was as sad as she was pathetic.

The remainder of the day was spent coaching Grace to correctly pronounce words and make sense of how they all came together in a sentence. Grace interrupted the lesson many times to relay her own stories and ask questions about absolutely anything that happened to pop into her head. Anna listened with patience, but a few times had to redirect Grace to the task at hand.

Henry's absence was noticed, but not unexpected. Anna was sure he was doing what he thought needed to be done in his pa's place. She'd give him some time to get adjusted to her being the adult in charge and his teacher. She doubted Grace cared that Henry wasn't alongside her at the table, book open, pencil and paper at hand. Anna didn't think for one minute that Grace was selfish for her attention. It was Grace's desire to learn that she found intriguing. Not at all unlike herself when she was young. She supposed that's why she became a teacher. She not only loved to learn new things, but now the ability to pass it on to someone less knowledgeable was exciting for her. Grace was the first Indian she had ever had as a student. Well, her first student if she were honest.

One of Anna's college courses had involved the process of teaching what her instructor had called, savages. He had presented a guide to how to overcome their stupidity and stubbornness. How wrong he was in all aspects. In the short time she'd been with Emma and her children, she'd been surprised at the intelligence, good heartedness, and generosity. In fact, Anna reckoned the instructors, as well as the majority of people back East, wouldn't be able to hold a candle to the superiority of these people, and were the ones whose beliefs should change. She knew she had a lot to learn about their ways, and her zealousness for knowledge re-emerged from a dormancy she hadn't realized until just now.

Henry walked through the door holding a skinned rabbit. "I got us some supper."

Anna rose and took the carcass from him. "That's quite thoughtful, Henry. Thank you." She put it on the bench and picked up a knife to portion it into smaller pieces. "Grace, please clear the table. Henry, would you mind digging a few potatoes for me, please?"

Henry stared at her for a moment, gave her a nearly imperceptible nod, and walked back out the door. He returned a few minutes later with three large tubers, tossed them next to the rabbit, and vanished into his bedroom.

Anna sighed. Henry was going to be a hard nut to crack. She had to somehow convince him that book learning was in his best interest. A sudden flash of realization hit her hard, and she scolded herself. Wasn't that what had been drilled into her head? She closed her eyes and took a deep breath. She couldn't believe her opinion had so quickly flown in the opposite direction of what she had recently concluded a short while ago. It wasn't fair to approach Henry with strict discipline just because he believed in something else. She decided to turn the tables and try to learn from him. Henry, if he was willing, would be her teacher. But she had to figure out how to gently break down his walls so it would seem more his idea than hers. Then maybe, hopefully, that would spark a curiosity about what he could learn from her. And, she had to make sure Grace understood Henry had a voice, as she had a tendency to talk over and for him. Being the quiet type, or likely more on the shy side, Henry simply let her.

Grace helped her clean up while Henry checked on the horses.

Anna placed some homemade lye soap in the sink and poured hot water over it from the tea kettle to make suds. She then pumped cold water on top to make it a comfortable temperature for her hands. Grace, balancing on a stool, added the dishes and, they washed and dried them together.

"We'll have to get wood in tomorrow," Anna said after scooping the ash from the fireplace and into a bucket.

"We don't have any more. That came from a tree Pa found by the river. He reckons it got washed down during the rains."

"Oh. Then what do you usually use to burn?" Anna had heard of people using dried buffalo and cow chips, but she hadn't seen any buffalo around and only the milk cow. Both of those fuels seemed as scarce as wood.

"We use prairie grass twists."

Anne frowned in confusion.

"They're little bundles of long grass tied in a knot," Grace said.

"I've not heard of that."

"We have to cut more," Henry said from the doorway. He carried an armload of said grasses to the fireplace and dumped them into a high woven basket.

"All right. Henry, will you please hitch a wagon in the morning, and we'll go."

"No. We have to wait until the grasses are dry in the afternoon. They won't burn if they're brought in wet."

Anna smiled. "Well, you just taught me something, Henry. Thank you."

"Besides," Grace jumped down from the stool, "in the morning, you have to learn to ride."

"Right." Anna sent up a silent wish for rain and then changed her mind because no fire meant no coffee.

Both children retired shortly after a quick scrub of face and hands. Anna imagined they were both emotionally exhausted. She wasn't far behind them and, following a glance around the cabin, headed out to the tepee.

Once she'd stepped away from the cabin, she couldn't help but notice the fields were bathed in moonlight and shadows that danced across the landscape. The night was alive with a gentle stillness, broken only by the whisper of the wind through the grasses and a quiet snort of a horse. In the distance, the outline of mountains rose against the night sky, their peaks silhouetted against the moonlit horizon. The moon was nearly full, a calming presence in the sky. Anna wondered how Emma and Betty were traveling.

ANNA HEARD HER name being called from the depths of her sleep. As she became more awake, she also heard scratching on the tepee flap.

"Anna, are you awake?" The flap was lifted and dropped.

"Yes, yes, I'm awake now." Anna wondered if this family ever slept in past dawn. She yawned and stretched, enjoying the vestiges of remaining sleep and the comfortable weight of the buffalo hide warding off the morning chill that Grace was letting in with her antics. "I'll be there in a few moments."

"Okay." Grace soundlessly disappeared.

Anna rubbed the crusty sleep from her eyes. She reluctantly flung the warm hide to the side and with effort, rose to her feet. Her body complained, but it was typical. She shivered against the morning chill as she pulled her dressing gown over her head and replaced it with a clean, yellow, cotton one and a wool sweater.

The day had dawned crisp and clear. Anna rubbed her arms to generate the warmth she'd left in the tepee. The sunrise was pastel-colored from the mix of light and small patches of clouds that had crept in overnight. A sense of peace and serenity settled in her mind. Anna closed her eyes and lifted her face to the quiet sun and felt the first vestiges of warmth. How long had it been since she'd appreciated and basked in the beginnings of a new day? Probably not since she was a child, before becoming and acting like what she expected an adult would act.

She couldn't help but smile when she walked into the cabin. The earthy aroma of coffee, salted bacon, and toasted bread tantalized her senses and made her stomach growl loudly.

Grace giggled. "You're hungry."

Henry was nowhere to be seen, as usual. But a hot fire was burning in the fireplace, and a few more bundles of prairie twists had been added to the basket.

"Has Henry eaten?"

"Yes. He's tending the horses." Grace grinned broadly. "You have to eat now. After breakfast, it'll be time for your first riding lesson."

Anna's appetite abruptly disappeared. But she still needed caffeine. She dragged her meal on for as long as possible, taking little bites, chewing slowly and moving the food around on her plate. This, despite several impatient sighs from Grace, who'd finished her meal within minutes.


FINALLY, SHE COULDN'T prolong it any longer. The remaining food on her plate had gone cold. Anna felt mildly guilty for the waste, but what she had eaten was sitting like a hard rock in her stomach.

Grace snatched the plate and utensils from in front of Anna as soon as she put her fork down. Her plate was the only thing left to wash. Grace in her impatience, had already done the other dishes and quickly took care of the last of it. She wiped the table, shooting glances at Anna all the while, then stood expectantly at her side with her hands planted on her small hips.

"Okay, okay. I guess I can't put this off any longer." Anna drained the last of her coffee and stood up.

Grace couldn't contain her enthusiasm. She grabbed the now empty cup, gave it a quick wash and jumped down from her stool. "Let's go. Henry's waiting."

Grace dragged Anna from the cabin toward the barn. Halfway there, she stopped short.

There, Henry sat aboard his beloved buckskin with comical smirk on his face. At the end of the rope in his hand was easily the biggest horse she'd ever seen. It dwarfed Henry and his horse by at least three feet.

"His name is Pitsih. He's gonna help teach you to ride. He's a good boy. I learned on him too." Grace tugged on Anna's hand. "Come on. You should meet him."

The closer Anna moved toward the horse, the bigger he seemed to grow. Kind, intelligent eyes looked out from under a bush of forelock. It nearly covered his broad forehead and his slight Roman nose. He placed his wide muzzle into Anna's hand when she offered it and moved his lips as if expecting to be given some food.

"My oh my, he's some pumpkins," Anna muttered, consciously avoiding the plate-sized hooves. She ran her hand over his arched neck, feeling the strong muscles beneath his deep mahogany brown coat. He wore a black mane that hung like a waterfall over his neck. His white face perfectly matched the white crawling up his legs as well as the feathering flowing over his hooves.

Grace fearlessly walked under his belly. Neither she nor the horse flinched. "See? He's very tame."

"Yes, I can see he's very placid, but there's no way I can get on him. He's just too tall."

"Pa built a ladder for me for when I was learnin'."

"I'll go put a saddle on him while you're getting that ladder, Grace." Henry's eyes twinkled with amusement.

Anna stood there, not knowing what to do while Grace went one way and Henry the other. "Dear, oh dear, what have I gotten myself into?" She felt the sudden urge to pee. Knowing her bladder would only get more insistent with nerves, she walked with quick strides to the outhouse to relieve herself.

By the time she returned, Grace, Henry, and the saddled behemoth were waiting for her. A ladder, made of two sloping parts that were connected at the top, stood up by itself near them.

"Ready?" Grace raced to her side and grabbed her hand.

"Mmm." Anna grimaced and had the sudden urge to run to the outhouse again. "Grace, are you sure about this?"

"We'll both help you, won't we, Henry?"

Henry's eyes danced with mischievous amusement. "Sure. We'll help you get on him, but then I have chores to do. Grace will tell you what to do from there on."

Anna closed her eyes and took a deep breath. "Okay. Let's give it a go."

Grace moved the ladder closer to Pitsih's side. The horse didn't react or even acknowledge the activity around him. If Anna were to guess, he looked bored and half asleep, but it was hard to tell, given his forelock was now splayed haphazardly over his eyes.

"Come on. Just climb up on the ladder and I'll tell you what to do." Grace tapped the top of the ladder and smiled.

Anna had seen people get up on horses too many times to count, but she'd never been interested enough to do it herself. Being all too aware of her largeness was enough to kill that curiosity. She moved to the horse's side and put a tentative foot on the first rung, which was made of a wood pole. Placing a hand on the horse's shoulder for balance, she put her entire weight on the ladder. It seemed sturdy enough.

"You're doing good," Grace said as she gently patted Anna's thigh, which was at her eye level.

Anna reached the top of the ladder. She'd have to somehow lift her leg a good two feet to reach the stirrup. "I don't think I can reach it, Grace." The muscles in her legs were already starting to quiver and threatened to cramp. An entire gathering of giant butterflies beat against the inside of her stomach.

"Reach up and grab the horn, Anna. Then put your left foot in the stirrup. You can do it. Easy."

"Easy for you," Anna said through a puff. But she made an attempt for Grace's sake. She reached up and took hold of the horn. To her surprise, it elongated her torso enough that she reached the stirrup with her tip of her toe. Nearly. Her bosom was in the way . . . as usual. Subtly, she hoped, she pushed them up higher and pressed harder against the saddle to keep them in place. At that point she wasn't sure what to do.

Grace came to her rescue and shoved the stirrup onto the ball of Anna's shoe. "Henry, help me push."

Anna suddenly felt four hands on her bum, pushing upward.

"Stand up," Henry grunted.

Anna put all her weight into the stirrup, her right leg dangling because she wasn't sure exactly how to do what she so obviously needed to do.

"Okay," Grace said, clearly out of breath. "Lean as far forward as you can and bring your right leg over his back." Grace pushed Anna's leg up and toward Pitsih's back end, while Henry strode to the other side of the horse.

With lots of effort and grunting, Anna squashed her belly against the saddle, and using her right toe and heel, crab crawled over Pitsih's back. She was nearly there, when Henry grabbed her foot and pulled it down and toward the front of the horse. With a bit of a hop and a big grunt, she settled her bottom into the saddle, completely breathless and elated that she had made it. She clasped her hands to her chest as heat radiated through it. She was sitting on a horse. She really was sitting on a horse.

"She's all yours, Grace." Henry shook his head and walked away.

"You did it." Grace bounced on her tiptoes and clapped her hands. "That was the hard part."

"You're telling me." Anna was still struggling to catch her breath. But she had made it and rewarded Grace with a smile. "So, what's next?"

Grace backed away from the horse and scrutinized her. "Sit up straight, hold the reins in your left hand, and give him a little kick with both your feet."

Anna took another deep breath and did as told. But nothing happened. "Is he sleeping?"

"No, he's just being stubborn because there's someone he doesn't know on him." Grace grabbed a rein and pulled. "Come on, Pitsih." The horse stood still as a statue. Grace rolled her eyes, picked up a rock, and threw it hard. It hit Pitsih in the hind quarters. His head shot up and his body tensed.

Anna's heart nearly stopped at the sudden movement. "Grace, please don't scare him into moving."

"I'm trying to get him to move at all." Grace picked up another rock. That seemed enough encouragement for Pitsih, and he took a step forward. "Keep kicking him, Anna."

Much to Grace's delight, and Anna's trepidation, the horse kept moving, his steps so slow, it seemed eons before he took another. But he was moving.

Anna gripped the reins hard, her knuckles going white. She felt drops of nervous sweat trickle from her hairline and continue down to the front of her chest. She swept the back of her hand across her forehead to get rid of the sweat heading toward her eyes.

"Turn him by pointing your hand in the direction you want to go." Grace skipped alongside as he walked. "First point to me."

Anna's hand, clenched into a fist was nearly numb, but she did as Grace instructed. To her amazement, Pitsih responded by easing to the left.

"Yay. Now do it the other way, but give him a good kick. He's slowing down again."

Anna kicked with minimal affect.

"Try clucking to him. That might help."

Anna put the front of her tongue against the top of her mouth and tried to suck air over it. But no noise came out. Her mouth was too dry. She worked her tongue around to try to generate some spit. After a minute or so, she was actually able to make a noise. Pitsih's ears turned back to listen to the unfamiliar sound, but his walk did seem to change from sloth-like to a slow amble.

Grace picked up another rock, and before Anna could react, she threw it against Pitsih's rump. The horse's head jerked up once again, but this time it stayed up and he broke into a trot.

It seemed to Anna that all her body parts were moving in different directions. Her legs flapped against the horse's side, her belly jiggled this way and that, and her bosom threatened to give her a set of black eyes. She quickly grabbed the horn with her right hand. Her left hand holding the reins waved wildly as if conducting an orchestra.

"Grace. Make. *grunt.* Him. *grunt.* Stop. *grunt.* Now." Anna could barely get the words out.

"Just pull back on the reins," Grace said, between barely contained giggles.

Ann lifted them higher, to take the slack out. The action caused her to lean back in the saddle and for not the death grip on the horn, she would've toppled off the back of him like a tumbleweed. But thankfully, Pitsih did slow, and after a few more steps, came to a stop.

Her heart still pounding wildly, Anna closed her eyes and took in deep breaths.

"Anna. You did it. And you didn't fall off." Grace danced below her from what seemed like a mile on the ground.

"I'm not exactly certain how I managed to stay up here." Anna knew damned well it was the fear of falling off that enabled her to keep a death grip on the saddle horn.

"Come on, try again." Grace searched the ground for another rock. Pitsih saw what she was up to and sidestepped his hindquarters over to face her.

"No, no. I think I'm done for today, child. We have other work to do."

Grace looked mildly disappointed, but brightened quickly. "Okay, we'll have another go tomorrow."

"We'll see." Anna looked from side to side, unsure of how to get off this monstrosity of a horse. The obvious would be to reverse the motions of how she got on. But, at the moment, it all seemed a blur and confusion of movements.

Ever the confident one, Grace released Anna's right foot from the stirrup. She returned to the left side, shaded her eyes with her hand, and gazed up at Anna. "Just do everything backward."

"Yes, I figured, but would you please remind me?" Anna dropped the reins on Pitsih's neck and tried to concentrate.

"Lean forward and swing your right leg over his bum."

Grace made it sound so easy, but Anna had no choice but to try. She effectively laid all her upper body weight forward. The saddle horn pressed painfully into her sternum, so she jiggled herself around to make it less so. With a lot of effort, she swung her leg over in one motion. The momentum of that one action caused her left foot to slip out of the stirrup, She clawed to stay up, but realized quickly, she wasn't going anywhere. Her brassiere was hooked onto the saddle horn. Anna hung helplessly from the saddle. She tried to pull herself back up, but her efforts were futile. She couldn't reach the saddle horn and there was nothing else for her to grab. She wasn't strong enough and couldn't get enough leverage even if she had been. She bent her knee and tried to get her foot back into the stirrup, but it was hanging at thigh height, making it impossible to do anything but dangle helplessly. She peddled with both feet to no avail.

Pitsih moved sideways to accommodate all the weight hanging off his left side. Grace moved quickly to gather the reins to prevent him from going anywhere.

Futile to keep struggling, Anna hung there like a limp load of laundry. It was beyond hope that her bra would succumb to her weight and tear. Because of her size, it had been designed with rigid material in the center. Strong material capable of holding up her heavy bosom, the ties were made of equally tough fabric, which were sometimes hard to release because of the pressure her bosom put on it.

Anna felt Grace's hands against her bottom, trying to push her up. But after a few tries, she gave up.

"Hold on, Anna. I'll get the ladder."

"Like I have a choice," Anna muttered against the leather. Suddenly, the entire situation seemed ridiculously funny. She giggled. Pitsih bent his neck to identify the muffled and unfamiliar sound and slowly spun around to get a better look. "Oh, dear, god, how could this get any worse?"

"Whoa, Pitsih." Grace had thankfully returned. "Um. I don't think this will work either, Anna."

"Why?" Anna swirled her left leg around to find purchase on the ladder. But all she found was open air. "Oh."

"I'll go find Henry. He'll know what to do."

"Grace, would you please tie this horse up so he doesn't go anywhere?" Unsettling visions of him galloping across the prairie with her flopping against him ran through her head."

"Okay. Hold on. I have to walk him to the tie rail."

Anna felt like a sack of feed hanging on a wall of moving horseflesh. As Pitsih walked, he kept trying to turn to have a look at her, despite Grace's yanking on him to stay straight. It seemed like hours before they finally reached the rail in front of the barn.

"I'll be right back. I don't think he left to check the herd yet."

"This seriously cannot be happening." Anna had never felt so helpless in her entire life. At that very moment, she vowed to work on shedding pounds. She felt she might have already lost a few ounces since she'd been here. The availability of sweets was nonexistent. That helped. What she also thought would expedite losing weight, was the fact she was always busy, be it helping Grace with her lessons, milking the dreaded cow, or completing other work that came with living here and caring for two children. Sure, she was always hungry at mealtimes. They all were. But her diet had changed markedly from the fat rich foods she was so accustomed to feasting on. Since arriving in this god-forsaken place, meat and vegetables were the mainstay. Bread, corn, jerked and fresh meat, beans, rice, and dried fruit and vegetables were kept stocked. Her habit of overindulging was slowly disappearing.

The sound of running feet and horse hooves pulled Anna from her thoughts. There hadn't been much else to do but hang there anyway.

"See?" Grace said in between gasps. "I didn't know what to do. Can you help?"

Henry cleared his throat and said with a raspy voice caused no doubt by laughing, "Undo the girth. There ain't much else we can do." He moved to Anna's side. "I'm gonna have to get my hands in there somehow."

"Oh, just do it, and get me down, please." The time for vanity had been gone since Anna had gotten hung up in the first place. She was completely aware that the normally easy routine of loosening the girth of a saddle was complicated by her rolls of fat.

Several minutes later, Henry said, "Got it."

Suddenly the saddle let loose. Anna dropped like a stone and her feet hit the dirt. Unbalanced, she fell backward, bringing the saddle with her. There was no sound other than her gasps for breath and the pounding of blood in her ears. Thankfully the horse didn't move a muscle once relieved of her weight.

She tried to sit up, but the saddle now straddled her. She looked up at the children. Grace's eyes were wide and her mouth was set in a perfect "O." Henry's dust covered face was tracked by tears. They were no doubt tears of laughter shed when Grace had told him of her predicament. At least he had sobered up by the time he'd arrived.

They both moved at the same time, Henry grabbed the saddle and pulled it off her, and Grace grasped her hand and tried to help her up.

Anna raised up on her elbows and said, "Give me a minute to catch my breath, thank you." Although her fall was cushioned by the fat on her bum, she was more committed than ever to get rid of it.

# Chapter Eleven

THE GUSTS OF wind bent the grasses over, making it hard for Anna and Henry to cut it near the ground and not in half or smaller. Anna found swinging the scythe fairly simple, but definitely work in keeping it level with the ground. The curved razor-sharp iron blade attached to the wooden staff was cumbersome, except in motion, when the two handholds made it easier to control. Henry had shown her how to keep the blade at a slight angle and pull with her leading arm as she swung. After many haphazard attempts, she finally mastered shuffling her feet forward as she went. By keeping the blade tip slightly up, as Henry explained, she was able to cut and drag the grass to the left and effectively form a windrow. Although hers were anything but straight, the grass was still in clumps, making it easy for Grace to pick it up behind her.

Grace's job was to gather and pile the cut grass onto the canvas sheet, which was now nearly full.

"Anna, would you help me drag this back to the barn, please?"

Henry glanced up and kept up his methodical sway and cut motion.

Anna left her scythe at the end of her row and walked over to Grace. "I'm confused. Why don't we use the horse and the wagon to move this?"

Grace tied the two sides together as best she could to form makeshift walls to keep the grasses from creeping off and then picked up a corner of the canvas. "Because if we put it on the wagon, it would all blow off, silly."

"Ah, because it would be higher."

Grace nodded and leaned into the canvas, readying to start. "It's not heavy. You'll see."

Anna grabbed the other corner, and together they slid the lightweight load the quarter mile along the ground. By the time they got to the shelter of the barn, Henry was just a hazy speck on the horizon.

Once inside, they rolled the grass off and headed out to the field again.

Five trips later, the three of them started the trek back to the homestead. Red streaked through the deepening sky from the mountains, where the sun had tucked just behind them. A vast silence reigned over the land, the only sound was the shooshing of the canvas as Grace and Anna pulled the last load of the day. The wind had died down shortly before they turned toward home, but their faces all burned from the abrasiveness of it, having stood out in it all day. Henry carried both scythes, one over each shoulder. Although he handled them easily, it was obvious he was exhausted, as his usual saunter was absent. They all were tired, as evident by the lack of conversation.

A chill had crept into the cabin as the shadows grew long. The fire had gone out long ago, leaving no vestiges of heat. It would've been a waste of fuel to keep it going anyway. Despite their fatigue, Henry brought in two armloads of prairie knots while Grace worked to build a fire. In short time, Anna felt the heat radiating from the fireplace. She lit two oil lamps, set one on the table and placed the other next to her at the bench.

Anna added corn flour and water into a bowl and stirred until it was thick and pasty. She then transferred it over to one of the pots hanging over the fire to bake. While she had been busy making that, Henry brought in a portion of cured venison from the smokehouse. Anna cut three generous slices and laid them on top of the cornbread to warm.

"You two get washed up," Anna said as Grace started setting the table. "Dinner will be ready by the time you get back." She took the plates from Grace and shooed her away with a smile. Henry looked somewhat surprised, but didn't utter a word. Both walked out the door.

After setting the table, Anna pumped water into a large bucket and set it near the fire to get warm. They all deserved a little spoiling after the day they'd had, and a more thorough washing with soap and warm water would feel wonderful. After the children washed, she'd carry the bucket with the remaining water to the tepee and clean herself in private.

She grabbed an oil lamp and jug and made a quick trip to the springhouse for some milk. The hatch type door was set into a mound of dirt, which opened to a set of stairs. It was the first time she'd gone into the structure. Cool air met her as she swung the door onto the cellar. She wasn't sure what she had been expecting. The roof was low enough that she had to duck her head, but light from the door allowed her to see the makeup of the room. Stacks of peat lined all four walls right to the ceiling. Baskets held potatoes, some with knobby sprouts, bumpy cabbages, and dry beans. A few were empty. On makeshift shelves were cloth wrapped parcels, she assumed were butter and cheese. In the corner, closest to the cool dirt wall sat the covered bucket of milk. Goose flesh peppered her arms as she transferred milk into the jug with the ladle. The air smelled of moist earth and ripening apples.

Anna stopped short when she opened the cabin door. Grace was spooning the corn bread onto plates as Henry cut the venison into smaller pieces. Emma's children amazed her. They were nothing like the lads and lasses back East who would've been idly sitting at the table, waiting to be served. The aromas made her mouth water and spurred her to close the door behind her and pour the milk into the three cups sitting at the edge of the table.

"Thank you both for working so hard today, including this," Anna said as the waved her hand towards the table. "It's a nice surprise."

Grace cocked her head as she chewed a piece of meat. "What's it like back East?"

"Nothing like this, I can assure you. You two do more work than I've ever seen children do."

"If something needs doing, we do it," Henry surprised her by saying.

Anna smiled. "You sure do. I can't tell you how much I appreciate it. I'm learning a lot from the both of you."

Henry averted his eyes and continued eating. Anna supposed that might be the last he spoke for the night.

"Back East, we call young people 'kids.' You two are nothing like them." Anna chewed thoughtfully.

"What's a kid?" Grace put her fork down and sat with her hands in her lap. It was a gesture she did when Anna had her full attention.

"In the old country, it means 'young goat.'" Anna knew the history of the word was a much more heinous than that. She recalled the shock when she learned that the word first referred to children who were sold by criminals to sea captains who then took them to British colonies as slaves.

"I don't think I'd want to live there," Grace said, looking thoughtful.

"No, I don't expect either of you would. It's much nicer here." Anna stifled a yawn, then noticed Henry slumped in his chair. "All right, you two. I think you need sleep more than a bath." She pushed away from the table and stood up. Every single muscle in her body complained. She was going to be some stiff tomorrow, that was for sure. "I'll clean up."

Anna smiled as Henry and Grace said good night and went to bed. She'd never met any children like them. She used some of the warm water to wash the dishes, trying to keep as quiet as possible. After stoking the fire, she looked longingly at the warm water. A face and hand wash would have to do tonight. She was too tired for anything else. Afterward, she extinguished the oil lamp and closed the door behind her.

The milky way stretched white and bright across the sky. Locusts and cicadas had already begun their cacophony of sound and would do so until dawn. A horse nickered from the paddock and was answered by another. Anna walked confidently to the tepee, her feet already familiar with the bumps of sod and small dips in the ground.


BEFORE ANNA OPENED her eyes, she heard the birdsong. It seemed the lark sparrows, redwing blackbirds, robins, and killdeer were all greeting the morning at the same time. She lay still, afraid to move for fear she wouldn't be able to. Yesterday's events, first with her tragic experience with riding and then the long hot hours in the sun and wind as they cut grass, would surely have rendered her body stiff and sore overnight. She experimented by tentatively stretching. Her stomach and shoulder muscles complained the most, but she didn't reckon she was completely incapacitated. She wiggled out from under the hide and carefully stood up. She was tired, but that wasn't entirely surprising. She could only imagine how the children were faring.

She realized that she'd woken on her own accord. There'd been no Grace scratching at the flap. She dressed quickly and exited the tepee. Right away she knew it was mid-morning. The sun had risen halfway to noon. She walked as fast as her legs could carry her toward the cabin. She'd gone about fifty feet when she heard voices from the barn. She changed direction and eventually found Henry and Grace sitting amongst the cut grass and a pile of tied prairie knots.

"Good heavens. How long have you been up?"

Grace looked up from the handful she'd been straightening and smiled. "We get up at the same time every day."

"Oh." Anna fiddled with her dress sleeves. "You should've woken me like usual."

Henry looked up and chuckled. "We were going to, but you were snoring so loud, we didn't think you'd hear Grace scratch."

Anna put her hands on her hips. "I do not snore. That's unladylike."

"You did this morning," Grace said. "That's okay. The cow was so busy listening that she didn't move. Henry didn't even have to hold her while I milked."

Anna laughed outright. "You fibbers. Did you have breakfast?"

"No. We thought we'd wait for you." Grace looked around. "We got a lot tied while we were waiting."

Anna rolled her eyes and sighed. "Yes, I see." She clapped her hands. "All right you two jokers, let's get something to eat before you blow away in the wind."

Breakfast consisted of cold leftovers from last night's dinner. But with the addition of hot coffee for her and fresh warm milk for the children, it was enough to fill their bellies and give them energy for the day ahead.

"What do you have planned today, Henry?" Anna stabbed a piece of venison onto her fork.

Henry glanced toward Grace. "Same as yesterday, I reckon." Finished with his meal, he took his dishes to the sink, donned his hat, and went outside.

"But I thought we couldn't cut until the grass dried," Anna put her cup down. A feeling of dread realizing itself, the food in her stomach began to churn.

"We can't. Henry is getting Pitsih ready for you." Grace drained her milk and wiped the white moustache from her upper lip with the back of her hand.

"Oh, Grace, I can't go through that again." Anna rubbed her sides, awakening the sensitive areas that her brassiere had viciously chafed while she'd hung helplessly from the saddle horn. She pushed away from the table and picked up her plate.

"Don't worry. Henry has a good idea." Grace rose and joined her at the sink.

"If I don't like this new idea, we'll do lessons this morning." Anna was already planning what reading she'd have Grace work on.

They washed and dried the dishes together and twenty minutes later were ready to meet Henry. And his new idea.

Anna had no idea what to expect, but it wasn't at all what she'd envisioned. Henry stood at Pitsih's head. Next to the horse was the sorting table she'd seen hides piled atop inside the barn. The top of the table was only a few inches below the stirrup. Next to the table was the ladder. The step up to the tabletop was not much more than the ones she climbed to the cabin.

"Hmm," Anna said as she mentally pictured herself using this new apparatus. "I suppose we may as well give it a try."

Grace bounced up and down on her tiptoes. "You'll see, Anna. It'll work."

Anna took a deep breath and glanced at Henry, who nodded toward the table. She put her foot on the first rung of the ladder. "Are you sure the table is strong enough?"

"Pa had a elk on it to cut up one time." Grace stood at the ladder's side. She offered her hand when Anna lifted herself onto the table.

The table wobbled and creaked, but seemed sturdy. Anna took a tentative step and then another. Once she stood at the horse's side, she realized she'd been holding her breath and slowly let it out. She reached up and grabbed the saddle horn, put her left foot in the stirrup, and placed all her weight in it.

"Just like yesterday. Swing your leg over his back." Henry let loose of the reins and moved to the offside.

Anna's back and butt muscles complained but it seemed easier to do today for some reason. She wondered why, but wasn't able to dwell on it because Pitsih started walking in his slow plodding strides.

Henry quickly slid Anna's right foot into the stirrup as she grabbed for the loose reins.

"At least I won't have to throw stones at him today," Grace said from behind her.

Anna settled herself into the saddle and concentrated on moving with the horse, which wasn't hard because his steps were such a gentle trudge. She reached down and gave him a pat on the neck. "Good boy. We'll get along just fine at this pace."

Pitsih responded to her tugs on the reins to go left and right. She was afraid to try a halt because if he didn't start to move again, Grace would start throwing stones. Feeling a little more confident, Anna circled the cabin, then the barn. Pitsih seemed happy to go someplace different, and not just walk in small circles.

Suddenly Henry and Grace were beside her, both on horses. She'd been concentrating so hard, she hadn't noticed their absence.

"We thought we'd ride with you today," Grace said from atop a scrawny bay. She rode bareback with nothing but a lead rope attached to the horse's halter.

Anna suddenly realized how relaxed she felt. Pitsih's walk was a gentle sway, much like she was in a rocking chair. He hadn't twitched a muscle when the other two horses rode up beside him. Maybe Grace was right. This horse was unflappable.

She smiled and surprised herself by saying, "Okay."

As they rode through the tall grasses, Anna happened to look down and noticed flowers growing low and close to the ground. Purple, white, and yellow dotted the dirt, while the taller black-eyed Susans waved gracefully in sporadic patches.

"I never realized how beautiful the prairie is," Anna muttered, mainly to herself. She'd thought it was just a sea of grass, but the different flowers and textures opened her eyes to its uniqueness. A tall, showy, yellow plant with hairy stems that looked like a fern caught her eye. The flowers had a number of yellow petal-like ray flowers.

Henry must have noticed her interest. "That's a compass plant."

"Oh? And why is it called that?" Anna smiled inwardly at Henry. This was a good step.

"Because the leaves follow the sun. Pa taught us that it's a good thing to watch for if you get lost out here."

Although the tall grasses were as high as Anna's feet as she sat on her horse, they reached to the children's knees and some higher. And indeed, it would be easy to get turned around on the flat terrain with no trees or discernible landmarks.

Their horses' pricked their ears forward. Grace's horse whinnied and was answered by another in the distance.

"That's Muddy's mother talking." Grace rubbed her horse's neck with affection.

"Your horse is named Muddy?" Anna laughed. The little mare's reddish-brown coat shined and was covered in dapples. Her black mane and tail flowed in the gentle breeze. "I don't see a spec of dirt on her."

"That's because Grace never lets her get dirty in the dry season," Henry teased.

Grace giggled. "We call her Muddy because when it rains, she always rolls in it. Even when it looks like the ground is all dried up, she can find a puddle to roll in. Sometimes I can't ride her because when it dries, it's like rock. Pa said when he first laid eyes on her when she was a foal, he thought she was a buckskin. He thought her mom had the wrong foal when he saw her again because she was brown."

ANNA'S KNEES AND bum were beginning to feel the effects of being straddled on a wide horse by the time they circled back. Back at the farm, she guided Pitsih next to the table, her knees and shoulders aching. She carefully dismounted, thankfully without any of the drama that'd occurred the day before. When she was safely on the ground, she rubbed Pitsih's neck. He lowered his head and sighed against her chest. She rubbed his face and whispered, "You're a good boy, aren't you. Thank you for that lovely ride."

Henry waited for Anna to finish before taking the reins. "Tomorrow, I will teach you how to put his saddle and bridle on."

"Yes, that sounds like a good next step," Anna said as she shaded her eyes and looked up at him. "Thank you, Henry."

Anna watched him casually lead the mountain of a horse next to his own much smaller one. The confidence at which he sat his horse melded with the gentleness he had with them. Grace and Emma both as well seemed to be able to wordlessly communicate with the horses. She found that fascinating. Before she had arrived at this homestead, she'd mostly seen horses used as tools and often roughly handled if not abused.

Grace was suddenly at her side. "Come on, Anna. I'll show you how to tie grass." She grabbed her hand, and they walked to the barn. "You did real good riding today."

"Really good," Anna corrected.

"Yes. Really, really good." Grace let go of her hand, sat down, and gathered a bunch of the dried grass. Another lesson began.


ONE MORNING, AS Anna was getting dressed, she noticed her dress didn't fit as snuggly. In fact, it felt rather loose, especially around her waist. And it wasn't near as much of a struggle to get her bra on either. Thinking the fabrics must have stretched or deteriorated from the dirt and sweat, and numerous washings over the past few weeks, she rummaged through her bag and pulled out another brassier and dress. But, as with the other clothing, the dress sagged pitifully and there was more than enough room in the brassiere, where before her breasts had stubbornly bulged from ever which way they found a void. Could she possibly have lost weight? True, she'd been more active than ever in her life, and the food she and the children subsisted on was not at all sweet, but rather meat, potatoes, and bread. But she'd been so busy with daily rides and afternoon chores, she'd forgotten all about her determination to lose weight.

A rumble of thunder pulled her out of her thoughts. She pushed the tepee flap back and was met with a gusty wind that smelled of rain. Dense black clouds hovered over the horizon and flashes of white danced across the sky.

Lightning cracked, loud as a whip, and a huge fork of jagged light split the sky into shattered pieces for an instant. The thunder followed immediately on its heels, battering Anna's ears as her eyes still recoiled from the after-image of the blaze. Small drops of rain fell quietly on the dry ground. The wind picked up and blew loose grass across the field in front of her.

Anna heard the horses nicker to each other for reassurance. But as quickly as it had come, the storm changed direction and was now touching the western horizon. The thunder followed it like an obedient puppy. The rain stopped abruptly. Not enough had fallen to do more than put pock marks in the dust.

Henry and Grace stood on the cabin porch watching the storm. Anna joined them after a few moments.

"I can't believe that storm moved off," Anna said, as she walked into the cabin.

"They do it all the time." Grace frowned. "We won't get rain for a while."

"We have to be careful when those storms come through. Even if they do go away, the lightning starts fires on its path." Henry poured milk into two cups and placed one where Grace sat.

"I hadn't thought of that. Has fire ever come through here?" Anna poured coffee into the kettle of hot water. Grace had taken it upon herself to hang the kettle over the fire as soon as she got it going in the morning.

"Once. Pa was building the barn, and it got struck by lightning and started a big fire. The prairie burned all the way up to the river. He lived in a peat house before he built this cabin for us. That saved him from the fire."

"Aren't you scared it could happen again?" Anna sat down, stunned and suddenly worried.

Henry shook his head. "Nah. Pa put a lightning rod on top of the barn when he rebuilt it."

"But what if the fire starts someplace else and comes this way?" Anna drew her eyebrows together and smoothed and re-smoothed the front of her dress.

"Pa said, we'd be okay." Grace shrugged and nonchalantly sat down.

Henry must have noticed Anna's rising anxiety. "If it did, the fire wouldn't come close to the cabin or barn. That's why we've been cutting the grass in a big wide circle away from everything."

Anna mentally slapped herself. Of course. And here she thought the oval pattern was so they wouldn't have to haul it far. The ingenuity for survival was already deeply ingrained into these two and this astounded her. The children back East, herself included when she was young, now seemed so soft and ignorant to nature's ferocity. If anything did happen, such as a big snow storm, the adults dealt with it, while the children took advantage of a new playtime medium. Henry and Grace were old beyond their years in comparison. Instead of worrying about the possibilities of a disaster, they learned precautions and no doubt knew actions to take in such an instance. She'd seen curiosity on their faces while watching the storm, not concern. Knowing what she knew now, it'd be hard for her to not feel dread. She realized yet again, how much she could learn from both of them.

After breakfast, Henry announced he was going to see if there were any rabbits, pheasants, or grouse around. He took the rifle, planted his hat on his head, and walked out.

"Anna, can I read some more today?"

"Yes, you surely can. I've found I have some sewing to do. You can read aloud to me while I work."

Grace cleared the table and washed up while Anna returned to the tepee to retrieve her sewing kit. She poured another cup of coffee after deciding on Grace's reading material.

"You're not as fat," Grace said in her normal directness.

Anna laughed. In the past, she would've have been slightly insulted by the insinuation, but she'd discovered early on, it was normal for Grace to speak her mind.

"No, I guess I'm not. It's all the hard work you two are making me do." Anna realized she appreciated Grace's acknowledgment. It wouldn't have mattered if she hadn't said anything. For the first time in as long as she could remember, Anna was starting to feel good about her body. She was stronger, and riding had definitely increased her confidence and helped tone her stomach and leg muscles most notably. The "what if's" rarely entered her mind these days, thus lowering her anxiety.

A few hours later, Anna was satisfied with the outcome of her dress. She taken it in an astounding three inches. Her brassiere was a little more difficult to manage, but she thought it would keep her bosom safely encased.

Grace had grown tired of reading, but it was the longest stretch that had kept her attention. She continued to improve almost daily, which clearly showed her intelligence. Anna was quite proud of her accomplishments.

Henry walked in a short time later as Anna was preparing a midday meal. He carried two rabbits and a pheasant, all cleaned and skinned.

"You did well, Henry," Anna said as she took a loaf of fresh sourdough bread from the hearth oven.

He shrugged and turned away to set the game on the bench, but not before Anna caught a glimpse of a self-satisfied grin.

"Your ma and pa would be proud. You've done well in keeping us fed." Anna sawed off a thick slice of bread and handed it to him.

"I need to put a couple deer up soon." Henry took a big bite of the bread.

"I've not seen any deer while we've been riding," Anna said thoughtfully.

"Pa and I go to the foothills for a few days."

Anna shook her head, aware of what he was implying. "You're not going alone. Grace and I will go with you."

"Finally. I get to go too." Grace clapped her hands together. "Henry, will you teach me to shoot your gun?"

"No, I will not. You're too little. It would knock you on your bum." Henry looked to Anna. "Do you know how to shoot?"

"My brother and I used to shoot rats at the pig farm when I was young, but I haven't handled a gun in years." Anna cut a few more slices of bread.

"Did you use a rifle or a pistol?"

"I remember it as a small rifle."

Henry went into Emma's bedroom and came out carrying a smaller version of the Winchester that seemed to go everywhere with him these days. He handed it to Anna. "Was it like this?"

Anna hefted the much lighter firearm and examined it. Instead of the lever action the Winchester had, the bullets had to be loaded singularly. In appearance, it resembled a toy, but she knew from childhood experience it was anything but.

"Yes, I believe it was a similar one." Anna tried to hand the rifle back to Henry.

He shook his head. "No. Keep this with you when you're outside. You'll take it with you when we go to the foothills."

"All right. When do you want to go?" Anna held the rifle with a confidence she carried from her past.

"When I decide on another horse for you."

"Why? I'm happy with Pitsih."

"He couldn't outrun a bear."

Anna realized he was quite serious. And probably right. "Whatever you decide. I trust you."

Henry gave her an easy nod.

To Anna, it seemed he'd grown up a little more just then. He held his shoulders back, scrawny chest out, and his chin high.

"Besides, I can't haul that big table around for you." Henry grinned at his own joke.

Anna chuckled. "So, you'll get me a short horse then." She casually anchored a hand on her hip.

Their eyes met for a few seconds. She wasn't sure Henry had ever looked her in the eye, in fact, more often, he avoided or diverted his quickly. In those few seconds, Anna felt a camaraderie born between them.

"I will find your horse." Henry gave her a half shrug and casually walked out. The door closed behind him with a soft click.

True to his word, Henry returned late that afternoon. He led a dark bay mare by a makeshift rope halter from atop his buckskin.

"You brought Belle," Grace exclaimed. She'd been standing on the porch next to Anna, but ran down and put her arms around the mare's neck. The horse nuzzled her then playfully nipped her shoulder.

Anna looked on from a few feet away. Belle had probably been jet black in her younger years, but now faded with flecks of white throughout her shiny coat. Her muzzle and forehead were speckled with grey. Her eyes were wise and spoke of years of surviving the harsh conditions of the prairie. The pendulous belly was indicative of the many foals she'd carried. But her body looked strong and most importantly, able to carry a chubby rider. The best part was the fact that she was half the size of Pitsih, and Anna didn't think she'd have any problems mounting without the aid of ladder or table.

# Chapter Twelve

THE FIRST THING Betty noticed as they pulled the horses to a halt on the rise, was how peaceful the village appeared. Horses grazed or stood dozing quietly by the river, nearly motionless except for an occasional tail flick at an apparent pesky fly. Tepees were scattered over the expanse of many acres, all with their openings facing east. Streams of smoke trickled out of the tops of them from cooking fires within. The air was still, but cool. Racks of drying meat were suspended over several fires, tended by children, who were busy keeping hungry dogs from snatching quick mouthfuls. A few women wandered from tepee to tepee, carrying baskets or bulky hides. All movements seemed casual and unhurried, like they had not a care in the world. A group of men sat in a circle, in what appeared to be a meeting. Two of them smoked from long pipes.

Emma raised her hand in greeting at two men on fast horses, who suddenly appeared to their left. Their black hair flowed behind them as they galloped toward them. Wearing nothing but deerskin leggings, their tanned chests bore the scars of battles and life in general. Necklaces which held a single bear claw hung from their necks.

One, in particular, looked familiar to Betty, and she wondered why.

"pehnaho," Emma called and smiled brightly. "babi!"

As they both slid their horses to a stop next to them, the one closest to Emma grabbed her into a bear hug, and they touched their foreheads against one another. That's when Betty put it together. He was clearly Emma's brother. They shared the same facial features Betty had thought so beautiful when she first saw Emma in the doctor surgery. But, of course, his had developed into a much more masculine version.

"We had word you were coming in three sleeps," Emma's brother said as he released her. He backed his horse alongside the travois. "John is sick."

Twelve sleeps into their journey, a patrol of warriors had come upon them. They were Paiute and a friendly neighboring tribe to the Shoshone. They had quickly sent for their medicine man upon seeing John's condition. They camped in place for five sleeps until John had stabilized enough to travel again. In the meantime, the men had provided food and protection for the three of them.

"Yes. He's had a bad fall. The white doctor couldn't help him. Sharp Stone gave him willow bark and pussy willow. But he needs Crow Old Man's medicine to heal him."

"Betty, this is Dancing Fire, my brother," Emma said quietly.

Dancing Fire urged his horse forward and stared appraisingly at Betty, as if seeing her for the first time. He pointed with his chin. "Who is this?"

"She is a friend. The hummingbirds brought her to me. She goes by the name of Betty." Emma smiled reassuringly at her.

Betty nodded, not sure of what to say to the imposing warrior. His eyes were wary, but a gleam of gentleness exuded from them. They spoke of power and extreme intelligence, able to pass judgement in an instant. She was suddenly very self-conscious as he evaluated her. She'd been judged by her looks in the past, but this was something else. As if he was gauging her value as a human. Betty sat stock still in the saddle as he circled his horse around her. She knew he was trying to intimidate her, but when she glanced to Emma, her soft smile told her she was safe.

Dancing Fire reined his horse to Emma's side. "I will ride with you." He looked to the other warrior whose horse pranced in place. "Tell Bear Hunter that Aka is home. Send for Crow Old Man."

Betty watched as he galloped away, sending wads of flying sod behind him from hooves gaining purchase in the ground.

"bii has put a tepee near them for you."

Emma smiled at Betty. "Gentle Doe is 'bii,' who is our mother."

"Bear Hunter is your father?" Betty already felt overwhelmed with names. In her past life, there was no need to keep track of who was who, other than those who worked for her.

"Yes.' Emma read her well. "You will be fine. It is not so important you remember names. Respect and politeness is what is expected."

Betty nodded. "That, I can do."

Dancing Fire slowed his horse level with the travois. "It is good you are awake, John. The People are gathering to welcome you back."

"It's good to see you, my friend," John replied in an unused, croaky voice. "Although I'd rather be beating you and your slow horse in a race."

Dancing Fire laughed. "This stallion is the fastest I've ever had. You would get lost in his dust. Right now you must rest. There will be a time for a match."

"They are good friends, I take it," Betty said quietly to Emma.

"They are like brothers. One wishes he could grow a beard and the other wishes he didn't. Sometimes they are worse than two children."

Betty sighed. As a young woman, her responsibilities revolved around taking care of her ailing parents. There had been no other focus. She'd had no time or energy for socialization, let alone making friends. After they had passed, a sense of freedom, more than grief had spurred her to leave her birth home and venture to parts unknown.

She envied the relationship between the two men. But if she were honest with herself, the camaraderie she had with Emma was developing into something special. The long weeks on the trail had given them time to get to know each other. Emma carried with her a wealth of knowledge about the world she and her family lived in, as well as her People. Their simple lifestyle was hard work in order to survive, but the adaptability and strength it took to get through challenges was remarkable. If a problem arose, it was dealt with, without all the angst, worry, and endless discussions that she was so accustomed to.

As they neared the village, Betty found herself looking forward to a rest from travelling. Sleeping under the cover of a tepee would be a luxury. Gazing at the night sky until she fell asleep was nice, she had to admit. But a tepee allowed her some comforts of home, and how grand it will be, to put her head down in the same place every night, for however long they would be among the Shoshone.

A crowd had gathered, apparently waiting to greet them. Betty saw the group part and two people move to the front. As they drew closer, she could see it was a man and a woman. Although she couldn't see their faces clearly because of the sun's angle, she was able to ascertain their sex based on their garments. The woman wore a long deerskin dress, adorned with porcupine quills, animal teeth, and beads. Long braids of black hair streaked with grey, grew to just below her shoulders. Her feet were protected by beaded moccasins. The man, on the other hand, stood out with much more eloquent clothing. Besides his breechcloth, high leggings, and buckskin shirt, a headdress composed of a headband made from leather draped with an ornate beading pattern and decorated with feathers and fur sat on his head like a crown. His grey, straight hair fell loosely against his chest. Betty could only guess he was a person of great importance within the tribe.

"Is he the chief?" Betty looked to Emma who wore a bright smile.

"Yes. Bear Hunter is my father, and my mother, Gentle Doe stands beside him." Emma touched Betty's arm. "You needn't worry. We are a friendly people and have had many whites pass through our village."

While she appreciated the reassuring touch, nerves, anticipation, and curiosity swept through Betty as they were forced to stop because of the circle of people surrounding them. All were chattering excitedly in a language foreign to Betty.

Emma dismounted and was immediately engulfed in the arms of both her parents. Betty could see both their faces clearly now. High cheekbones sat below almond-shaped dark-colored eyes. Wrinkles accentuated their brown skin. Despite their age, she thought them very attractive.

At Emma's urging, she stepped to the ground, and joined Emma, Bear Hunter, and Gentle Doe. Their nods and smiles upon introductions eased Betty's trepidations.

John quickly became the main focus of attention. A medicine man, based on his garments, chanted over him. Betty guessed he was Crow Old Man.

Dressed similarly to Bear Hunter, his headdress was a bison skull cap. Feathers, bear teeth, and the mane of a bison hung feely from it. His long hair had bright cloth and fur braided into it. Six young men loosened the bindings of the travois and gently lifted John.

Emma went to John's side and kissed his cheek. "You will begin to heal now, natainappettsi." She brushed the hair from his eyes and rubbed her fingers through the beard along his jaw and chin. "I will see you soon."

John nodded, squeezed Emma's hand, and closed his eyes.

Accompanied by Crow Old Man, John was carried toward the center of the tribe's tepees where he disappeared into the shaman's lodge.

"After you get settled, you join us for a meal," Gentle Doe said. She turned and left them with Bear Hunter.

"I can see the worry on your face, baide. Crow Old Man's medicine is strong."

"The white doctor could only put wood on John's legs and give him pills to make him sleep. He is broken and sick. I can only hope the journey has not made him worse."

"John's spirit is strong. It will battle the sickness, and he will come back to you." Bear Hunter placed his hand on the small of Emma's back. "Come. I will show you to your tepee."

Emma and Betty removed the packs from the tired horses. They'd not had a lot of time to graze and had lost weight. Their ribs and hip bones jutted against their hides. As soon as their bridles were taken off and the travois dropped off the one that had hauled John, they wandered to the river, drank their fill, and eagerly grazed the lush grass along the banks.

The round-shaped tepee was very spacious. A warming fire already burned in the circle of stones, and the smoke found its escape through the open off-centered hole at the top. The majority of the floor was covered with buffalo hides, but there were also deer, bighorn sheep, and elk skins.

Betty laid her pack at the back of the lodge and tossed her hat onto it. As she did, she noticed pouches made of buffalo hide hanging from the poles.

"My mother has made sure there is always food available, even if it is not next to the fire." Emma opened a few of the pouches, revealing dried meat, berries, water, and sage. She removed a sage sprig and placed it in the fire. "This will clear out any unwanted energy that has followed us and create a blank space for resting. Crow Old Man will use sage to heal John, as well as other things no one knows about."

The acrid smell reached Betty's nose. She was quite familiar with the pungent aroma. A lightning strike had burned through many acres of sage outside of Eagle Rock, sparked by the train that had carried her there. She'd had to wait a few weeks for transport to Oro Fino and had been subjected to the smoke. Thankfully the small amount that now burned in the cooking circle didn't mess with her head like before. She recalled many of the town residents experiencing short psychedelic changes in their visual perceptions and moods. They were all thankful when rain had extinguished the rampant fire. But all the same, the smell of burning sage had lingered for many days afterward.

"Your parents speak English quite well." Betty unbuttoned her dusty over-shirt and shrugged out of it, noting that it needed a thorough washing. The majority of her clothing did, but she was able to find a cleaner one in her bag.

"My People have traded with yours for many moons. There have been many different ways of making the talk. My grandfather has a head piece from a Spaniard, and a white bear robe from a French man. And John, of course, used to bring trinkets and cloth when he passed through." Emma sat down on the hides and put her head in her hands. "I was so worried I would lose him on the trail. Now I'm worried he won't be the same after Crow Old Man heals him."

Betty sat down beside her and put an arm around her shoulders. "You said yourself that John is strong. It's natural to worry. But he is in the best place right now. You did well getting him up here safely and without making him sicker. His bones will heal. You know that. I see the way he looks at you. There's not a chance in this lifetime that he will change."

Emma nodded and swiped tears from her eyes and cheeks. "I know. I'm sorry. I'm just very tired."

"Of course you are. It takes tremendous strength to remain strong. You're entitled to a rest and a good cry if you need it."

"You are a good friend, Betty. I wouldn't have been able to make this journey without you. Thank you."

Betty smiled and pulled Emma closer. "I am honored that you say that. I feel the same about you. And you've taught me so much, and I thank you. I know now what I've been missing while lying on my back in that saloon. I can say this. I have never felt more alive or myself. And I have you to thank for that."

Scratching on the side of the tepee interrupted them. For ease of access, they'd left the flap lying open against the side of the tepee when they brought their belongings in. Their visitor remained standing, unable to see inside until acknowledged.

Beyond the leggings, Betty was surprised to see that the day had drawn on, the sun slowly giving way to dusk. When the village had first come into sight on the rise, the sun had been high in the sky. Not for the first time did she ponder how fast the days seemed to go since she had left Oro Fino and all it represented to her.

Emma got to her feet and peered out. Once their caller crouched down, Betty recognized him. Dancing Fire smiled brightly at his sister.

"bii is waiting."

Emma laughed. "Of course she is." She looked back at Betty. "My mother has no patience when she is excited. Are you ready?"

Betty nodded. "Can't keep her waiting then, can we?"

Accompanied by Dancing Fire, they walked to the chief's tepee. It was ornately painted with black bear paw prints and streaks of yellow that Betty assumed were rays of sun.

Familiarity allowed Emma to scratch once at the side of the flap and enter in one motion. Betty followed, aware of Dancing Fire right behind her as she bent over.

A fire burned brightly in the center, and delicious aromas of meat made Betty's mouth water. She sat down next to Emma and stole glances around.

The tepee was laid out exactly like the one they were staying in, with many pouches hanging on poles. Birch bark boxes sat on the floor beneath the bags. An elaborately painted warrior's shield, a lance, and bow and a quiver of arrows hung to the right of it. Buffalo hides lay piled beneath them, and Betty assumed it was the sleeping area. A fur bag and another small pouch hung right above where their heads would be. The tepee was efficiently laid out. Not for the first time did Betty think that the absence of typical furniture did nothing to detract from the feeling of hominess.

While Gentle Doe busied herself putting the finishing touches on the pot of boiling meat, Bear Hunter sat next to the fire, smoking a pipe. He raised his eyebrows high as if surprised, as Betty and Emma joined him.

"You have hair like burning sky." Bear Hunter laid his pipe on his lap and studied Betty.

Betty self-consciously pulled at strands of her red hair. It had been hidden beneath her hat when they'd ridden up. "I don't suppose you see this color often."

"My people have heard stories. But I have not seen it myself." He grunted as Gentle Doe handed him a wooden bowl of steaming meat.

Betty gratefully accepted the bowl handed to her. Unsure of how to eat without utensils, she gently blew over the brim and glanced to Emma who smiled knowingly.

"Drink the broth first, then use your fingers to eat the meat."

Betty muttered thanks and put the bowl to her lips and sipped. The flavors that played over her tongue were like no other she'd ever tasted. She was able to detect mint, rose hips, juniper, and the sweetness of gooseberries. The meat proved to be just as delicious. It was tender and with a slight hint of sage. Betty had to work to keep from gulping it down. She hadn't realized how famished she was until she'd entered the tepee and smelled the cooking meal. In a few minutes time, she felt sated and slightly heady. The day, as well as the entire trip had caught up to her in a single meal and she fought to stifle yawns.

"It has been a long day and journey for you both. You should close your eyes before the moon rises," Gentle Doe said as she gathered the finger-cleaned bowls.

Betty followed Emma's lead and rose. "Thank you for the delicious meal." She made sure to meet the eyes of Bear Hunter and Gentle Doe.

Bear Hunter grunted and waved them away. Gentle Doe smiled and rolled her eyes at her husband.

Outside the tepee, Emma said, "I will see John now. Can you find your way to our lodge?"

"Yes, of course. It's just over . . ." Betty turned in a circle. "Well, I thought we came from there." She pointed. It amazed her how she'd lost her sense of direction in the sea of tepees.

"Let your eyes adjust. You will see everything in a moment." Emma stood patiently beside Betty.

Sure enough, Betty was finally able to make out the subtle shapes of the things around her. "I thought I would be able to see right off because of the moon."

"We have been sitting around a bright campfire for too many moons. You will get used to the dark."

Betty ventured a look toward the direction she thought their tepee stood. "Ah yes, I see it now. You go see John. I'll be right from here."

Emma tapped Betty's shoulder and disappeared into the maze of the camp.

Coals still glowed in the fire circle when Betty entered their tepee. She threw a few more pieces of wood onto it to ward off the chill, although after doing so, she noticed how warm the tepee had remained even with the low fire. She also knew without a doubt how warm the buffalo hide would keep her as she slept. She quickly undressed into a long shirt that extended to her knees. It was a garment she used to wear to bed at the saloon but hadn't had the opportunity since she'd left Oro Fino.

Betty woke early the next morning to birds singing and the rustle of a breeze in the grasses. She'd hadn't heard Emma return. In fact, she was quite sure she'd fallen asleep as soon as she'd pulled the hide up to cover her neck.

She rose up onto an elbow, keeping the warm hide draped over her shoulder. Emma was still sound asleep as evidenced by the steady rise and fall of the hide. Betty stood up, keeping the buffalo hide wrapped around her. There was some residual warmth left in the fire. She stirred the coals and added some dried grass and kindling. Within a few minutes, after coaxing it to ignite, the sparks caught and a flame rose to claim the small branches. While the fire grew, Betty gathered what she needed for coffee and breakfast, trying to be as quiet as possible so Emma could have her rest. She had no idea how long Emma had been with John.

While on the trail, they'd often be up at dawn. In their haste to get on the way, they'd make sure the fire was completely out and have a cold breakfast of jerky and pemican.

Betty realized there wasn't enough water in her canteen to make the coffee. She looked round and saw the water skin hanging from one of the poles. As she hefted it, she realized it was nearly empty as well. She slid her feet into her boots, not bothering with her hat because the sun was still low in the sky. Draping the buffalo hide snuggly over her shoulders, she pushed the flap aside and stepped out.

She passed a few women carrying two or more bags of water, already on their way back from the river. They avoided her eyes and said nothing. The morning apparently was to be kept quiet in respect for those who needed sleep, Betty thought. Just one more thing many people she knew could stand to learn.

Betty reached the river's bank. A few horses were drinking on the other side while their herd mates grazed or dozed in the early sun. It was easy to pick out Snowdrift, the horse she'd spent so many hours on. As if sensing her presence, the mare lifted her head and nickered softly. Betty smiled. It warmed her heart to know that the horse had recognized her so easily.

The river was wide and shallow enough to clearly see the bottom. An old tree hung dangerously over the edge, its roots dangling toward the water where part of the base had been washed away. It had survived many years, and Betty wondered if the next spring rush of water from melting snow high in the mountains would be its final demise, sending it downriver to who knew where.

She held the bladder with the opening pointing upstream and it filled quickly. Looking around, she was happy to see she was still alone and splashed water on her face, gasping at the coldness. If she hadn't been awake before, she surely was now. She cupped her hands again and brought them to her lips. The glacial water tasted like snow, light, clear, and incredibly fresh. She drank in the fragrance of the cool water, never having tasted water quite like it.

Yesterday had been so intense with their arrival and meeting Emma's people, that she realized she'd not taken in her surroundings, other than the camp of course. Both ends of the river seemed to wander the valley and eventually disappeared into high snow-capped mountains. Grass grew aplenty all around her, supplying the huge herd of horses with ample feed. The sheer number of horses astounded her. There had to be over a hundred if she had to guess. Some had foals at their sides, others were wide in pregnancy. There seemed to be a group that stayed close together, and when she looked carefully, she saw a few had been hobbled. These horses bore remnants of images on their hides where they'd been painted. They were obviously animals belonging to warriors or influential members of the tribe at any rate. They were muscular and fit and seemingly always on alert, watching the camp in between mouthfuls of grass, as if looking for their person. She imagined that quality would come in handy for a warrior whose life might depend on having such a loyal steed.

Betty picked up the water bladders and crawled up the riverbank, careful not to slip and lose them. When she got to the top, she stood up straight and stretched her back for a moment before putting her shoulders into it and walking on. Making sure she had a good grasp on the skins, she made her way back toward the camp. She raised her head briefly to make sure she was headed in the right direction. She stopped dead in her tracks when she saw a young man marching in her direction. His face was youthful and beautiful, but was clearly contorted in anger. The fringe from his buckskin shirt and legging flapped wildly around him as he strode toward her.

He stopped short in front of her and roughly grabbed her chin and looked deep into her eyes. Betty stood frozen in place, uncertain of what she did to deserve this, and unsure of what to do.

"Ba-T?"

Betty suddenly realized the person confronting her was a young woman. Her choice of garments confused her. The women typically wore dresses, not shirts and leggings.

"Ba-T?" The woman shook her chin, the fierceness in her eyes never wavering.

"I'm sorry, I don't understand." Betty's legs were so weak she was in danger of collapsing. She tried to control the trembling that overtook her body. Blood pounded loudly in her ears. She averted her eyes, but the woman forced her to look at her by pulling her chin higher.

"Ah you Ba-T?"

Able to understand a bit more, Betty nodded. "Yes, I am Betty."

The woman roughly released her and stared. She abruptly turned and just as quickly strode away.

"What the hell was that all about?" Betty said and rubbed her jaw. She looked around, but she was still alone. A few men milled about now, but no one looked or came in her direction. It was almost as if the incident hadn't happened. But she could still feel where the woman had held her. She shook her head and slowly walked back.

Emma was awake and was warming some strips of venison over the fire when Betty entered the tepee. She now wore a full-length deerskin dress instead of her traveling shirt. "What's wrong? Your eyes are disturbed."

Betty handed a skin to Emma and hung the other. "I'm not sure. I was approached by one of your People who asked me if I was Betty. I have no idea what it was all about."

"Did she hurt you?" Emma rose to her feet. She studied Betty carefully.

"No. Not really. She scared the dickens out of me though." Betty sat down next to the fire and relished the relief of having the weight off her arms and shoulders from the heavy water. Her legs were still a bit unsteady from the encounter. She let the hide slide from her shoulders, the hot fire already warming her stressed body.

"I will ask around," Emma said as she mixed coffee grounds and water. She put the kettle in the middle of the fire. While they waited for it to brew, they chewed on pieces of meat.

"How is John?" Betty said, as she cut another piece of cooked meat.

"I sat with him for a few hours while he slept. Crow Old Man has given him strong medicine. But I was happy to not be causing him pain."

"Yes, I know how you worried. But as I said yesterday, he is right where he needs to be. And you need to rest as well." Betty poured them each coffee.

"I wonder how my children and Anna are doing." Emma sighed. "I'm torn between staying here for a little while and rushing back to them."

"Look, Henry and Grace are forces of their own. Along with Anna, I'm sure they are fine."

"Grace wants to teach Anna to ride," Emma said with a chuckle.

Betty shook her head and smiled. "I wonder how that's going." She had a vision of the overweight woman on a horse with a sagging back. She guiltily pushed it away.

"How long do you think we will stay?" Betty poked at the fire with a stick, causing sparks to stream upward. Emma looked up. "I'm not in any rush to get back. The decision is entirely up to you of course. I'm just curious." After the morning's incident she had begun to wonder how welcome her presence was among these People. Confusion still wracked her brain. Emma had told her that the tribe had seen many whites and had been friendly toward them. So why this?

"Crow Old Man said John will show signs of getting better in ten moons. But it's really depends how patient John is." Emma shook her head. "He is most definitely not the most patient man when it comes to his own abilities. I think that's why he and Gentle Doe get along so well. They understand each other." She studied Betty. "I can see you're very troubled by what happened. I will find the answer."

Betty couldn't help but warm further to Emma. "Thank you. I'd like to know if it was something I did unawares. But gosh, we've only just arrived, and I've never seen her before."

Emma shrugged, drank the rest of her coffee, and stood up. "Don't worry, my friend. I will be back in a little while. I would like to see my husband if he is awake."

Betty rose to her feet as well. "I'd like to wash some clothes in the river, if you think it's all right."

"Yes. And you will be safe. There are many more awake now, so you will not be alone." Emma offered her a reassuring smile, quickly ducked out, and was gone.

While gathering her armload of laundry, a couple of dogs raced passed, yapping as they played. Other than that, she didn't hear any other signs of human life. But as she stepped through the tepee opening, she was taken aback to see what looked like the majority of the tribe going about their daily tasks. What a peaceful existence, she thought. And so tranquil, which was a stark contrast to the constant noise and hustle and bustle of the town.

She made her way back to the river without incident. True to Emma's words, there was more activity by the river. Women bathed their children and washed themselves and clothing. The horses who had been hobbled were being groomed one by one and set free to roam, however they didn't seem to want to stray far. A few watched the camp, heads raised, ears perked, clearly expecting their person to arrive.

Betty found a quiet area under a tree where she could hang her cleaned clothes after washing while she worked on the rest. No one acknowledged or even seemed to notice her presence, which oddly was a relief and a worry. Would someone come to her aid if that woman came back? She could only hope.

She went to work, glancing warily toward the camp, and soon had shirts and trousers on branches. She was very conscious that her drying clothes were obvious indicators of who was at the river. But she sure as hell wasn't about to let her underwear make that proclamation, so she scrubbed them last and laid them flat on the grass. Betty thought she'd had a safe go of it, but as she wrung the water out of her last pair of panties, she saw two figures approaching in her peripheral vision. Based on the familiar angry stride, her blood froze as she realized the angry woman had brought help. She quickly waded into the river and closed her hands around two fist sized rocks. She would defend herself if need be, even if no one else would. In addition to being apprehensive, a part of her was angry. She'd done nothing to warrant any aggression.

Betty stepped to the top of the bank and stood tall and rigid, trying to ignore the images of what-could-be flashing through her mind. She licked beads of sweat off of her lips and looked for an escape if she had to. She stared hard at her aggressor, hoping to convey that she wasn't going to put up with any other nastiness she might dole out.

As they came closer, the second woman smiled broadly. She said something to the other woman and a look of uncertainty and anguish crossed her face. Betty glanced at the grinning woman. She was dressed identically to the other, her hair, brown and braided, but her complexion seemed lighter than any of the People she'd met. In fact, her facial structure seemed wrong for an Indian.

"Betty. It is you."

The voice was familiar, but Betty couldn't place it. Her dialect seemed to mix with white and Shoshone. Betty studied her face and eyes. She had only known one person with that beautiful smile.

"It can't . . . it can't be. Mayme? I thought you were dead." Betty shook her head and dropped the rocks she'd been gripping so tightly. Her hands felt stiff with the effort. She flexed them quickly before throwing her arms around her lost friend.

"No, it's me, and I'm quite alive," Mayme said as she hugged her back.

"You've been here all this time?" Beth said, releasing her.

"It is quite a long story. But I will tell you over a meal." Mayme looked to her companion. "This is Muha ai-wa, which means Moon Fawn."

Betty noticed how Moon Fawn's body language had changed from aggressive to nearly defeated. "Why does she look so sad now? I thought she was on her way to kill me."

Mayme gazed adoringly at Moon Fawn. "She thinks you're here to take me away from her."

"I don't understand."

"She shares a tepee with me." Mayme tugged on Moon Fawn's shirt fringe and was rewarded with a brief smile.

"I have so many questions." Betty shook her head in confusion.

"And I have so much to tell you. Please sit at our fire when the sun is low."

Betty nodded, speechless as they turned and walked away. Seeing her friend alive and living amongst the People was so surreal she still had a difficult time believing it.

# Chapter Thirteen

"MOON FAWN'S FATHER, Osh-Tisch was part of a hunting party on their way back through the mountains when they found me." Mayme sat cross legged across the fire from Betty, in their tepee, Moon Fawn at her side. "I had got caught in a bad snow storm and was nearly frozen to death by that time. They brought me here and held me as their captive. Once they figured out I was a girl, they were more lenient and kind."

"How did they find out? As I recall you were quite a convincing boy. Otherwise, you wouldn't have gotten the job riding for the post."

Moon Fawn's shoulders shook in silent laughter. Mayme bumped her shoulder with her own and chuckled. "Osh-Tish cut my clothes off."

Betty covered her mouth in surprise at how close Mayme might have come to losing her life.

"And then they laughed." Mayme shrugged. "I eventually won them over by saving this one's life."

"Oh my. What happened?" Betty couldn't help but keep shaking her head in amazement and shock of the events that led Mayme here.

"She got swept down the river and almost drowned. So, I jumped in after her."

"That is how she got her name," Moon Fawn said. She looked at Mayme and Betty did not miss the look of adoration that passed between them.

"I am now called 'Pop-pank' which means jumping fish." Mayme sat up a little straighter. Her pride was evident.

"That was years ago. Are you still a captive?" Betty bent her neck forward and stared openly at Moon Fawn.

"No. I was eventually allowed to leave. But I realized I didn't have much of a life in the white man's world. I didn't think a disguise would work anymore as I looked more like a woman. I knew I would find myself yearning for the mountains, listening for the wolf, and missing the softness of a buffalo hide. And most importantly, my heart pulled me back to Moon Fawn." Mayme placed a hand on top of Moon Fawn's. "She has taught me what it is like to not want to live without a mate."

Betty bit her lip and stared at the fire. "Are you sure?" she finally said quietly.

She glanced around the tepee, looking for answers. There were no signs that Mayme was being kept against her will. In fact, there were a number of weapons at her disposal if she wanted to try an escape. Two bows and arrow filled quivers hung on the poles. Various lengths of knives hung in protective sheaths. Smooth colored pebbles sat in wooden bowls among a small collection of dried flowers and herbs. Sewing items sat next to a stack of tanned deerskin hides. The tepee had a definite air of how a man and woman couple would arrange their belongings. But, unlike in Bear Hunter's tepee, where there was a distinct segregation of items between man and woman, it was absent here. More, it looked like a combination of the two women. She couldn't have guessed where the presence of Mayme ended and Moon Fawn began, or visa versa.

Mayme must have read her confusion. "I know who I am now, Betty. Moon Fawn and I are two-spirit. We live as man and woman, and woman and man. We are the same and different. At first, we were not sure what was happening. But Crow Old Man sent us into the mountains to pray for visions. Moon Fawn was the only thing in mine, and I, only in hers. Crow Old Man said our connection is spiritually powerful and that even in death we will remain together."

Betty nodded, suddenly understanding Moon Fawn's actions. "No wonder she was afraid. I would be as protective if I had a love such as what you share. You needn't worry. I am envious of you both and hope nothing ever comes between you."

Moon Fawn covered her mouth with her hand and gazed at Betty with shining eyes. She reached for Mayme's hand and squeezed it. She uttered something too soft for Betty to hear. Mayme pressed her forehead to Moon Fawn's and smiled.

Betty watched on, tears escaping her eyes and creeping down her cheeks. She'd never had a love as strong as theirs. In fact, she could honestly say, she'd never known an intimate love, only an intense fondness for Mayme. Betty realized how much she had missed her. Mayme had left an unfilled a hole in her life when she'd mysteriously disappeared. That aching wound had begun to heal the moment Mayme had said her name near the river. Age old questions and painful doubts had been answered and relieved. Mayme was alive and obviously happy.

"I can't tell you how relieved I am that you're alive, Mayme." Betty wiped her eyes with the edge of her sleeve.

"Surely you didn't think I was dead? I sent a message to you and Mr. Smart."

"What else could I think? There were rumors you'd been killed like Billy Prescott. But no one ever found your body, so it seemed you had just disappeared without a trace."

Mayme sat up straight, anger flashing in her eyes. "When I made the decision to return to the Shoshoni, I waited for a post rider to come through on the trail. I stopped him and told him who I was. I gave him the watch Mr. Smart had given me and told him to show it to you and then give it back to

Mr. Smart. The thief must have kept it." She scrubbed her face with her hands. "Oh, Betty, I am so sorry. You must have been incredibly worried."

Betty nodded, fresh tears forming. "I think I know what happened to that rider. He was found by a gold miner. He washed up dead on a riverbank where he had his claim. They say he and his horse must have been caught in the high river and swept away. It was several months before the miner came to town with his gold. He said he buried the boy, but nothing about if anything was found with him." Betty raised her head and smiled. "But I've found you very much alive. And I can't tell you how much joy I'm feeling now."

WHEN BETTY RETURNED to her tepee, she found Emma staring into a fire that was now only red embers. She sat with her legs crossed and hands lying limply in her lap.

"Emma?" Betty said softly. "Are you okay? Is John okay?" She put some wood on the fire and then sat next to her.

"Crow Old Man said it will take many moons for John's body to heal."

"Oh, sweetheart, I'm not surprised. He is pretty broken up. Has his sickness gone?"

Emma nodded. "He cannot move until his bones have knitted."

Betty sensed there was more to Emma's mood and patiently waited.

"The People will be moving to their winter camp in half that time. They will not return to this valley until buhisea'-mea'."

"When is that?"

"It is the budding moon."

Betty thought about the different seasons and calculated the timing. "That means springtime. May? But that's nearly a year."

Emma sighed. "I don't want to leave John. But I cannot stay away from my children that long."

"Of course not. Have you talked to John about this?"

"Not yet. Crow Old Man walked with me. He said I should pray for a vision to help me decide." Emma leaned forward, stretching her back and neck. "I am very happy to be among my People again. But two parts of my heart are not here."

Betty sat quietly, knowing Emma's heart was warring with her mind.

"It is not for me to decide. Tomorrow I will ask *Puha* for guidance." Emma breathed a huge sigh.

She looked up, and her eyes were clearer. Her jaw seemed set in quiet determination, and her body looked settled.

"How was your visit with Jumping Fish and Moon Fawn?"

Betty grinned and raised an eyebrow. "It is wonderful to see my friend alive and happy. But I'm a bit unsettled by her choice of mates. Were your People not initially put off?"

"No. They are looked upon with great honor. It is rare that two women can share such a strong totem. They do not join the men on patrol, but have been known to watch over and bravely defend the village if need be. They also provide food, finding deer when the men cannot, especially during dommo-mea', um, winter. Crow Old Man says their medicine is almost as powerful as his own."

"I'm not surprised. Mayme has always shown me to be fearless and adventuresome. She would've had to be to hold the post rider job. When she was young, she was put on a train by her father. Even now I'm still angry that her family would've abandoned and sent their own child into the unknown."

"She has done well. They have a herd of fast and agile horses that are looked upon with envy. My brother has stopped challenging Jumping Fish to races because he always loses." Emma chuckled. "But he is proud to have her as a friend."

"Would you ever bring your family back here to live?" Betty stirred the fire and added another piece of wood. Sparks rose lazily and disappeared through the open flaps above.

Emma stared into the fire for such a long time, Betty wasn't sure she'd heard her. "When a *nabusai* comes to me in my sleep, it is always with my People. But my home is with John and my children. Sometimes we talk about it. There are hardships in each place because of the many haters in the white man's world. My People are living in peace for the moment, but John thinks it will not be long before soldiers come. Because of that, he thinks we are safer living where we do."

"I suppose you're right. There's been talk of regiments arriving in Elk City, but thankfully they've not shown up in Oro Fino. And if they do venture this far, hopefully they won't find this place."

"They know my People are here," Emma said softly.

"John didn't . . ."

"No. Long before John found us, two men came when I was young. They were guided here by a trapper from where the bright star rises. John told me it is a place called Canada."

"Did they make trouble?"

"They caused great suspicion among the warriors who thought they were agents for our enemies, the Blackfeet. Or maybe others. They carried weapons my People had never seen before."

"Guns?" Betty could imagine the fear invoked by such strange items.

"Yes. Long rifles, pistols, and a gun that used air to shoot balls of lead. It was very quiet, and the men did not trust it."

"I've never heard of such a thing. Are you sure it didn't use gun powder?"

"It did not. I remember it was a very long rifle, but as I said, I was very young and things always seemed bigger. But I remember the man called Lewis said we didn't need to cover our ears."

"Did they hurt anyone?" Although Betty had only known the People for a short time, she felt oddly protective of them, likely because Mayme lived among them.

"No. I do remember they were quite impressed with themselves. They marched in, wearing colorful jackets, sparkling swords, odd hats, and polished guns and bayonets. They flew flags and blew whistles. The women and children hid in the tepees, while the men met them, ready for a fight. But soon the women saw the gifts they had with them: colorful cloth, beads, and other trinkets, and were allowed to come out."

"They wanted to trade?" Betty couldn't believe they had carried such weapons on such a trip.

"My grandfather was told they were explorers. They had a Shoshone woman with them who made the talk so my People could understand. It was said they were looking for a way to the north and west by water. They wanted to connect the east to the west and find other land across the great water."

"I think they were referring to China and maybe other countries. Your People were left alone after they were gone?"

Emma yawned. "There were good and bad people who came to trade over many moons. The bad were taken care of. I married the good one."

WHEN BETTY OPENED her eyes the next morning, she realized Emma had already gone. She looked through the upper flaps of the tepee as she lay under the comforts of the buffalo hide. The sky looked grey and moody this dawn hour. Specific time was irrelevant for the People. They stirred when their eyes opened and slept when they were tired. Although meals seemed to be timed with those that lived under the same tepee, they ate when they were hungry. It seemed time was governed only by their individual needs, daily activities, the sunrise and setting, and the seasons. Not by the constraints of the white man's clock, where hands pointing at numbers delegated certain actions. Where she came from, youngsters were trained very early in life that the watch was master and were forced to commit to it.

Emma must have gone well before sunrise, but had fed the fire before she'd left. The coals were glowing fresh, and a few flames flickered and danced above them. Betty rose and prepared coffee while chewing on a piece of smoked venison and a handful of dried berries.

She sympathized with the decision Emma was faced with. If she were to leave, she wouldn't see her husband for close to a year. But could she leave her children in the care of someone she barely knew? True, Anna had proved she was capable, and it was easy to see she was fond of Grace and Henry. No doubt she would keep them occupied with school lessons. But for them to be without their mother for that long would be intolerable. For the children and Emma. She was glad to not have to make the choice herself.

Scratching at the flap alerted her to a visitor. Surprised, she quickly said, "Yes. Come in."

Mayme threw the flap aside, and with a smile, sat down across the fire from Betty. "Do you know how long it has been since I've had a cup of coffee?" She eyed the kettle heating in the coals and drew in a long breath through her nose.

Betty chuckled. "Best be careful then. You'll be bouncing on your tiptoes all day." She poured each of them a cup and gazed fondly at Mayme and blew over the top, before venturing a sip of the hot liquid.

Mayme took a sip and closed her eyes. "This is one of the few things I miss about back there. Aside from you and Mr. Smart of course. I used to stash bags of coffee inside my mochila to balance the mail and have a couple more in my saddle bags. I could've cried when it was all gone."

Betty shook her head, amused. This was the Mayme she'd known so well. She'd seemed a bit formal last night while sitting next to Moon Fawn. She wondered if that was the norm or if Mayme had been trying to show strength to the woman she lived with.

"You are welcome to a cup every morning for as long as we're here." Betty set her cup on her lap.

"I hope you can stay for a long while then." Mayme looked at the kettle, then Betty, and raised an eyebrow.

Betty laughed. "Help yourself."

Mayme's face was tanned a beautiful brown. If it weren't for the shape of her face, she would easily be passed over as a naturally born part of the Shoshone. She moved easily in her buckskin shirt and leggings. Both were adorned with fringe. The shirt had a row of different colored horse hair, bound with leather ties, attached on the right. Small pieces of antler hung on the other side, pinned to the shirt with porcupine quills.

"Do you remember my horse, Duster?" Mayme ran her hand over the grouping of horsehair.

"Yes, of course. Is she still with you?"

"She has many more grey hairs these days, but has given me six grey foals from a black stallion. She leaves the herd at night and sleeps near my tepee."

"Your bond with her has always been strong."

"I ride her when I can, although it is much slower these days." Mayme's eyes brightened, and she sat up straight. "Would you like to ride with me today?"

"Given I have no engagements planned, yes, I would like that very much."

Mayme emptied her cup in one gulp and got to her feet. "I will bring Duster and your horse up while you get dressed." She quickly disappeared through the flap.

Betty chuckled to herself. Yes, that was her old Mayme. Spontaneous and excitable, but quiet and calm when she had to be. Although she'd grown into a beautiful woman, there were still bits of the young girl Betty had met years ago.

By the time she'd pulled on her trousers and long-sleeved shirt, and put her boots on, she heard hooves slowly plodding in her direction. She ducked and exited the tepee to find Mayme already mounted on Duster. Indeed, the mare was nearly white, with only a dusting of the blue-grey that had covered most of her hide in earlier years. But although she wasn't as muscular as she was when Mayme rode her to deliver mail, she looked fit and happy. Her bulbous belly spoke of the foals she'd carried.

Betty's white mare stood calmly next to Duster, held only by a rope around her neck. "It'll take me a few minutes to saddle her."

"Just put her bridle on," Mayme said as she slid off her horse. "You can ride bareback. We won't go fast."

Betty furrowed her eyebrows. "I don't know, Mayme."

"You'll be fine. Trust me."

Snowdrift accepted the bit without issue as usual. Betty moved to her side and wondered how she'd get on. The problem was solved when Mayme wove the fingers of both her hands together for Betty to place her foot in. Betty bounced once then was lifted up, and she easily swung her right leg over the horse's back. She watched in awe as Mayme grabbed hold of Duster's mane in her left hand and seemingly without effort, vaulted onto her back.

"How long did it take you to learn that trick?" Betty shifted her bum from side to side, looking to find a secure seat. Snowdrift's withers were covered in flesh, and therefore not painful to sit against. But she still missed the assurance of the saddle horn and stirrups.

"A while," Mayme said with mischievous merriment in her eyes. "I had to practice on a shorter horse first. I hit the ground on the other side a couple times because I jumped too hard. Then poor Duster had to put up with my heel in her side and back more than a few times until I got used to her height." She scrubbed the horse's neck affectionately. "Ready?"

"Can we take it slow? I already feel like I'm going to slide off." Betty grabbed a handful of mane and crouched down.

"Sit up straight and push your legs down like your feet are in the stirrups. Your muscles will remember and help you stay on."

Betty found herself relaxing as they walked along the river. True to Mayme's words, she began to feel much more comfortable. She gripped her horse lightly with her knees and moved in time with her strides. She discovered she felt Snowdrift's movements more directly and before long, was able to ride in easy rhythm with her. The gliding, ground covering feeling was like none other. Betty felt more a part of her horse, the warmth of the animal and the muscles working beneath her, exhilarating.

A vast silence reigned over the land as they turned away from the river. Rolling hills led up to huge outcroppings of underlying granite and gaunt pines that towered somberly everywhere. There were large swaths of birch trees and poplar, their leaves quaking in the invisible breeze high above. They rode through them, hooves made silent by the layers and layers of shed leaves that had been pressed flat by the heavy snows, now only a memory, but a certainty in the not-so-distant future.

"How did you come to meet Aka, um, Sunflower? Sorry, it's been such a long time since I've spoken English." Mayme broke the silence for the first time since they'd left the camp.

Betty drew in a big breath, wondering how much to tell her. "I first saw her when she and her children were at Doc's surgery when John got hurt. Then a few days later, I interrupted some cowboys harassing her and found myself in the middle of it."

"How did you end up here?" Mayme pulled Duster to a stop and slid off.

"It's a bit hard to tell. Even I have a hard time believing it sometimes. I had decided to not participate in the business anymore. So, I . . ."

"Did something happen? Did some heathen hurt you?" Mayme interrupted. Duster sensed her change in mood and pranced around her.

Betty averted her eyes, not wanting to watch the anguish on Mayme's face. "Yes," She said quietly.

"Who?"

"It's not important."

"Who, Betty? Tell me."

"Mayme," Betty said, finally meeting Mayme's eyes. Her eyes blazed with rage. She stood rigid with her fists clenched. "It doesn't matter anymore."

"It does to me." Mayme wiped a stray tear from her eye.

Betty quickly slid off and wrapped her arms around Mayme. She smelled of the earth and water and wood smoke. "I know it does. I love you for that. But it will all be taken care of eventually."

"You're right. It will. When I find out who it was, I'll track him down and kill him myself." Mayme's body was rigid against her own.

Betty looked up and didn't recognize her for an instant. She'd taken on the hard glint of a warrior, her face taunt and ready for a massacre.

"No, you will most certainly not. Emma and I, and the woman who is caring for Emma's children, have a plan in the works."

"Whatever it is, I want in." Mayme fingered the sheathed knife on her hip.

Betty stepped back from Mayme, her hands resting on her shoulders. "Emma had a vision. Apparently there were three eagles which signified Emma, Anna, and myself. We have to trust that vision."

Mayme seemed to search Betty's eyes. Her body became less rigid under Betty's hands.

"Things will work out." Betty hoped she sounded more convincing than she felt.

"I will help if you ask."

"I know you will. Now, can we continue our ride? I'm kinda liking this bareback thing you got me doing." Betty gave her a reassuring grin.

Mayme nodded. "Would you like to try getting on by yourself?" She cocked a teasing eyebrow.

Betty laughed. "I'm quite sure I'd make an utter fool of myself or hurt myself in the process. Both probably. So, if you wouldn't mind giving me a leg up again."

"Suit yourself." Mayme chuckled and stood at Snowdrift's side.

Once mounted, they followed the tree line for a while and then turned onto the grasslands in the direction of the river. Mayme held up her hand in a motion to stop. She loaded an arrow onto a bow Betty had only just now noticed. The quiver of arrows and bow had hung so close to her back, they had blended in with the brown buckskin shirt she wore.

Mayme let the arrow fly and quickly jumped off Duster. She ran swiftly and claimed her quarry. She walked back clutching the limp body of a prairie grouse. "Are you hungry?" She dropped to her knees and field dressed the bird.

They rode to the river and found a flat, rock covered wash. Wood was abundant from the recent spring's melt so it took no time to gather enough.

Mayme collected a handful of dried grass and tiny sticks. She withdrew a piece of flint from a small bag around her neck, and the knife from its sheath. She knelt next to her small pile and struck the steel down against the flint. The grass caught the resulting sparks and it soon glowed. Mayme blew on it gently. Smoke floated up and the tinder burst into flame. When the fire burned bright, Mayme placed the bird, feathers and all into the center of the fire, where the flames quickly engulfed it and turned it black.

Betty watched on as Mayme turned the bird a couple times with the aid of a forked stick. Finally, she flicked the now burnt bird out of the fire and onto the cool damp rocks where she pulled back the charred skin, revealing the juicy meat beneath.

In another world, Betty would have found herself looking for place settings and utensils. But she sat down wordlessly next to Mayme and accepted the meat offered to her with the blade of her knife and ate it with her fingers. The flavors of the dark meat and juices danced on her tongue.

"Oh, my heavens, I don't think I've ever tasted a bird this delicious." Betty wiped the juices that had escaped down her chin with the back of her hand.

Mayme grinned and shoved a large piece of breast meat into her mouth. "I used to crave salt on my food. But Moon Fawn taught me how to season with things like sage, onion, garlic, sumac, and ginger."

"This doesn't need a thing," Betty said between mouthfuls.

Shortly thereafter, the fire extinguished, the remains of the bird left for a fox that had been studying them from a short distance away, and with full stomachs, they began the ride back to the camp. The horses were content, sighing as they walked. They had grazed heartily on the long, lush grass that lined the riverbanks.

"Emma left early this morning to pray for a vision. Our time here is largely dependent on what she sees," Betty said quietly.

"Crow Old Man has said that. Whatever her totem guides her to do will be the right decision."

Betty frowned. "Yes, I know. Either way, I'll be sad to leave because I've just found you again. But at least I know you're alive and happy."

"It will not be the last you see of me, I promise."

"How can you make that promise with all the unrest that is brewing?"

"The People have survived hardships and battles for centuries. They will continue to do so."

"Oh, Mayme, please tell me you're not that naive. There are more soldiers and guns out there than you can count." Betty recognized the anger and frustration in her own voice. "The danger is real. You and the tribe should be afraid."

"And what will constant fear bring us? Sickness and anxiety. The men are watchful and are good warriors. They will keep the women and children safe and well. Bear Hunter will take us deeper into the mountains where no one can find us."

"I hope you're right." Betty raised her eyes to the horizon, almost expecting to see soldiers lining the hills. But other than the few lone, windswept trees that had bravely driven their roots into the unforgiving ground, the knolls were bare. She blinked and squinted into the radiance rising from the landscape. Slowly the wavy images of the tepees materialized. Although she wasn't anything like the worshipping type, she sent a quiet prayer to whatever spirits were listening, that the People would know peace for a very long time.

As they drew closer to the lodge Betty occupied, Mayme said, "Would you like to ride again tomorrow?"

"I would like that very much." Betty slid off Snowdrift. Her groin ached and her legs were tired from the constant effort it took to stay astride the horse. Until now, she hadn't noticed. She took a few tentative steps on jelly legs and looked up at Mayme. "If I can walk tomorrow, that is."

"You will feel stiffness tomorrow, but riding will help."

Betty groaned. "Are you sure about that?"

Mayme chuckled. She slid the bridle off of Snowdrift, replaced it with her rope, and tugged gently. The mare dutifully followed Duster as they turned in the direction of the grazing herd.

The tepee was empty and quiet when Betty entered it. The fire had long since died, the coals burned to ash and gone cold. There was no sign that Emma had been back. It was late afternoon, and the sun was starting its decent. It would be dark soon.

Betty lit the fire while nibbling on a piece of jerky and washed it down with several large swallows of water. She added a few large pieces of wood and watched the small flames lick them. Suddenly tired, she laid back on her bedding, drew the buffalo hide over herself, and fell fast asleep.

# Chapter Fourteen

EMMA WOKE A few hours before dawn. She quietly pulled on her buckskin shirt, trousers and high moccasins. After adding some fuel to the fire, she slipped out of the tepee with only a flint and knife. She wouldn't need anything else.

The sky was lit with millions of stars, and one that glowed brighter than the others. A slash of opaque white covered a part of the sky to the south, engulfing its share of stars. The moon had chosen to be absent this night.

Dew had moistened the grass, making her passage among the other lodges largely silent. Once she'd gotten closer to the river, she whistled low and was answered by Coal's nicker. The black horse was largely invisible in the dark, but she could hear him walking in her direction, blowing softly as he worked to scent her whereabouts.

She whistled again and, having located her, he trotted the last several yards.

Coal lowered his head against her chest and blew softly while she rubbed his neck and cooed to him. She slid to his side, grabbed a handful of mane, and vaulted onto his back. Using her legs and slight shifts in weight, she guided him north. Far beyond the grassy knolls, she would find the high rocky cliffs used by so many of her People in their quests for visions and guidance from the spirits and their totems.

A breeze teased the tall grasses, bending their stems low, before easing and allowing them to briefly straighten again. The sun showed a hint of glow, still hidden below the hills to the east. Mountain bluebirds sang from grass tops, flashing their sky-blue plumage as they plunged into the grass after insects. A small flock of white-crowned sparrows flew toward her and split to avoid horse and rider. Emma smiled, knowing their presence was a blessed omen of protection, and would ward off evil spirits. A red-tailed hawk called from above her, its distinctive reddish tail flaring as it navigated the sky in circles, in search of an unsuspecting mouse or rabbit.

The sun grew more intense, the higher she rode. The sporadic trees became scarce and finally absent as the thick grass covered ground gave way to intermittent patches amongst outcrops of rock. A trickle of water flowed into a deep stone pool. Its source a mystery, hidden deep within the depths of the compressed slabs.

Emma slid off Coal's back. His hide was slick with sweat from the effort of the climb. She would leave him here. The horse would have sufficient feed and water to last a few days if that's what it took, and a large overhang offered shelter. The rock dust beneath it was littered with the tracks of hare, mice, coyote, and the horses of other vision seekers. The absence of doyaduku, the cat who prowled the rocks was a relief. Coal would be safe. Lone horses often fell victim to predators. Without the protection of the herd, where many eyes and noses alerted them to danger, he would be vulnerable. More than likely he would descend to the safety of the grasslands at night and come back during the day to drink and wait for her return.

Emma drank deeply from the pool. It would be the last water she would have until she came back down.

Coal came to her side, dipped his head, and quenched his thirst. When he finished, Emma leaned her forehead against his neck and breathed in his dark, rooty fragrance mixed with the pungency of sweat. He smelled of strength and security.

"I will return soon, my friend. Be safe." Emma faced the wall of rock and boulders and took a deep breath. She wended her way through the outcrop. As she climbed, she heard only her own breathing and heartbeat and felt the burn in her arms and legs. The rocks were sharp and loose beneath her feet as the pebbles shifted with every step. She slid back a step for every two she took. Small rocks clattered down in her wake. Finally, she had climbed high enough to find secure footing on a narrow ledge and paused to catch her breath. Sweat ran freely down her face and neck, and she swiped it away with her sleeve. A wind blew softly over her overheated skin, and if not for the buckskin, it would have chilled her body. She listened to it whistling along the slopes, creating its own music. A falcon screamed at her, unhappy with being disturbed from its hunting perch.

The rest of her ascent, although steep, and with sharp finger holds, took less time. Grit drifted onto her face with every movement. A natural route full of switchbacks gave her some relief from the fatigue plaguing her legs. She finally spotted her destination. A huge crag formed a small cave that offered protection from the constant wind yet faced the southwest to take advantage of the sun. The rock absorbed the heat and would stay warm well into the night. With no ability to make fire, this was the best alternative.

Emma slid her knife from the sheath. She was in more danger than ever of confronting a lion, who may have claimed the cave as its own. As she crept closer, she scanned the sparse ground for footprints, scat, or remains of a kill. If a male cat were in the area, he would mark his domain with his urine. But the area smelled fresh. Still on guard, she approached the opening warily and didn't relax until she was sure it was safe. Relief flooded through her, and she sat down at the opening of the cave. A feeling of intimate tranquility settled into her chest as her eyes swept over the peaks in the distance, and the vast grasslands below. The clouds were high and constantly shifting, causing great shadows of movement on the ground.

The cave's floor consisted of a few loose rocks sitting on top of soft, dusty sand, created from thousands of years of wind erosion. The air was cool despite the sun beaten rocks at the entrance. Cryptic etchings of bison, arrows, deer, the river, and bear claws were scratched into the rock, probably with knives or sharp rocks. Emma wondered how many had come before her in search of guidance, and if it had been only her People.

One particular drawing toward the back of the cave caught her eye. She tilted her head and ran her fingers over the rock etching. Eight stick figures carrying what looked like spears had surrounded a creature she'd never seen or heard of. It was a massive animal compared to the figures seemingly hunting it. Oddly, it had two large, curved teeth escaping its mouth, and its nose was long and droopy. From the long lines drawn vertically over its body, it must have been a very hairy animal.

Intrigued, she searched for other odd drawings, but there were only those on the one side of the cave. Emma leaned against the opposing wall and felt a breeze that was absent on the other side. It seemed any others had been worn away by the prevailing wind.

Shadows crept into the cave as the sun set. Weary from her long journey and climb, Emma searched for the best place to lay down. It would have to be where the loose footing seemed deepest. The night would be black, long, and chilly, for lack of a fire. She scooped out and mounded the sand as best she could, taking advantage of the retained warmth. Satisfied with her makeshift bed, she settled into it. She lay with her hands clasped over her chest and gazed at the ceiling. She widened her eyes as images came into focus. Hand prints colored in the red ochre clay of the river covered the ceiling. In between the clusters were colored paintings of deer, horses, and bison with a huge hump and long horns that curved upward.

The light faded quickly thereafter, making it impossible to see anything else. She turned her head to look out onto the moonless landscape and saw nothing discernible. The stars had yet to appear, but even their presence would keep the night dark. Emma pulled the knife from her sheath and laid it on her chest as a precaution. It would be there in case she had to use it quickly. She closed her eyes and took a deep cleansing breath. There was little sound beyond her breathing. The wind had dropped off to little more than intermittent movements of air. She smelled dust and the faintness of pine from miles away. As she lay unmoving, her head pounded and spun. A leg cramped painfully, and she rose quickly, fighting the dizziness, to straighten and massage the tangled muscles. She pushed a fist into her ribs as a side-stitch formed. She accepted it. It was part of the process.

Emma blindly looked for the knife that had slipped off when she got up. On her knees, she swept her hands back and forth, but they came up empty. She widened her search from the hollow she'd been laying in. Finally, just short of panic, her fingers felt the cold steel. She gripped the handle. She sat back and held the knife to her chest, and drew a deep breath threw her nose, and quietly exhaled. She decided to re-sheathe the knife to avoid losing it again. She chastised herself for the stupid mistake. Had she become too complacent living in John's world? In the white man's world? Sharp instincts and common sense, once always forefront in her mind had seemed to become soft. John had once called her jumpy when they'd arrived at his home. Everything had been strange except his comfort. She had been wary of everything. The solid enclosure of the cabin had been dark and claustrophobic. John had found her asleep on the porch or with the horses many a time. When had she given in to that? After the children were born? No, a mother's protection and intuition would naturally grow stronger. When then? Had it been the routine John had instilled in her? Before the children, he'd insisted on staying in bed in the morning until they'd made love. They'd rise for breakfast and begin the daily upkeep of the livestock and farm. She decided that was when her mind and body had begun to dull. Thankfully *Puha* had not deserted her. She wondered if her parents had noticed the softness in her and felt ashamed. She was Shoshoni and would start thinking like one again. Her family's survival depended on it. *Puha* would give her guidance as he always had. In fact, it had been he that had bestowed the vision of John during her time of mourning. She had dismissed it, given her depth of grief. But twelve full moons later, when the trapper had been forced to spend the winter, she had realized what her spirit guide had been conveying.

Emma settled into her makeshift bed once again. Thoughts of her guardian had calmed her. She touched the sheathed knife for reassurance, closed her eyes, and willed her body to relax and ease the tension out of her tightened muscles. She emptied her mind of thought and listened to the cadence of her heart.

*The rustling of leaves woke her. Her back was stiff from leaning against a tree. She opened her eyes, and her breath caught. Puha, in the shape of a great elk stood in front of her. He lowered his majestic antlered head and took one step toward her. She sat frozen, eyes wide, but oddly at ease. The elk turned away, its body blurring and morphing. It took on the shape of a bear and rose onto its hind feet. Fog rose up from the ground and it became a white wall of moving snow. Emma watched as John's accident unfolded. She saw the horror on Henry's face and subsequent grief and desperate attempt to be brave as he shot the horse. After he raced off to get her, she heard John talking.*

*"kamangande, I love you. If I don't make it through this, take Henry and Grace and go back to your People. I am strong. I will do my best to stay with you."*

*Emma relived the birth of each of her children. She felt the pain of labor, smelled the blood, heard their first cries. She blinked. Henry and Grace stood before her as toddlers, both wearing the traditional dress of her People. She watched as their bodies changed and grew into the children she'd known before she'd left them. Their smiles were bright as they looked into her eyes. But tears formed, ran in rivers down their cheeks, and dropped onto the ground at their feet. Grass and trees sprung up and grew high, obscuring Henry and Grace. A herd of horses, many with foals at their sides thundered past, terror in their eyes, chased by men with scarves hiding their identity. The dust in their wake dispersed. The prairie was silent and clear but for a trickle of smoke rising from a mound of blackened rubble. Emma realized she was looking at what remained of the cabin and barn. She frantically looked around for Henry and Grace. She finally saw them riding their horses. Another rode with them on a horse as well. Her home, still in one piece, stood strong on the horizon behind them. The wind swept the images away, and John reappeared.*

*"We will come back to you, Aka."*

*John blurred and the elk returned with three eagles perched on its back. They opened their wings and engulfed the elk.*

*Emma slowly opened her eyes and blinked in confusion. The images of the hands above her rippled as if waving. A low growl and hiss brought her attention to the cave opening. A huge lion crouched, ready to spring. She reached for her knife, but it wasn't in her sheath. She risked a glance down to look for it. But it was too late. The lion launched itself.*

Emma woke with a start, looking for her knife. Her hand closed on the antler handle. In one movement, she pulled it, and jumped to her feet, ready to defend herself. But the cave was empty. There was no sound but her quickened breath and the pounding of her heart in her ears. She cautiously approached the entrance, looking for footprints, listening for the lion, smelling for his odor. But the dirt contained only her footprints and the large imprint of wings as only an eagle could make. A movement on the cave wall caught her eye. She moved closer, still wary of the lion in her dream. Three feathers, all golden in color, all eagle, were caught in a crevice in the wall, the morning breeze gently lifting them up like a bird ready to take flight.

Legs suddenly weak from relief, Emma sat down and licked her chapped lips. She realized the lion had been part of her dream. The feathers fluttered quietly. Those three feathers. What did they mean? Henry, Grace, and herself? Betty, Anna, and herself? She would have to ask Crow Old Man.

The morning sky was clear and streaked with red and shades of blue. It was time to leave. Emma rose and toured the cave one last time, committing to memory the images the walls bore. She mentally thanked the invisible spirits who had guided her brother, father, grandfather, and many before them. At the cave opening, she shivered in the morning cold, for the sun had not fully risen enough to offer heat. She gently collected the feathers and guided them into the knife sheath, where they'd be safe.

The descent was more difficult. Her legs were stiff, her body's energy stores depleted from overexertion and dehydration. Her movements were lethargic, and her mind was dull. She worked to concentrate fully on where to place her hands and feet to avoid a catastrophic fall. She constantly adjusted grip and footing. Sweat ran into her eyes from the effort, despite the coolness of the air and rocks.

By the time she reached the bottom, she had nothing left. Her stomach had long since given up asking for food. She hadn't eaten since the prior morning. Water was her priority. Her muscles cramps were agonizingly painful. She forced herself to focus on her task despite the threatening hallucinations at the corners of her mind.

She crawled on hands and knees to the pool and drank until she couldn't drink anymore. Her stomach revolted and forced the water back up. She wiped her lips and drank slower, take sips more often. Exhaustion overcame her. She lay back on the rock and fell asleep in the sun. There were no dreams this time.

Soft breath and a fuzzy muzzle against her cheek woke her. Emma smiled without opening her eyes. Coal. She knew without a doubt he would stay with and guard her until she was ready to rise. After quenching her thirst again, although much more slowly, she closed her eyes and slept again.

The sun was starting its descent when she woke. Coal grazed on the sparse grass just feet from her. He glanced her way and nickered. Streaks of sweat coated his hide. He'd obviously stood over her during the hottest part of the day, protecting her from the harsh heat.

Emma sat up on her elbows and debated the journey back. Her long sleep would keep her restless during the night. But without the moon's light, the ride could be treacherous. She decided to stay put for a couple hours. She would know after dark if the moon would rise. In the meantime, she would take advantage of the warm rocks after a much-needed bath. The excess water flowed over a ledge, creating a sedate waterfall. She undressed and carefully climbed down. The stream wasn't much, but it was enough to rinse off the sweat and dust. Small particles of sandy dirt allowed her to give her body a refreshing scrub. One last rinse and she climbed back up.

Coal stood at the edge, watching her, and nickered a greeting as she returned to the top. Emma leaned her forehead against his and rubbed his cheeks. She loosened her braided hair and let it fall down her back to dry and then set about gathering mature grass heads that were tucked amongst higher rocks. Coal hadn't been able to reach them despite his long neck. Using their stems, she wrapped them together to form a crude brush.

Her body dried quickly and as the sun dipped further still, a chilly breeze rose gooseflesh over her body. Although she welcomed the sensation, she put her clothing on, the soft hides so familiar against her skin. Once her moccasins were laced up, she called Coal to her. His coat was rough with sweat and dirt. Using her brush, she firmly swiped his hide in the direction the hair grew. Coal sighed in contentment, his nose wiggling, clearly enjoying the sensation.

As a young girl, she had spent hours brushing her father's horses. She had groomed the mares and introduced the foals to the sensation of human touch. Even the moody stallion succumbed to her touch and let her whisk away the dirt, before indignantly trotting away from her, tossing his head with pride. She'd known it was only an act to keep up appearances.

Emma ran her hands over Coal, making sure she'd loosened every last streak of sweat. If the sun had been higher, she knew his coat would be gleaming. Her stomach growled and lurched, wanting food. Her activities had made her even hungrier. She knelt at the pool and drank to temporarily squelch its complaining.

Despite her hunger, when the moon failed to rise, she decided the risk would be too great to go down the mountain in the dark. She recalled having to carefully navigate him over treacherous rock on the way up. The descent would be even more difficult and taxing. The dangers were too real. Coal could lose his footing with her aboard and fall. That, in itself, could be fatal for both of them. Rattlesnakes were abundant in the rocks, although she'd not seen one on the way up. But they often hunted at night, taking advantage of the warm ground to keep them mobile. Should they make it down to the grasslands unscathed, hidden gopher holes and even unfriendly humans moving in the night were possible dangers. No, she would wait until dawn.

In an attempt to squelch the empty, gnawing feeling in her belly, she chewed on grass stems. They were fairly tasteless, but with frequent drinks of water, they quieted her rumbling stomach. They failed however, to eliminate her headache and the slight trembling in her hands. Finding a comfortable place to lie down on the rocks was impossible. In the end, she leaned against a large boulder and closed her eyes. She heard Coal move closer to her, once again preparing to stand guard over her. She focused on his deep, methodic breathing and matched her own with his.

Coal's grazing woke her as he yanked the remainder of the dried grass from the hard ground. There was only a hint of light in the sky. Emma didn't remember falling asleep, and was in fact, quite surprised that she had. Using the boulder as a prop, she pushed herself to stand. Her bum was numb and there were still vestiges of stiffness in her limbs. When she felt her legs were steady enough to support her, she walked behind a rock and relieved herself. From there, she went to the pool and drank. It would be her last, and she sent a silent thanks to the spirits who had kept it full and clean. She whistled for Coal to join her at the pool. She placed the handful of grass heads she'd collected on top of the water to encourage him to drink. Coal was familiar with this trick. He lipped the grass into his mouth, then drank. He lifted his wet muzzle and nuzzled Emma. Drops of water trickled onto her cheek and ran down her neck.

"All right, my boy. Let's go home." She grabbed his mane and in one motion, jumped and threw her right leg over his back. It felt good to be on soft flesh as opposed to hard rock.

The day grew brighter as they rode down the mountainside. She let Coal grab mouthfuls of grass as they went. She was in no hurry. They'd be back to the village by dusk. She took a deep, satisfied breath and enjoyed the warm sun on her face. A breeze brushed her hair, and she pushed it behind her ears. Tall grass slid against her legs as she rode.

The dream still confused her, but it was for Crow Old Man to interpret it for her, as he had done for so many other vision seekers. She would make her decision based on his words. For now, she would enjoy the peacefulness that filled her.

The swish of the grasses blowing in the wind didn't mask the drone of bees on the many flowers that had opened since her earlier passage. Dragonflies and other insects flew up, disturbed by Coal's hooves. She breathed deeply, taking in the smell of grass, warm earth, and sweet flowers.

Coal stopped and pricked his ears forward. He snorted in annoyance and tossed his head. Emma placed a hand on his neck and leaned forward to try and locate the source of his agitation. Ah, yes. There it was: A harmless, yet large, five-foot prairie gopher snake. Its striped, thick body lay in an *S* shape around the mouse it had just killed. It hissed and flicked its tail like a rattlesnake, clearly not happy its breakfast had been interrupted. Emma guided Coal in a wide berth around the snake, leaving it to eat.

Shadows drifted over the land as clouds passed overhead. Shafts of sun lit up the prairie in between them. The miles seemed to pass quickly. Coal quickened his step and lifted his head. Emma squinted and saw the vast herd of horses in the distance. She squeezed her legs, leaned forward, and encouraged Coal to gallop the last couple miles. Her loose hair flowed in waves behind her, the fringe on her shirt and trousers flapped wildly. As they drew closer, many of the horses raised their heads and watched, some whinnied a greeting, and still others seemed indifferent. Emma guided Coal to the river and slid off. A great blue heron took to flight, squawking irritably as it pulled itself into the air.

Emma twisted her long hair and dropped it over one shoulder. She drank deeply and then cupped her hands together and washed her dust covered face. She blinked the water from her eyes and wiped her upper lip with the back of her hand. She watched as Coal returned to the herd, reacquainting himself with squeals and strikes to the ground. The horses soon grew uninterested, and they all returned to grazing, Coal included.

Despite her hunger, Emma was determined to see John and speak with Crow Old Man. She walked with a fast-paced stride to the medicine man's tepee. While very eager to see her husband, she needed the old man's insight.

She stopped outside his lodge and scratched the hide in greeting. Upon hearing Crown Old Man's characteristic huff, which sounded more bison than human, she drew the flap aside and entered. She glanced to the right, where John lay. His eyes were closed, and he seemed to be sleeping.

Crow Old Man sat cross-legged next to his fire. A long pipe, decorated with eagle feathers and the skull of a crow, dangled from his bony fingers as he inhaled from it. He looked up at her with rummy eyes through the smoke and motioned her to sit with him. He offered her the pipe with two hands and nodded. Emma accepted it and bowed her head in recognition of the act. She placed the end of the pipe into her mouth and drew smoke into it. She tasted tobacco mixed with red willow, sumac, and birch. The smoke was light and pleasant. Thankfully Crow Old Man had foregone the kinnikinnick this time, which was heavy and apt to leave one in a stupefied condition.

Emma returned the pipe to Crow Old Man and stared into the fire.

"*Puha* has visited you." Crow Old Man placed the pipe at his side.

"Yes." She withdrew the three feathers and held them in her lap. "He sent me a dream and left these. But I don't know what they mean."

"Eagle feathers are powerful medicine. It is a strong message and a difficult meaning to bear."

Emma raised her eyes and met his. "I don't understand."

"My child, you have always been one to whom the spirits speak freely. Many men live their entire lives without having been visited by their totem after their naming. *Puha* has a task for you to complete."

"Yes. But what? I am torn between the decision of staying here with John and going back to my children."

"That decision has no basis on the sign you have been given." Crow Old Man stroked his chin and watched the fire for a moment.

Emma knew better than to interrupt the medicine man's thoughts. When he was ready, he would speak directly. If interrupted, his thoughts would fork like the branches of a tree, and she would be no further ahead.

The fire crackled, and sparks rose and disappeared into the night through the lodge's opening. She could hear John's soft snore as he slept on the hides behind her. Tension built in her neck, shoulders, and back as she waited. But she remained motionless in respect for Crow Old Man's pondering.

Finally, he spoke without looking from the fire. "*Puha* has chosen *pites*. You and two others who have recently entered your lodge. Three of you. There is another of this tribe who will join you for a short time."

Emma held the feathers up in sudden realization. How could she have been so naive? It was so plain to see what *Puha* desired. The feathers were yet another sign that everything decision she made from here on out must include three people. She must focus on the task, not the moons before or after. John would be mended here. Jumping Fish would accompany she and Betty back to the ranch. *Three.* Jumping Fish would bring Henry and Grace here. *Three.* They would stay with their father. *Three.* She, Betty, and Anna would continue with their plan. *Three.*

There was a scratch on the tepee. Crow Old Man grunted, and the flap was pushed to the side and Jumping Fish stepped in. Without a word, she sat down and accepted the pipe from Crow Old Man. Using a small twig, she lit the pipe and smoked for a few moments, while gazing into the fire. She then handed the pipe to Emma, who also smoked before returning it to Crow Old Man.

"We will leave when the moon is full." Emma stood up and went to John. She moved his long hair off of his forehead and brushed her hands over his beard. Although asleep, he sighed in contentment. She gently kissed his lips and after wiping a tear from her cheek, she left him, noting there were three now in the tepee.

# Chapter Fifteen

"LET ME HELP you with that, ma'am," the mercantile clerk said. He took the trolly handle from her and pulled it through the doorway.

"Thank you. I appreciate it," Anna said as she followed him out of the store, clutching the small purse containing the last few cents she owned. She raised her dress and tentatively stepped down the steps that led to the muddy road.

It had been raining nearly nonstop for over a week, preventing a trip into town for supplies. While there was a sufficient supply of meat hanging in the curing shack, given their success on the hunting trip over a month ago, they'd had to ration the dried goods. Flour, corn meal, molasses, lard, salt, beans, rice, and heaven forbid she forget the coffee, were loaded onto the back of the wagon.

Grace and Henry turned on the wagon seat to watch.

"You shoulda made that Injun boy help you. Hope he does more work for you than sit on his red bee-hind." The clerk tossed the remaining sacks into the back of the wagon.

"I beg your pardon?" Anna flared her nostrils and put her hands on her hips. Heat flushed through her body as she tensed, anger building as the seconds marched by.

The clerk nodded toward the children. "Where'd you git 'em anyway? A pretty lady like you shouldn't be near them unarmed. I wouldn't trust 'em." He spit tobacco juice at his feet and wiped the corner of his mouth with his fist.

Anna strode up to the man, intentionally invading his space. "I hardly think it is any of your business. And for your information, these two work harder than any grown man I've ever met." She kept her voice low, but she made her meaning clear. "Now if you don't mind getting out of my way, I have a farm to run."

She turned in a huff, leaving the man speechless. He'd obviously never had a woman return words. She climbed effortlessly onto the wagon, grabbed the reins, and clucked gently to the horse. She wouldn't take her rage out on another hard worker.

"Put your hats on and don't look at anybody. This town is starting to fill up with mean people." Anna put an arm around Grace and pulled her close.

"Why are they like that, Anna? We didn't do anything to them." Grace grabbed some of Anna's dress and bunched it in her fist.

"Because they're afraid of what they don't understand. And that makes men mean. The color of your skin scares them because they don't trust what they don't know. And instead of trying to be kind and learn, they think they need to overpower and take control."

"Like a wild horse." Grace sighed.

"Yes, like a wild horse." Anna glanced at Henry. His eyes were hard and gleamed with anger.

"I'm not ashamed of who I am," he said through gritted teeth.

"Nor should you ever be. But don't ever lower yourself to being mean and nasty like that man back there. You're much more valuable as a human being by being the kind, gentle man that you are. Understand?"

Henry glanced over at Anna and nodded.

Anna didn't relax until she'd driven the wagon past the outskirts of town. She deliberately let out a quiet exhale. She didn't want the children to know how nervous she'd been about any possible retaliation the store owner might send their way. The nerve of that man, she thought. She uttered a quiet curse and jiggled the reins. The horse raised its head and broke into a trot. The harness slapped softly against its body. Anna relished the lull the sound made. The wagon rattled and rocked over the uneven road, made worse from the rains.

Several miles on, Anna steered the horse off the road and followed the trail that would eventually lead them back home. Grass slapped against the wheels, stirring up grasshoppers and other bugs. Henry reached down and grabbed a few stalks of sweetgrass. He stuck one in his mouth and handed one to Grace and Anna each. Anna stuck hers between her teeth and thought they must look quite the sight. She looked over and smiled at the two youngsters.

As the weeks had drawn on, a very special relationship had formed between the three of them. Henry had finally let his guard down, and oftentimes they'd share a laugh or secret. The afternoon he had finally approached her and subtly suggested he'd like to learn to read and write marked a milestone. The dreary days had found all three of them sitting at the table for hours, Anna listening to them read or answering questions. Henry had spent many a day with a frown and furrowed brows as he struggled to make his fingers create letters and numbers. But with encouragement, most notably from his sister, he had mastered the alphabet and quickly took to reading. Sometimes hours would pass without a sound from any of them, so engrossed in the books she always carried in her bags. Anna always felt badly when she had to break the solitude and prepare a meal. But even then, Henry and Grace would both eagerly give her a verbal synopsis of what they'd read and their opinions on the characters and plot. When they'd finish, they'd clear the table. Henry would head out for chores while Grace set the table and helped prepare their food.

The roof of the barn came into view as they began the small incline that would bring them to the homestead. The slabs of wood it had been constructed from were weather worn and grey. It matched the gloominess of the sky. While the sun had broken through earlier, inspiring the trip to town, the sky was now closed up with heavy clouds. In the distance, far to the west, angry thunder clouds boiled and churned. Lightning skittered nonstop through them as they made menacing progress toward them, filling the horizon with a blue-black promise that in all likelihood, would deliver another big drenching.

"Here it comes again," Grace said with a sigh.

"There might be some snow in that storm," Henry said. "The temperature is dropping."

"You're right. After we get the wagon unloaded, best put it in the barn and close it up tight." Anna kept her eyes on the storm as she drove.

"We've got company," Henry said as he reached behind him for the rifle.

Anna looked toward the mud-chinked cabin that had just come into view. Three horses were tied up in front of it. Three unidentifiable shadows stood under the overhang of the cabin's roof.

"I think that's Coal and Snowdrift," Grace said excitedly.

"We don't know for sure, Grace. I don't see the big wagon. And I sure don't recognize that spotted horse." Anna pulled on the reins and stopped the horse. "Henry, can you make out who it is?"

"No. Not from here." Henry pulled the lever of the rifle down and loaded a bullet. He held the barrel in the crook of his elbow and rested the stock against his hip. He settled his hat on his head and nodded to Anna.

"We'll go in slow until we can see better. If they're not friendly, at least we have a bit of headway to try and make a run for it." Anna clucked and the horse leaned into the wagon. "Hopefully, they haven't seen us yet."

"I reckon they've probably been watching for us."

"Anna, I'm scared." Grace grabbed her arm and snuggled close.

"I know, child." Anna chewed her lip and felt the tightness around her eyes. An empty feeling settled in the pit of her stomach. The desire to flee, to keep the children safe was one slap of the reins away. But where would they go? She scanned the sky and blinked hard. The storm was getting closer. Lightning reached for the high hills and thunder rolled menacingly.

"We can't stay on top of this ridge. The weather is getting too dangerous." Anna leaned forward and met Henry's eyes. "Keep that rifle ready."

Henry nodded. He repositioned the rifle so the stock rested in the crook of his shoulder. All he'd have to do is raise the barrel and aim.

As they drew closer, two Indians and a man stepped off the porch and walked past their horses.

"What do you think they want?" Grace clutched her arm painfully.

"Horses maybe," Henry replied. "But Pa usually brings them to town to sell. No one ever comes out here. Pa makes sure of it so there isn't any trouble."

After today's events, Anna knew the real reason. John had avoided any conflict between the Indian haters and his family. Seemingly, it had worked. Until now. She wondered if these men had heard that John was hurt and were out to take advantage of it.

One of the Indians waved and broke into a run toward them. Henry raised the rifle and aimed. Suddenly he put the rifle on the floor, sprung off the wagon, and ran toward the Indian.

"Henry! Wait!" Anna's heart jumped into her throat.

Henry called over his shoulder. "It's my ma!"

Grace loosened her grip on Anna's arm. "Let me off, Anna. Please!"

Anna pulled the wagon to a stop so Grace could scramble off. She watched helplessly as they both ran toward Emma, who knelt and held her arms wide to embrace them.

Anna shook her head and closed her eyes, as relief spread through her body. She sagged against the seat and uttered a soft curse.

"Anna!" She looked up at the sound of her name and smiled. Betty climbed aboard the wagon and hugged her with one arm. "Let's get this wagon unloaded. This storm isn't going to wait."

Between the five of them, the goods were quickly carried into the cabin. Henry drove the wagon, and Grace led the three horses into the barn just as raindrops hit the dirt. Out of respect of the man Henry had become and to avoid the barrage of questions from Grace, Emma wanted to wait for their return. But hers and Betty's focus was on Anna at the moment.

"Anna, I truly wouldn't have recognized you. You look absolutely wonderful." Betty shook her head in disbelief.

Anna waved off the compliment. "Let's just say losing the inches became a necessity the first day Grace gave me a riding lesson. I'll let the children tell you that story."

"You must have been quite busy with taking in your clothes. I dare say, you are not even half the size you were when we left." Betty playfully picked at Anna's dress material.

"Grace told me I have enough linen now to make her a dress. At the very least, I have a lot of patching material."

"Henry and Grace look happy and healthy. I cannot tell you how much that means to me." Emma formed a steeple with her hands and pressed them to her lips. Her eyes were soft and filled with an inner glow.

"It took a little time, but we all settled in well. They're both very special to me," Anna said as she began putting together the makings of bread.

"Did Henry give you any problems?"

"Oh, look, I was a complete stranger back then. So, I just let him watch me and do his own thing until he began to talk and trust me more. I eventually won him over, and didn't he surprise me by asking to be included in the learning. I dare say his writing is prettier than Grace's." Anna chuckled. "He doesn't mind hearing it either. He was prouder than a peacock when he lettered his first sentence."

"I was hoping he would come around. Grace wanted schooling so badly, but even if we lived closer to town, I wouldn't have wanted her to go alone."

"The town has become very volatile," Betty said quietly. "From what I've seen, and I think we've all experienced, there is no tolerance and few friends in that place."

Henry and Grace came through the door just then, drenched, but beaming smiles lit up their faces. They disappeared into the back room to change into dry clothes. A few minutes later, they reappeared and hung their wet gear next to the fire to dry.

Both came to Emma's side and talked at once.

Emma held her hand up. "There will be time for stories. Right now we must talk about something very important."

"Is Pa okay?" Henry said quickly.

"He is mending. Every day is a little better day for him. Please listen now." Emma pulled Grace onto her lap. Henry stood beside her, one hand resting on the back of her chair and the other on her shoulder.

"Your pa is going to stay with Crow Old Man until he is well. That means he will be traveling with the People to the wintering grounds. I need you two to go be with him. You will leave tomorrow with Jumping Fish."

Betty motioned for Mayme to come forward. She had been standing motionless and soundlessly in the shadows against the wall. Anna had completely forgotten about her.

"Jumping Fish will take you to the village. She is an old friend of Betty's."

"But . . ." Grace twisted around.

"Shhh, little one. This is important. We rode through some snow high up. This means Bear Hunter will move the village soon. You must be there when that happens. He has promised to wait for you as long as he can. I will come find you when the oak leaves come in."

"But you just got home," Grace sniffed.

"I know, little one. But I must do this. *Puha* sent me a dream. Anna, Betty, and me must complete a task. The only way I can get through this is by knowing you're safe."

"But Henry and me could help." Grace twisted around and smiled hopefully at her mother.

"We could," Henry chimed in with an air of readiness.

Emma took Henry's hand in her own and smiled softly. "You both have grown up so much since your pa got hurt. You are strong and smart. Your pa and I have wanted you to spend time with Bear Hunter and Gentle Doe, and now it will happen. You will learn and see and do things that will make you both more valuable to us and the spirits that guide us through our lives. You must trust in that. And me. Okay?"

Both nodded, although Grace's eyes shone with tears and Henry wore a stoney expression. His lips were pressed tight in a grimace.

"You will leave before the sun rises tomorrow. After dinner you must gather some clothing and the bedrolls. You will travel light and fast, so only take what you need for the journey. Once you're at the village, you will be given everything you need. You will share a lodge by yourselves. When your pa is able, he will live with you. After the snow melts and the trees begin to bud, you may start looking for me. I won't be long, I promise."

Resigned to their fate, Anna thought both seemed to have relaxed. "You two spend as much time with your mom as you can. I will take care of tonight's meal."

"It has stopped raining. Let's go for a walk. You two can show me what you've been up to since I've been away." Emma rose from her chair and the three walked out the door.

"I'll help you, Anna." Betty stood up. "Just tell me where you need me."

"Me as well." Mayme spoke for the first time.

Anna cocked her head. "You're not a full blood, are you?"

Mayme chuckled. "No, not even a drop. I live among the People because I choose to. I am very fortunate to have been accepted as one of their own."

Anna's mouth fell open. "Are you the little girl Betty met on the train all those years ago?"

"She sure is," Betty said as she put an arm around Mayme's waist. "She's not so little anymore."

"I'm sure you have some stories." Anna finished kneading the dough and patted it together. She carried it over to the bake kettle, a deep cast iron pan with three legs, set it in, and covered it with the rimmed, close-fitting lid. The kettle had already warmed from the fire, so the bread wouldn't take long to bake. "I'll just put some beans on to cook and then we can go out to the smoke shack and get the meat. You all must be starving." Anna wiped her hands of flour and opened the newly bought bag of beans. She poured a generous amount into another blackened kettle, covered them with water from the bucket, and hung them over the fire to cook.

"Come with me, and you can decide what you'd like to eat." Anna pushed her hair behind her ears and took a plate from the stack by the sink. "What?" She caught Betty's amused look.

"You have changed so much, Anna," Betty replied. "You walk with your head held high and a bounce in your step. Even your attitude seems easy going and carefree."

Anna laughed. "Did you consider it might be because I now have adult company?"

Betty giggled and shook her head. "No, I believe it's more than that."

"I will tell you, since I've lost all the fat, except for my bosom . . ." Anna hefted her breasts. "These don't seem to have changed much." She sighed comically. "I have been able to do things I never imagined myself doing. I can get on and sit a horse, shoot a gun, and skin a deer. And none of it seems like work. It just feels so good to be able to move around without getting in my own way."

"Your inner radiance has met your outer beauty," Mayme said quietly. "Your obvious joy shows it was a wonderful reunion."

Betty and Mayme followed Anna out to the shack. The tantalizing smell of smoked meat exuded from the wood it was built from. Anna lifted the bars that held the door closed from the wooden hooks. She watched with amusement as Betty's eyes widened in bewilderment as she led them in.

The carcasses of two elk and five deer hung on ropes from the ceiling along the walls. Strips of rainbow, brook, and cutthroat trout, as well as eighteen dressed prairie chickens were suspended on racks above the smoking ring.

"Wow. Where did you get all this?" Betty spun slowly, taking it all in.

"We harvested the elk and deer on a trip into the foothills. The fish came from a few trips up and down the river, and the birds from our morning rides."

"Amazing." Betty looked at her with a mischievous smirk. "Which of these did you shoot?"

"Three of the deer. Henry shot the other two and both elk. He's much better at imitating an elk's bugle than I am."

Betty responded with raised eyebrows and a slow, disbelieving shake of her head. "I was really only kidding."

"This is mostly the winter meat. We were planning a short trip out in a few days to try to get a Pronghorn, but . . ." Anna's throat suddenly ached. Sadness cloaked her. Things were about to change dramatically. Although admittedly she had missed the company of adults, Henry, who was quickly developing into one, and Grace, had become part of her family. She had enjoyed their daily routines, and aside from today's fiasco in town, had lived a quiet, mostly enjoyable life in this secluded part of the world. She sniffed and scrubbed her face with her hands.

"You've done well, Anna," Betty said in a soothing voice and patted her arm in comfort. "Emma told me often that she missed her children. But she never, ever said that she worried about them. She knew they were in good hands." She waved at the hanging carcasses. "And look at all you've achieved. The Anna I knew when we left would've had a difficult time dealing with anything other than teaching."

Anna bowed her head and nodded. She swiped the tear rolling down her cheek, sniffed, and looked up. "We should probably get this meat on the fire." She picked up the knife used specifically for the cured meat and took hold of the nearest deer. She skillfully carved off a half-length of backstrap.

The mood around the table while they ate was surprisingly light. Grace and Henry both regaled everyone with tales that often had them laughing. Anna marveled at the resilience Emma and John had instilled into their children. They seemed to easily take life one day at a time, dealing with whatever the day presented them with. To look at them, one wouldn't ever guess they would be soon be separated from their mother once again.

If she were honest with herself, that adaptable toughness was exactly what she had learned to incorporate while living here. Gone was the insecure, undecided, introverted woman she'd been since her early years. She used to find such fearless determination intimidating and was even turned off by it. Her actions now seemed to mirror Emma and her children. She found she committed quickly, but on the other hand, because of her newly learned convictions, which she now shared as their force of three, she had a hard time backing away from what she believed to be the most direct course of action. She pushed her own limits and boundaries daily, and because of that, she found she was not held back by fear or uncertainty anymore.

Soon after the meal, Emma directed Henry and Grace to bed. Their fatigue was clearly reflected in their faces. They'd had emotional ups and downs throughout the day, from the verbal attack in town, to being reunited with their mother after so many weeks, and then to find out it would be short lived, and they would be leaving in the morning to be with John.

When Emma returned a little while later, her eyes were wet and dull. She sat down, crossed her arms, and held onto her shoulders.

Betty patted her on the back. "We need to get this done so you can have your family back together again."

"Emma, why don't you all ride out with us to where you left the wagon?" Mayme leaned forward, encouraging eye contact with her. She smiled empathetically.

"That's a great idea. We could make camp there, you'd have one more night with Henry and Grace, and . . ." Betty winked at Anna. "We can see how well Anna sits her horse."

Emma grabbed Betty's hand and reached for Anna's as well. "*Puha* has given me the best *tetteyannees* for this journey. Thank you. We will ride together tomorrow."

Anna looked up at Mayme. "I hope that means friends, and not what it sounded like."

Mayme chuckled and nodded.

# Chapter Sixteen

ANNA HAD A hard time watching Henry and Grace ride away with Mayme. She could only imagine how difficult it was for Emma, but from the feelings invoked in herself, she had a pretty good idea. Heaviness had settled in her chest when they'd started breaking camp and readying their horses. But like Betty, she focused on alleviating Emma's anguish rather than her own.

They cleaned the wagon of leaves and branches that had fallen on it over the months. A squirrel had stored nuts in a leaf-filled corner of the tray. Emma gently scooped it out, under the supervision of the complaining animal, and placed it in a small hollow of rock that was easily accessible to the squirrel. It had scrambled down to investigate and from then on was silent. The harness, although damp with bits of green and some bird droppings, had hung protected from a strong pole shoved into a crevice just under the rock shelf.

Coal stood patiently while the harness was fitted on him and backed without hesitation between the shafts of the wagon.

"You'll get a nice rest after this, my friend," Emma said. She pressed her forehead against his neck for apparent solace.

Betty lifted her saddle into the wagon and tied her horse to the back. Emma had ridden out bareback, but had carried a bedroll in front of her, which was now also put in the wagon.

"I'll ride back," Anna announced. Her new-found love of riding was a good excuse to keep from crowding the other two on the wagon seat. She would've easily fit, she realized when Emma and Betty climbed aboard. It still slipped her mind that she was half the size she used to be.

They travelled in silence for the first few hours, each seemingly caught in their own thoughts. Anna knew Emma, like herself, was yearning for the children's presence, and Betty was no doubt missing Mayme.

"It is time we start making hard plans," Emma said, breaking the silence and the overcast mood. She held her chin high with new resolve and determination.

"I have a few ideas," Betty replied.

"As do I," Anna said as she reined her horse closer to the wagon.

"That is good. We will talk around the table." Emma glanced at Anna and grinned. "Grace taught you well."

Anna shook her head. "Oh dear, it surely wasn't without trials and tribulations. That mountain of a horse she first put me on helped a treat. I didn't know it at first though. I believe I saw my life pass before my eyes on numerous occasions."

"Henry has very good things to say about you. He called you *pahah* when we talked alone. It means 'aunt.' He has never uttered that word until he spoke of you."

Anna parted her lips and closed her eyes to savor the happiness that she felt. "I didn't know." Her voice cracked.

"You are part of my family now," Emma said, then leaned into Betty, "As are you."

Betty tilted her neck and touched her head with Emma's. "Thank you. That's very special to hear." She bent forward and looked at Anna. "You've obviously made quite an impression with the boy. I think that's wonderful."

Anna was still too choked up with emotion to reply.

"Tomorrow we will go to the herd and find three clean horses," Emma said, after a while.

"With all this rain I would think they'd all be clean," Anna said, finally finding her voice.

"I think she means unbranded, sweetie," Betty said. Her lips twitched to contain the laugh that was threatening to come out.

"Oh." Anna looked at her friends and burst out laughing. "For being a learned woman, I can be a bit dense sometimes." She shook her head. and then recalled the ride the children had taken her on a month ago. Henry had wanted to check on the herd. They'd ridden among the horses, checking the broodmares and making sure the foals were big and healthy. The bay-colored stallion had raced up to them and whinnied a challenge. He reared and then pawed the ground, sending clods of soil behind him. Henry had called to him. The horse had glared at them before trotting back with a high head and raised tail. Henry had made sure they stayed at a safe distance from him. Stallions, especially those with mares and foals, were unpredictable he had told her. The horse had visibly relaxed at his voice, recognizing they were no threat to him or his herd. He had stood watching them, only lowering his head to quickly grab a bite of grass. The wind had lifted his black mane and forelock, giving him an even wilder look. Anna remembered being uneasy under his intense gaze, but also marveled at the power and freedom the stallion displayed.

"I wasn't looking at brands, but isn't your herd all mares with foals?"

"Yes. It'll be time for the older foals to be weaned. We will cut those mares from the herd and bring them into the paddocks. After John and I were joined, my father gave us . . ." Emma stopped and covered her mouth with her hand.

"What?" Anna said.

"What's the matter, Emma?" Betty grabbed the reins and pulled the wagon to a stop. Coal snorted at the sudden tension on his mouth.

Emma stared straight ahead. "After John and I were joined, my father gave us three horses."

Anna widened her eyes as the significance sunk in. Three. "Oh, my."

Betty wore a similar expression. "Does that mean your destiny was designed from the moment you and John met?"

"*Puha* moves in mysterious ways. We must use those three horses."

Anna leaned from side to the side to see if her horse was branded. She'd never noticed one, but that didn't mean much. She normally had other things on her mind while grooming and saddling her. But there it was, on Muddy's left hip. Shaped like a lightning bolt, that Anna had overlooked as a two-inch scar. But as she ran her fingers over it and parted the hair, she realized it was indeed a brand. She rode up alongside Coal and studied his coat. He bore no brand. She turned her horse around to face the wagon. "Aside from Coal, who are the other two horses?"

Emma met Anna's eyes. "The stallion and his lead mare."

"Oh." Anna's stomach flip-flopped. Henry had pointed out the mare when they'd ridden through. She had a huge black-as-night foal at her side. He explained it was her job to lead the herd to food and water, and that she controlled their daily movements. As they had watched on, the mare had pinned her ears, lowered her head, and approached another who was grazing at the edge of the herd. She had rolled her eyes and spun around, threatening to kick out. But the other horse had read her intentions and had sided away, quickly disappearing among the other horses. She remembered asking Henry why she had done that. His reply had surprised her. He'd said that the chased mare was probably young and not smart about predators. So, the lead mare had sent her and her foal into the middle where it was safer. But despite his logical explanation, Anna had thought the mare as wild and unpredictable as the stallion.

It was nearing dusk by the time they crested the rise overlooking the cabin and barn. All three were tired, and in agreement to start fresh the following morning. After tending to the horses and tack, they prepared and ate a meal of bread and milk. The cabin seemed unnaturally quiet without Grace's chatter, and decidedly empty without either of the children. Anna knew it would take some getting used to, for Emma especially. She and Betty retired to the tepee after cleaning up, leaving Emma to face the cabin's loneliness by herself.


BETTY WOKE AT dawn. She rolled onto her side, pulling the buffalo hide over her shoulders to ward off the morning chill. Anna slept soundly on her back, her soft breathing barely noticeable. She reckoned she wouldn't have even recognized Anna had she passed her on the street. Her appearance had changed so dramatically, as well as had her increase in strength. She'd watched as Anna rode her horse with confidence, then later had carried the heavy saddle over her arm and hefted it effortlessly over the wooden bar mounted high enough on the barn wall to keep it out of vermin reach. Although she was taller than Anna, she'd had to work to lift it nearly shoulder high. If only she'd had Anna's strength when that bastard Hopwood had beaten her up. Anna would surely have been able to ward off that little weasel of a man and probably have given him a good what-for as well.

An idea formed in her head. She'd had a few ideas to present to Emma and Anna, but this one might just keep them all from being hanged if they were caught. Hopefully it wouldn't come to that, of course. She'd just hoped Anna could be convinced.


AS SOON AS Emma opened her eyes, she felt the emptiness of the cabin. A longing so intense grew and ballooned in her chest. Her heart ached with it. She crossed her arms over her chest and hugged herself, imagining it to be the arms of her children around her. Soon, but not nearly soon enough. She sighed deeply and sat up. The smoke of a newly lit fire wafted into her room. She wondered who was up already. She stood in the opening of her room and dressed, using the dim light from the window next to the door. The blue of dawn hadn't started to fade. In fact, there wasn't any sign of the sun as of yet. It must be very early.

"I wondered who was up," she said to Betty. "I'll go tend to the stock and see if that cow has come in to be milked. I saw that it has a bull calf by its side now. First one that's survived."

Betty looked up from adding more fuel to the fire. "No need. Anna is already out there."

Emma raised her eyebrows. "Oh?"

Betty chuckled. "She's a different woman, isn't she?"

"Mmm." Emma went to the fire and warmed herself of the morning chill.

"This part of the world will make or break you, I think." Betty met Emma's eyes. "Anna was the last of us to learn that. We had a nice talk earlier. I think she's ready."

"Ready for what?" Anna said as she closed the door behind her. She carried a bucket of milk in one hand and a hunk of meat in the other.

"To make things right." Betty rose and took the bucket from her. She set it on the bench to settle. After a while, one of them would skim the cream off the surface, use it to top a meal or make butter or cheese.

"We've been giving what's left to the calf. Grace taught it to drink from a bucket." Anna fought down the pang of nostalgia.

"She gets along with that cow better than anyone. John and Henry tend to lose patience with that cranky old thing, but for some reason it took to Grace soon after we got it." Emma shook her head and smiled. "It even let her get on its back one time. But Grace said her back was too bony and hard on her bum so she ain't doing that again, she said."

Betty moved to the fire and, using a thick wad of material made from layers of Anna's dress, lifted the coffee pot by the handle and brought it to the table. As she poured coffee into three cups she said, "All right. Let's talk about what we need to do. Emma, you said the herd needs to come in for weaning and branding."

"Yes. But because we need to use the stallion and mare, we will just bring the herd in for now. They will feel safer here in their absence. The weaning can wait." Emma cut thick slices of the day-old bread, buttered them generously, and gave one each to the other two women.

"Once we have them in, Anna and I will need you to take us into town. We won't need the horses for a week or so."

"That'll give me some time to settle the stallion and mare," Emma said between bites.

"Yes, go to Doc's after a week. I'll leave a note for you. It won't seem odd that you're there, given what happen to John. I'll let you know if we need any more time."

Anna shoved the remainder of her bread into her mouth and washed it down with coffee. "Since Betty is familiar with the town and people, she figures we can watch more closely the movements of that banker. Once you come get us, it'll only be a day or so before we carry out the plan."

"What is your role in town, Anna?" Emma said as she drew her hair into a long braid.

"She's going to be"—Betty grinned at Anna—"an ornament. At first. Then bait when we set the trap."

Emma nodded her understanding. "Let's go round up those horses then."

THE PRAIRIE GRASSES had greened up considerably with the recent rains. The ground had greedily soaked up the water, giving life to existing and dormant plants. The blues and purples of the asters and lupines mixed with the bright yellows of the balsamroot as the wildflowers slowly opened their buds and revealed their flowers amongst the already spent taller wild barley and fescue.

They rode up to the herd slowly and stopped a short distance away. All eyes were on them. Emma slid off Coal, handed the reins to Betty, and approached the horses on foot. As expected, the stallion charged out quickly, snorting and tossing his head in a challenge. He stopped only yards from Emma and pawed the ground. She wasn't afraid of him. She respected his power and need to protect the herd. But he also needed to hear her. She pursed her lips together and whistled the sweet song of the chickadee, a *fee-bee* with the second note lower than the first. She patiently repeated the call until the horse quieted his stomping and finally took notice. The transformation was immediate. He nicked, lowered his head, and walked to her.

"Hello, brave man," Emma said quietly, as she scrubbed his face with her fingers. The stallion nuzzled her neck and drew in her familiar scent. He visibly relaxed under her touch. A soft whinny gained her attention as the lead mare joined them. Emma smiled and held her hand out, palm up. The mare placed her muzzle in it and breathed a heavy sigh. "How's my big girl? It's been too long, my friend." A smaller replica of the mare shoved his head between them, eager to see what his dam was so interested in. Emma whistled again, familiarizing the colt with the sound. His ears pricked forward with curiosity. He lowered his head, extended his neck, and opening his mouth, made an exaggerated chewing motion. Emma knew he was displaying the common behavior of a submissive youngster.

She turned to the stallion once again and stroked his neck, feeling the barely tamed power in the muscles beneath his hide. She grabbed a handful of mane and in one quick movement vaulted unto his back. He snorted in surprise and threw his head up, but made no effort to dislodge her. She leaned over and ran both hands on either side of his neck, then over the crest of his mane. Emma felt the pounding of his heart beneath her legs. She waited until it slowed and matched her own. She knew then their spirits had made allegiance.

Emma motioned for Anna and Betty to move toward the back of the herd. They would watch for any stragglers, but more importantly, not give the stallion any reason to think he was being challenged. He had only ever known her family and had accepted that they were the true guardians of his mares. She knew he would do whatever she asked of him. And now she urged him forward and whistled for the mare, who moved to his side, followed closely by her colt.

At first Emma heard only the breeze and distant bird song. Then a deeper sound arose, like a low thunder, a sound she could feel. It seemed faint at first as the front of the herd moved. It grew stronger and louder, the vibration resonating in her chest.

She pushed the stallion into a slow trot, not wanting to tax the foals behind her. But the mare knew where she was going. She picked up speed and cantered past. The herd passed her in a wave of mane, tail, and hoof. The thunder reached a crescendo and her heart, overcome with the beat, pounded in unison with the hooves.

Emma felt a wave of passion and freedom, of energy and power, wash over her as the herd dissolved around her, only to reassemble as a whole again once they passed her. Her eyes pricked with tears as the beauty and majesty of the horse spirits revealed itself.

As they approached the homestead, the herd circled around, black, brown, red, gold, white, platinum, tails flying like banners in their wake. The thunder's tempo quickened again as the sheer wall of force and will came barreling straight back toward her. She felt a moment of alarm for the safety of the women behind her. But it was quickly replaced with relief and exhilaration, as again and again, the horses circled and played, snorted and bucked, a cough, a sneeze, the air full of dust and the scent of horse sweat. The lead mare guided them to the hollow, filled full of water from the recent rains. After drinking their fill, the mares grazed while the foals lay down for a much-needed rest.

Emma had watched the herd settle from the stallion's back and now she slid down and released him. He trotted to the hollow and drank his fill before circling his herd, making sure all was in order.

Anna and Betty met her at the barn. Their faces and clothes were covered in dust, marked only by the streaks of sweat that had trickled along their necks. Their teeth shined white from the smiles beneath the dirt and grime.

"That was the most beautiful thing I've ever seen," Anna said.

Betty coughed and spit into the dirt. "I don't know how you saw anything with all the dust they threw up."

Anna laughed and patted Betty on the back. "True, but it was amazing when they first started to move." She swiped her face with a sleeve, revealing part of her face.

Emma chuckled. "You'd best both have a dip in that hollow. There's not enough water in the cabin to clean you off."

Betty and Anna burst out laughing as they gazed at one another's dirty selves.

"We certainly wouldn't make a good impression back in town. They'd think we'd just come down from the gold fields and wouldn't know we were women." Anna took her hat off and ruffled her hair, creating a small cloud of dust.

"Well, we can't have that, can we. We have work to do." Betty took Anna's arm and marched her off to the tepee for some clean clothing.

Emma suddenly felt lighter. Her worries and concerns evaporated for the moment. She adored those two. She felt the three of them were closer than friends, more like spirit sisters. On a whim, she quickly went into the cabin for a change of clothes, intent on joining them in the water.

# Chapter Seventeen

MILES WAS THE first to see Betty as she walked through the swinging saloon doors with Anna close behind.

"Holey moley," he said, abandoning the towel he was using to wipe the bar. He came around the side and quickly strode over to them. He grabbed Betty around the waist, lifted her off her feet, and hugged her. When he set her down, he held her shoulders and gazed appraisingly at her. "You look a picture, Miss Kitty. Truly a sight for sore eyes. The girls will be so happy to see you."

Betty rested her hands on Miles' chest. "It's good to see you too, Miles. I want you to meet a friend of mine. This is Anna. She will be staying with me in my room, so if you would please put another bed in there, I'd be much appreciative."

Miles nodded and smiled broadly at Anna. "Pleased to meet you, Ma'am." He centered his attention on Betty once again. "Are you back for good?"

"Only for a little while this time. I'll explain it all after we get settled and before the place gets busy." Betty let her eyes roam the saloon. Nothing had changed physically. What she did notice was the smell. Body odor, cigarette smoke, horse manure, and, of course, the stale smell of whiskey and beer. It hadn't turned cold enough for Miles to fire up the wood-burning stove. The smoke from it sometimes was able to dampen the stink that undoubtedly had permeated everything within. How had she lived with it? She supposed it was something she'd grown used to when she lived under this roof. But, at the moment, it accosted her senses. She wondered how Anna was coping.

"Miss Kitty!" Clara cried as she ran down the stairs. "Oh my gosh. Girls. Miss Kitty is here."

Betty smiled broadly at her dear friend. Doors opened and closed above and soon the other four girls were hurrying down the stairs. Most were still in their sleeping attire, with mussed hair and no makeup, having had worked their usual late night.

Clara flung herself into Betty's arms. "It's you. It's really you."

Betty laughed. "Yes, yes. It's me."

Moments later she was surrounded and taking turns giving hugs. "You all look well. I see Miles has been taking good care of you." Out of the corner of her eye, she saw Miles puff his chest out proudly. She winked at him and grinned.

"Now look. I'm only here for a short visit to check up on you all."

"How long, Miss Kitty?" The girls' voices mingled and rose.

"A week or so." Betty turned and grabbed Anna's hand. "But there's someone I'd like you to meet. This is my friend, Anna. Please treat her kindly. Don't worry. She's not here to work. I have something else in mind for her."

The girls' faces seemed to fall at first when they noticed Anna. Betty knew they'd feel threatened at first, that they'd lose customers to Anna's obvious good looks. Hopefully, she thought, I've reassured them.

"Girls, girls," Miles said, above the din of voices. "There will be time to visit with Kitty later. Let's let them get settled. You all need to get ready for work." He clapped his big hands together. Aside from some disappointed moans and disgruntled comments, the women quickly dispersed and returned to their rooms.

"Give me a few minutes, Miss Kitty. I'll get your room set up. We've left it empty in hopes you'd come back one day." Miles pulled at the ends of his moustache. "I'll be back shortly."

"Thank you, Miles." Betty pulled a chair from one of the tables and sat down, indicating to Anna to do the same.

"They all seem very nice." Anna tucked her dress beneath her and sat down. They both wore dresses now that they were back in town. She didn't own anything very grandeur, but Betty had insisted that she had something that would fit her in her wardrobe.

"Yes, they're very good girls. I'm pleased they're looking so well." Betty had taken the opportunity to discreetly examine all their faces. Without their makeup, bruises, and cuts from unruly customers couldn't be easily hidden.

"Do you think he'll come?" Anna said in a stoney voice, referring of course to Clarence Hopwood.

"I'll have to ask Miles if he's been here. I can't imagine he hasn't been given his circumstances at home. Don't worry. If he doesn't show, I'll pay him a visit and drop a hint that there's a pretty new girl in town."

Anna suddenly looked nervous. "You'll keep me safe from the other men? I've never done anything like this before."

Betty placed her hand over Anna's to reassure her. "Darlin' all you have to do until you have to deal with Clarence, is talk to the men, dance with them if you like, and otherwise just keep them in the saloon buying drinks and playing cards. The other girls will take care of their other needs."

Anna nodded quickly. "I'll be okay, and can put on a good act with that weasel because I'm mad enough. But I've never really been around men before."

"You'll be fine. Most of them come in here to unwind, have a couple drinks, and meet up with others to tell their stories. The others come in for female company. They have their favorites and don't often deviate from them unless their girl is sick or otherwise indisposed."

"Do you miss it?"

Betty threw her head back and laughed. "Oh hell, no. These past few months have taught me there's something better out there for me. I'm not sure yet what it is exactly, but soon I'll have the money to go searching."

"I don't know exactly what I'll do after all this is over." Anna frowned and rubbed her hands down the front of her dress.

"You'll find your place, Anna. We both will. We just have to be open to possibilities."

"Miss Kitty, your room is ready," Miles called from the top of the stairs.

Betty winked and smiled at Anna. "Come on. Let's get this thing started."

They climbed the stairs and met Miles at the top.

"Miles, may we have a word in private?" Betty indicated her room with her chin.

"Sure, Miss Kitty." He waited politely for Betty and Anna to enter her room before following and closing the door behind him.

"Has that weasel Hopwood been a customer as of late?" Betty crossed her arms over her chest.

"No, ma'am. After you left, he's not been in."

"Damn. Pardon my French." Betty frowned and tapped her lips with her finger. The plan had hinged on his continued patronage. It could all go to hell in a hand basket if they couldn't find a way to lure . . .

"Sarah goes to the bank," Miles said.

"Excuse me? What does that have to do with anything?"

"What I'm trying to say, is that every Tuesday and Saturday, Hopwood closes the bank early. That's when Sarah visits him. He made those arrangements shortly after you left, Miss Kitty. I think he was worried he may have a few fingers pointed at him about what happened. Even worse, it mighta gotten back to his wife."

"Ahh." Betty nodded and paced the room, staring at the floor. She looked up and patted Miles on the shoulder. "Thank you, Miles. You've been very helpful."

Miles stroked his moustache down a few times, clearly nervous. "I'm not in trouble, am I, Miss Kitty?"

"Oh, for heaven's sake. Of course you're not in trouble. When was the last time you and I had words?"

Mile's eyes twinkled. "I believe it was when I tried to kiss you after you bought this place."

Betty snorted. "It would've been like kissing a big brother. Now go on. Anna and I will be down after we've freshened up."

After the door closed behind Miles, Betty sat on the bed next to Anna, who had remained silent during her conversation with him.

"This turn of events will work more in our favor than I would've thought."

Anna gave her a curious look. "What do you mean?"

"It means that you don't have to entertain here at the saloon. And, more importantly, no one will see a thing." Betty stood up quickly and opened the doors to her wardrobe. "Let's find you something to wear." She pawed through the hanging dresses, muttering about the different styles until she laid her hands on a stylish earth-toned garment. It was a gown with a bustled skirt and a jacket-styled bodice. It had a low bust-line, giving it a sexy look, but not outrageously so. The sleeves flared at the wrist and the entire ensemble was intricately decorated with lace and folds. Betty held it up for Anna to see.

"It's beautiful. But of what use will it be?" Anna stood and ran her fingers down the lace.

"This is what you'll be wearing when Clarence lays eyes on you for the first time." Betty pushed the dress into Anna's arms. "Put this on, and we'll go test the waters. Well, you will, anyway."

ANNA BRUSHED THE dust off the bottom of the dress as she stood in front of the bank. She entertained a fluttery feeling in her stomach. The success of the plan hinged largely on the impression she presented when Clarence first laid eyes on her.

After she'd changed into the dress, Betty had done up her hair and added a bit of lipstick to complete the look. She'd hardly recognized herself when she'd looked in the mirror. An unfamiliar, yet very attractive woman had looked back at her, and she'd gasped in astonishment. Betty had smiled with approval.

Anna took a deep breath and stepped up onto the planking that led to the door. The town was quiet. A young man drove a wagon past her on the uneven and rutted road. He stopped at the dry goods store a few buildings away. Several horses were tied up in front of the livery to be shod. The high-pitched banging of a hammer on an anvil indicated there was already one horse being worked on. A group of men huddled around the entrance, talking and smoking. A young mother with a baby and toddler carefully navigated the road. A pair of well-dressed older women strolled down the walkway, caught up in deep conversation, not even affording a glance her way. She heard children in the schoolyard, playing and screaming, and then the voice of an adult calling, no doubt summoning them back to their lessons. *That should've been me in there.* Anger boiled in her chest, and she opened the door with renewed energy, nervousness forgotten.

A bell jangled above the door as it swung inward. She turned to close it behind her, thankful that, but for Clarence and herself, the place was empty.

"Be with you in a minute," Clarence said in grumpy voice. He sighed as if any business were too much bother for him.

Anna wondered why people didn't hide their money in a box and bury it in the ground rather than give it in trust to this horrid man. She approached the counter. As she stood waiting, and as the minutes ticked by, she had to work to keep from slapping the counter with her palm to get his attention.

He sat on the other side with his head down, scribbling something in a diary book, the scratching of his quill on the paper the only sound. The top of his head was balding, with little whiskers of hair poking through some of the bare scalp.

"All right. What do you want?" Clarence said, slamming the book closed and pushing it aside. He looked up with a scowl on his face. Then his eyes widened in surprise. He smiled brightly, showing yellowed teeth with a gap in the front. "Oh, my dear lady, please accept my humble apologies for making you wait." He stood up, licked his palm, and straightened what hair he had left on his head. He wiped his hands on his jacket and straightened his bow tie.

Anna swallowed her revulsion and said in a dry voice, "Yes, well, I hope it won't happen again." She knew she had his full attention now by the wanting look in his eyes.

"Please, please, what can I do for a lovely lady such as yourself?" His eyes wandered to the hint of cleavage that Betty had made sure was prominently showing.

"I'm not exactly sure you can fulfil my needs. Maybe I should just find another bank." Anna turned to go, knowing full well his objection would be forthcoming. And that there was no other bank within a hundred miles.

"No. I mean, I beg you. I've been quite busy with the miners arguing about their gold. I apologize profusely if I showed cross. I assure you, it won't happen again."

Anna hesitated as if still considering her options. "Very well. I have just arrived and will need some place to keep my money."

"Yes, yes. I can certainly do that for you."

"I have no idea how to begin to do business with your establishment."

"How much would you like to place in my, er, the bank's trust?"

"I don't have much at the moment, so I will keep what I have. However, I expect to be earning a good amount soon."

"Oh, yes, yes. May I ask what your occupation is?"

"I suppose you should know," Anna said with an air of superiority. "I have taken a position at Big Nosed Kitty's."

Clarence gasped.

"Will that be a problem?" Anna's heart pounded in her ears as she cast the bait.

"Oh, for heaven's sake, no. Not at all. I'm very well acquainted with Miss Kitty."

Anna raised an eyebrow and lifted her chin. "Is that so?"

Clarence blinked several times. "Yes, of course. We go way back. I have handled her assets for years. That said, opening an account can be rather tedious and time consuming. If you would allow me to give you all my attention, let's say, after hours, I'm sure we can come to an agreement." His eyes had yet to leave her bust.

Anna sniffed. She knew very well what assets he'd handled, and it wasn't just her money. Men like him, who blatantly took advantage of women, were the scum of the earth. She hoped her expression didn't relay that opinion.

"Very well." She raked him with a steely gaze. "I will come by the day after tomorrow." She turned briskly, nearly losing her balance. Recovering quickly, she grabbed hold of the door knob and made her exit. She stood outside the bank for a moment to gather her breath and calm her racing heart. She straightened her shoulders and patted her hair just in case he watched out the window. She could almost guarantee it. She carefully navigated the steps down onto the road and quickly made her way back to the saloon.

Betty was pacing anxiously in her room when Anna returned.

"Thank heavens you're back. I was beginning get worried." She pulled Anna into a hug.

Anna shrugged. "Everything's fine. He's just as much a cow plop as I remember."

"Come sit." Betty motioned to the bed. "Tell me what happened."

"He behaved just as you said he would, the lecherous weasel that he is. I told him I was beginning work here, which of course pleased him immensely. He wants me to meet him after-hours so he can assist with my assets." Ann stuck her tongue out and pretended to gag. "So, I said day after tomorrow." She gently crossed her ankles.

Betty gasped. "But that's too soon."

"Of course it is. Don't be daft. I'm not going. You should have Sarah tell him that I'm extremely busy, if you know what I mean. I don't think we should have her change her visits."

"No," Betty said, nodding. "You're right, that's a good idea. And should he come calling, I'll have Miles tell him you're reserved for very special patrons, and of course more expensive." She lightly stroked her throat in thought.

Anna chuckled. "It'll be amusing to mess with his head for a while. The ugly one on his neck that is."

Their eyes met and they burst out laughing.

"Anna, you're a devil. I would never have thought." Betty fanned herself with her fingers.

"I may have never been around men much, but I've heard things." Anna frowned. "The women used to talk freely around me. I don't know if they were trying to make me jealous of what they thought I would never have or were just ignorant bitches."

Betty leaned against Anna's shoulder. "Definitely the latter. I don't know those women, but I do know women like them. It has always amazed me that in this man's world, that women don't stick together more. We could get so much more accomplished, and peacefully at that."

"Truly." Anna pushed her shoes off with her toes, stood up, and began to remove the dress.

"We should walk the town a bit tomorrow." Betty rose and helped Anna with the garment. "We could even shop a little if you'd like."

Anna frowned. "I used the last of my money to buy dry goods for the farm."

Betty hung the dress up, turned, and sported a devilish grin. "Help me move the wardrobe, will you?"

Together, they pushed with their shoulders and with a lot of grunting, managed to move it a foot. Betty took a nail file from one of the drawers and crouched down. She inserted the file between two floorboards and pried one up. She reached in and retrieved a small pistol, which she placed on the floor next to her. She lowered her hand again and pulled a metal ammunition box out and handed it to Anna, who had to use both hands to hold it.

"Go ahead. Open it," Betty said as she replaced the board.

Anna placed the box on the bed and sat next to it. She undid the latch and lifted the lid. "Oh my gosh." She looked at Betty with wide eyes and mouth open.

"Close your mouth, dear. You'll swallow a fly." Betty grasped the pistol and stood up.

"Where ever did you get all this?" Anna stared down at the huge bundle of bills and gold coins.

"When I bought this place years ago, the lady who was in charge of the girls warned me about Hopwood. I still had to use the bank for obvious reasons. But I knew not to trust him. He became a regular client of mine, and would bring his own flask of whiskey with him. He had it imported, apparently. It was quite nice if I remember correctly. It was fermented with honey. Anyway." Betty waved her hand. "After . . . you know, he would fall asleep. And that's when I would search his pockets. I didn't take much, just a little so he wouldn't much notice."

"All this is his?" Anna chuckled.

"Most of it. Not the pistol. That was my daddy's."

"I can't believe he never wised up."

Betty sighed and her shoulders slumped. "Remember the first time you saw me?"

"At Doc's."

"Yes."

"You had a black eye and a bloodied lip if I remember correctly."

Betty nodded.

"That bastard."

"He woke while I was going through his pockets."

"And beat you."

"Yes. While I was angry as a hornet that he didn't give me all my money when I asked for it, I knew why."

Anna was silent for a moment. There in the box was more money than she'd ever seen.

"Why did you leave this here when you went to Emma's?"

"It wasn't going to do me any good there, so what safer place than under a floorboard in an old whore's room? Certainly not the bank. I still own this place and knew I could come back to get it if needed."

"But you still want to rob Clarence even though you have all this?" Anna fingered the roll of bills and swept her fingers over the gold coins.

"Absolutely. No man has a right to beat a woman like he did me. Even if I were stealing from him. I'm sure he skims money every chance he gets. Money he has no right to. But because he's the only banker, no one dares to question him. He wears the finest clothes and drinks expensive whiskey. He's also the silent proprietor of the sales yards and, well, you may as well say, except for my saloon, he owns the town. Now where would a man who came to this town with only a few dollars, get all that money? I remember a time when he could barely rub two nickels together. And now look at him."

Anna shook her head in amazement. "He owns this town."

"Yes. How do you think the townspeople are going to react when their money disappears, and he can't account for it?"

"They'll drive him out of town."

"More likely, they'll string him up."

"Deservedly so. But how will the town survive without a bank?"

"They won't have to for long. I've got some ideas about how to fix that and bring my saloon back into the good books with them." Betty pulled the roll of bills from the box and counted off several. She twisted the new roll into the coins and held the remainder out to Anna. "This is his money. Let's go spend some tomorrow."

ANNA SLEPT LATER than she had in quite a while. The saloon had come alive shortly after the evening meal and the drone of noise had kept her awake. Not to mention the constant traffic and giggles on the stairs. So, she'd entertained herself by watching the comings and goings through the window. When she felt brave enough, she'd open the door and peer out, observing a scene that had no doubt been going on for years and years. When the rising smoke stung her eyes, and the overwhelming stench of the men overcame her, she'd close the door and return to her vigil by the window.

Betty lay asleep in her bed. She'd gone down to work, although not with the intentions she'd had in the past. Anna had watched with fascination as Betty had donned layers of makeup, finishing the look off with bright red lipstick. She'd then rubbed bandoline, a clear sticky gum solution, through her hair to stiffen it. Her red hair looked like it was on fire after being sprinkled with gold hair powder. A spritz of lavender on her neck and dress, and she had disappeared out the door. Anna hadn't heard Betty return. She'd obviously wiped her face of its coverings and lipstick before she went to bed. Her dress lay haphazardly over the foot of her bed.

Anna drew back her blanket and rose quietly, not wanting to wake Betty. She dressed in the clothes she'd arrived in and carefully tiptoed out to the top of the stairs. The saloon seemed unnaturally quiet now in the morning light. She heard movement below, and hoping for a cup of coffee, descended to the main floor.

Miles was busily shoving chairs under the tables and wiping them, so he didn't notice her at first. Finally, he turned and smiled. At least Anna thought it was a smile. It was hard to tell under that huge moustache of his.

"Good morning, Miss Anna. I hope you weren't too disturbed by the noise last night. Unfortunately, it's a nightly thing, so you kinda have to get used to it." He pushed the last chair under a table and strode behind the bar.

"All good, Miles. Thank you." Anna slid onto one of the bar stools. "I was hoping there'd be coffee here somewhere.' She sniffed and thought she'd smelled a faint aroma beyond the normal odors.

Miles pulled off the towel he had draped over his shoulder and tossed it onto the bar. "I believe it's time for one myself. I'll be right back." He disappeared into an area behind the bar that Anna had not noticed. While she waited, she focused on the wolf skin hanging above the bar. It apparently had been a huge animal when alive, based on the size of it. A movement to the right caught her eye. A soft morning breeze had lifted the edges of some papers tacked to the wall, and they fluttered gently. Curious, she walked over to examine them. There were seven in total, all had "Wanted by the Law" inked at the top and crude drawings of the accused criminal below. Some had a bounty on their head, still others were wanted dead or alive. She scanned the names, unfamiliar with the likes of the Dalton Gang, Oscar Walter, York, Bass Reeves, and Pat Garrett. But she had surely heard of Jesse and Frank James. There was one notice that had the pictures of four women. Their names, Belle Starr, Laura Bullion, Etta Place, and Rose Dunn were listed as accomplices to outlaw gangs. The lettering at the top of the page listed them as wanted for questioning, although beneath Pearl Hart's depiction, it said wanted for attempted robbery. Anna was shocked to see how young these women were. She wondered if Betty, Emma, and herself would soon have their own wanted pages.

"See anyone you know?" Miles placed two cups of coffee on the bar and swung the dingy towel over his shoulder.

Anna chuckled and shook her head. "No, thankfully." She returned to her stool and gratefully grasped the cup of coffee. "Thank you, Miles. This is my morning delicacy."

"I almost always have a kettle warming on the stove in back. Help yourself anytime." Miles dunked a dirty cup into a bucket of soapy water. He lifted it out and wiped it with the ever-present towel.

"I will most assuredly take you up on that. Is there anything I can help you with? I feel like a proper slug just sitting around here."

Miles furrowed his brow. "I'm not sure if Miss Kitty would approve."

"Oh posh. She'll be alright. Now tell me what I can do." Anna drained her coffee and set the cup on the counter with resolve.

"Well, ma'am, I have to get some more whiskey from the barrels out back. It'd be mighty fine if you would wash the rest of these cups."

Anna playfully saluted. "Consider it done."

Miles picked up his coffee and took a sip. "I reckon I've seen you before." He scratched the side of his face.

"We met a few months ago. I came in here for a drink."

"Methinks I woulda remembered you."

Anna felt the flush that crept across her cheeks. "Do you recall the fat woman who had too many drinks and fell off her stool a while back?"

"Hmm." Miles pulled his moustache in thought. "I do believe." His eyes widened like saucer plates. "Wait. That was you?"

"I'm embarrassed to say, yes." Anna twisted on her stool and looked past the swinging saloon doors. There wasn't a single person or horse moving yet. She turned around and forced herself to meet Mile's eyes. She knew he was too polite to say anything about her new looks.

"Miss Anna, I have to tell you something." He flexed his hand into and out of a fist. "After you picked yourself up and headed to Doc's, I had to put a man in his place for laughing at you. Sometimes my hand still hurts, I hit him that hard."

"But you didn't even know me."

"But, ma'am, I do know right from wrong." He glanced up the stairs toward Betty's room. "I'd done do it again too."

Anna knew without a shade of doubt he was referring to what happened to Betty. "You're a good man, Miles." She picked up her cup. "How about we get this place cleaned up?"

# Chapter Eighteen

THE DAYS SEEMED to fly by to Anna. She'd wake early every morning and creep downstairs to share a kettle of coffee with Miles, then help get the saloon ready for another night of business. After breakfast, she'd listen as Betty discussed the previous evening with the other girls and conduct the business side of things. Each one would walk away with a fair share of the earnings, and not a one ever seemed dissatisfied.

After breakfast, she and Betty, but more frequently, just herself, would take a walk. When she was with Betty, women tended to pull their children closer and frown in disgust. Oddly, when she was alone, these same women would surprisingly smile and sometimes stop her in the street for a chat. Somehow word got out that she was a learned woman and a teacher. On more than one occasion, she had to listen to a disgruntled mother complain about the young teacher in place at the school. Apparently, she spent more time filing her nails and tending her blonde hair than teaching. The children wanted to learn, not watch her groom herself.

Anna knew the complaints had more than an air of truth to them. Her wanderings often took her past the school. She couldn't help but slow and watch the goings on inside. The children were made to sit like statues, hands folded on the top of their desks, books sitting unopened beneath them. The teacher sat at her desk, seemingly uncaring that she was ignoring a duty of care. It took every bit of control to not barge through the doors and restore the school to that of a learning institution instead of a prison. But, Anna knew, whatever she did would be short lived. And anyway, she couldn't take the risk of getting on the bad side of Hopwood. The inept teacher would certainly voice a complaint to him, and he might eventually remember their first meeting, which had not ended pleasantly.

Very early Monday morning, as she stood admiring the horses at the sales yards, three women approached her. She stiffened and her mouth went dry. Usually accompanied by their children on the road, they'd purposefully kept their distance and sent glares her and Betty's way. Why would they be seeking her out unless to cause her discourse? She offered them a smile that she knew didn't reach her eyes, but didn't dare speak. She needed to know what their purpose was before she reacted, which was to run like the dickens. She felt exposed and bit the corner of her bottom lip.

"We hope we're not disturbing you," said the youngest. She had brown hair pulled into a bun, which did not at all complement the long nose on her slim body. Her dress was plain and well worn.

Anna shook her head and looked past them, hoping to see a familiar face. But it was too early in the morning. The saloon wasn't open on Sundays, and therefore, after their coffee, Anna left Miles' company for a walk.

"Can I help you?" She managed to croak out.

"We have a proposition for you," another woman said. She was dressed nearly identically to the first woman, only her dress seemed better tailored. She had dark hair as well, chubby cheeks, and brown eyes, which looked rather accusing in Anna's opinion.

"We're willing to pay." The third woman, short and plumpish with a round face and pouty lips, held her hands out imploringly.

Anna shook her head in confusion. "I don't understand. What do you think I can help you with?" A few possibilities crossed her mind: maybe preventing their husbands from visiting the saloon's girls was one. The other was to leave town immediately.

"Look, we know you're not one of *those* kinds of women." Plump woman said it like she'd just tasted something rotten.

Anna raised her eyebrows at their presumption. "And how would you know that?" She put her hands on her hips in defense.

"Miles is my brother. My name is Millie," Nice dress admitted.

Anna studied Millie in the nice dress. If she imagined her having a moustache, it was a possibility she was related to Miles. She thought there might be a similarity in their eyes, but she wasn't really sure.

"I don't see Miles that often. My husband says it would set a bad example for our son if I were to be seen with him. But I was desperate and got word to him that I needed to see him. He says you are an upstanding woman and the only thing you've done in that place is help him clean up in the morning. He's quite taken with you, by the way."

"What?" Anna's head began to spin.

"We want you to teach our children," the first said.

"Please, Anna. The children need you."

Anna put her hands up. She suddenly felt overwhelmed. It seemed everyone now knew her name and what she didn't do. She was supposed to be a quiet presence in town and recognized as just another working girl at Big Nosed Kitty's. "But there is already a teacher in place." She shook her head slightly, trying to think of a way to let these women down with a gentle declination.

"She's a tart and dumb as a box of rocks."

"Our children are learning nothing from her. They're made to sit quietly at their desks and not make a move."

"Hopwood was apparently taken with the size of her bosom instead of the size of her brain."

The three women spoke all at once. But Anna clearly understood.

"There are other mothers who are as angry with the situation. But we thought just the three of us should approach you. It would've appeared a mob was to overtake you."

"We didn't want you to get scared and run." The third woman barked a laugh.

Anna sighed. "I understand your problem. But I can't just march in and take over." She looked from one woman to the other. They all wore pleading looks in their eyes, and their faces seemed drawn with worry.

Millie stepped closer. "The children never get a full day at school. She sends them home near after their noon meal. Miles says if we could get you to agree, you could use the old cellar. It's empty except for some old trunks. There's a hidden entrance behind the saloon that no one knows about. You see, Anna"—she took hold of Anna's arm—"no one would know."

"But what if one of the children talks about it?" Anna protested. "It would cause heaps of trouble for me, and possibly you as well."

The plump woman moved closer too. "Our children are bored. They want to learn to read and write. My daughter hates her wasted days and comes home quite moody."

"Yes, my boy is grumpy as."

"Mine as well."

"How many children are there?" Anna wiped the front of her dress with her hands.

"Right now, seven. But there could be more if we can convince the other mothers."

"Even with only those seven, what about books and pencils and paper? Aren't they kept in the school? Surely, she'd notice if any of those supplies go missing."

"I doubt it. But leave it with us. And we'll get the cellar cleaned up and ready for you. Agnes will talk to the others." Millie nodded to long nose, and Anna finally had a name.

"It'll take us maybe a week to get everything ready. Between cleaning the cellar and collecting the things you'll need," Agnes said. "We'll need to be discreet, but we will get it done."

Anna looked at each in turn. This could work, she thought. We really haven't thought much beyond getting the money from Hopwood. I'll need an alibi, and maybe these women could somehow provide it.

"Please think about it. My name is Edith, by the way." Short and plump finally had a name as well.

Anna raised her eyes to the sky and blew puffed air from her cheeks. The morning mist was dispersing, chased by the rays of the rising sun. "Okay. If you're sure there won't be trouble. But, be warned. If I hear of anyone talking about this, I will deny it to my dying breath."

The three women grabbed her in a group hug, uttering thank yous over and over. Anna felt a bit claustrophobic and pulled their arms away to break their embrace. "Quick. You must all go now before someone sees."

Anna watched as Millie, Agnes, and Edith split and walked in opposite directions. Their failed attempt to be inconspicuous was nearly comical but for Anna's fear of unwanted eyes watching. None of them used the path that they came in on, but waddled and stumbled in holes hidden in the wet grass, undoubtedly made by the livestock. She turned back to watch the horses for a few minutes, then decided to have a look at this proposed school room. By then, the three women were nowhere in sight.

"WHERE THE HECK have you been?" Betty said and laughed. "You look like you've been cleaning out an old closet."

Anna filled her in on her morning. "I asked Miles to show me where the cellar is." She chuckled. "Those women have no idea how much work is in store for them."

"I haven't been down there since I bought this place. I have no use for it, so you're certainly welcome to use it." Betty picked strands of sticky cobwebs from Anna's hair "Well. Are you going to do it? Are you going to start teaching?"

"I'm thinking about it. I can always back out or even quit if things don't work out. But one thing is for sure. Hopwood cannot find out before I meet with him. The entire plan would go to hell in a hand basket." Anna pushed aside the thoughts of guilt she'd have if she let down the women, but mostly their children.

"Yes, I agree." Betty brushed her fingers together. "I think you should pay him a short visit very soon."

"Hmm. You're probably right."

"According to Sarah, Hopwood has asked about you on every one of her visits. He finally told her that you should call in. In her place."

"Oh dear." Anna sat down on the bed and chewed the inside of her cheek. "It's nearing the time that Emma will collect us. I suppose it is necessary to make my first after hours visit."

"Tonight."

"Tonight?"

Betty frowned and nodded. "I'll have Miles draw you a bath. You can't go looking like that."

"What do you mean?" Anna stood up and looked at herself in the mirror. "Oh. You don't think he'd like the dirt and grime look?"

"Nor the cobwebs." Betty picked another dusty cobweb off of Anna's shoulder.

WHEN ANNA RETURNED from her bath, she found a dress lying on the bed. It was similar to the one she had worn on her last visit to the bank, but this one had plays of red in the fabric. She put her hair into place using hairpins, finishing it off with the mother of pearl comb carved from a mollusk shell.

Betty was busily rummaging around in the drawers of the wardrobe, slamming them shut in frustration. Finally, after searching the bottom one, she triumphantly declared, "Ah ha! I knew it was here someplace." She held a bone corset up by its tightening straps.

"What are you going to use that hideous thing for?"

"This should show off your assets quite nicely, methinks." Betty smiled devilishly and winked.

"Oh no. I'm not wearing that. I have nightmares about those torturous things."

"You've worn one before?" Betty sat down on the bed with the dreaded corset in her lap.

"My mother tried fitting me in one years ago. I can't recollect why, but I do recall the huge undertaking it required to get me strapped in. After several minutes of grunting and unladylike cussing, my mother resorted to bracing her foot against my back and pulling the tightening straps so tightly, I could barely breath."

"One does have to breathe a bit shallower when wearing one," Betty agreed, furrowing her brows.

"Trust me. The end result was not at all what my mother had expected. Instead of condensing all of my fat into place, I looked more like a bulging water bladder, ready to explode if I made any slight movement. Thankfully, she quickly gave up on that notion and let me wear the dress with only a brassiere."

Betty covered her mouth to hide her giggles, but her quivering shoulders gave her away. Finally able to collect herself without laughing outright, she said, "Darling, trust me. Your body shape is very different to what it was back then. Humor me, and have a go at wearing it. If you can't bare it, I'll find something else to hold them up the way he likes them."

"You do know how to make a girl feel sick to her stomach, don't you?" Anna turned her back to Betty and removed her dressing gown.

Betty wrapped the corset around Anna's waist from behind. Anna fumbled with the buttons on the busk, but managed to get them fastened. Betty helped her adjust the corset so that the smallest part rested against her waist.

"Okay, I'm going to start tightening. Hold the girls up so they don't get pinched." Betty began to pull on the loops.

Anna felt the air get squeezed out of her and she gasped. "Not so tight," she squeaked.

"Just a little more. Breathe in."

"I can't. I think my lungs have already collapsed."

"Hold on. I've only got to tie it now." A few moments later, Betty exclaimed, "There! Turn around and let me see."

Anna turned slowly, uncomfortably encased in a tube from below her breasts down to her hips. It dawned on her that her oxygen stores were being depleted at an alarming rate. It felt like she was being squeezed to within an inch of her life.

Betty must have noticed her bulging eyes. "Anna, breathe slowly. Take small breaths. That's it."

Anna glanced down and nearly touched her breasts with her chin. "My god, they're squished up so high."

Betty slipped the dress over Anna's head and straightened the garment as it fell. "Look at you. Two round globes. You've got dinner buckets for days."

"I'm not sure how I'm going to move."

Betty opened one of the drawers and pulled out two cups and a bottle of whiskey. She poured each of them a generous amount and handed a full cup to Anna. "Drink. It'll help you relax."

"Betty, truly. If I fall down, I shan't be able to get back up." Anna took a sip of the whiskey. It burned the back of her throat and all the way down. The fumes made her feel a bit heady. She raised the cup to her lips again and took another drink, this one bigger. The whiskey warmed her, and her body began to loosen. Either that, or it was just numb from the whiskey and unable to register any more discomfort.

"You'll be fine. Now let's get your face dolled up. You'll look a peach when I'm done."

True to her word, Anna again nearly didn't recognize the woman who looked back at her in the mirror. Amazingly, she looked even different from the last time Betty had fixed her face.

"How do you do that?" Anna went to pat her cheek, but Betty grabbed her wrist.

"Don't touch. And to answer your question, I've figured out that different layers will cause different affects. In my prior line of work, I had to do something to keep the men interested. I couldn't change the way my body looked, but I could alter the appearance of my face." Betty put a finger under Anna's chin and lifted. She examined her from side to side before nodding her approval. "I've made you up like Hopwood likes. He'll be butter in your hands."

"Yuck. I can't think about touching that. Besides, my objective tonight is to get information about where he keeps the money, right?" Anna tried to take a deep breath in an effort to calm herself, but the corset was too restricting. She had to settle with taking small ones and concentrating on keeping herself mentally intact.

Betty massaged her shoulders to help her relax. "Yes, and you'll do fine. Just remember that you're a much better person than he is, and he'll get his just due very soon."

The brass clock that hung on the wall opposite the beds indicated it was two-thirty in the afternoon.

"Land sakes, I'd best start thinking about going," Anna said. She took a deep breath and lurched to her feet. She heard two pops and suddenly her cleavage was gone. In fact, her breasts had disappeared completely within the dress, leaving only sagging fabric in their wake. The corset slowly slid down her body like a fallen soldier and landed at her feet in a tangled heap. She looked at Betty with panicked eyes. "Oh, no. What'll we do? The bank closes at three."

"I was hoping this wouldn't happen. I'm relieved it didn't while you were at the bank. That would've caused a scene no one should see. Don't worry," Betty said as she flung a drawer open. I have a brassier that should fit you fine. You're a bit bigger than I am, but that just means you can show off more." She unbuttoned the back of the dress.

Anna shrugged it down to her waist and waited while Betty freed her of what was left of the corset. She stepped out of it, noting a few of the ribs had broken in various places as well. When she was completely extricated of it, she slipped the brassier on, noting that her bosom was held just as high. Although, the straps were narrow and seemed to imbed themselves into her shoulders. But, she thought, at least I can breathe, and not feel like I have a tree stuck up my backside.

Betty rebuttoned the dress and moved to Anna's front. "Perfect. You have plenty of time." She tucked a small roll of bills into Anna's brassier between her breasts. "You'll need this. Now, off you go." She took Anna's arm, led her to the door, and gave her a reassuring smile. "You'll do great."

Anna made her way down the steps and out onto the road. As she walked toward the bank, she noticed Millie and Agnes on the other side, chatting with their heads bowed and nearly together. They glanced at her with stoney faces, then having recognized her, careful smiles grew on their faces. They lifted their hands in small waves, which Anna returned. She wondered where the third member of the trio was. A heavy wagon pulled by four horses rumbled down the road toward her. By the time it passed, the women were no longer in sight.

Anna focused her attention on avoiding the ruts and puddles in the road. She lifted the hem of her dress as she stepped up the stairs leading to the bank. The "open" sign still hung in the window, but as she neared the door, a hand grasped and flipped it. The lock clicked loudly. She quickly knocked and peered in. Hopwood scowled back at her, but when he saw who it was, his face broke into a wide smile. He promptly unlocked the door, poked his head out, and looked both ways as if he was worried the open door was an invitation for business.

"Well, well. It's wonderful to see you again. I was beginning to wonder if you were avoiding me." Hopwood took her by the elbow and urgently guided her in.

"Of course not. I've been preoccupied, if you will." Anna sashayed ahead of him, fully aware his attention was not above her waist. She turned abruptly when she reached the counter and turned. "I haven't come too late today, have I?"

"No, no, no. Of course not." Hopwood gazed openly at her bust. "What can I do for you today?" He licked his lips and continued staring.

Anna boldly decided to take matters into her own hands. She grabbed his chin, forcing down her revulsion at touching the man, and forced him to look her in the eye. "How about you focus on business first, Mister Hopwood," she said with as much authority as she could muster.

Surprise flickered in his eyes, and then the flash of a hard glint. Anna worried she'd made a mistake. But suddenly his face softened. His smile, once lecherous, transformed to a shy boyish grin. She surprised herself by thinking he had might have been somewhat handsome before the greed of money and stress of how to steal it, had aged him. She wondered if the fancy whiskey had contributed to it as well.

"Of course. And, please, I would appreciate it if you could call me Clarence."

"We shall see if you earn that courtesy." Anna moved to the counter and waited with raised eyebrows.

Hopwood seemed to have lost any sensibility.

"I'm prepared to open an account. Now. If you don't mind." Anna pushed her shoulders back and puffed her chest out. She maintained strong eye contact with Hopwood and kept her face neutral of any expression.

Hopwood finally responded. "Yes. Yes, I suppose you would. If you could please follow me around to my desk." He indicated the direction with his hand and a slight nod. He led her through the entrance to the banking office.

Anna rolled her eyes and tucked her dress beneath her bottom as Hopwood slid a chair against the back of her legs. She sat down and flicked imaginary dust off her clothes with the back of her hand as if she'd entered into an unclean room. In truth, the room was very well organized. There didn't seem to be a thing out of place. Paper was stacked neatly in one corner of the desk, and a blotter was centered in front of the chair that Hopwood now occupied. She dared to look around, noticing the absence of a safe.

Anna removed the money from her cleavage slowly with her thumb and index finger. "Before I hand over any of my hard-earned money, I'd like to see where you will store it."

Hopwood shoved his chair back quickly, the legs of it screeching loudly against the wood floor. "Of course." He removed two keys from a pocket inside his suit coat and held them up for her to see. "These are with me all the time." He removed a large-framed likeness of Abraham Lincoln from the wall.

Anna shoved the bills back into their safe place and rose to have a better look. A thick sided metal box had been built inside a wall cavity. She watched curiously as he inserted a key, turned it, and opened the door. Inside was another metal box. It was smaller, but appeared to be as soundly constructed as the first. She gasped when Hopwood opened it in turn and pulled on the door to reveal thick stacks of bills and two glass jars of gold coins. But most impressive were the jars of gold dust and gold nuggets.

"You see, there is no need for concern. The strong boxes are state of the art in security. All the banks out East use them. I can assure you, your money is safe with me." He resecured both boxes and hid them with Lincoln.

Anna returned to her seat. "Right. I'm satisfied. Let's get on with it then, shall we?" She was finding the air of authority easier to maintain with each passing moment.

Hopwood slid the keys back into his pocket and returned to the desk with a sheet of paper, which he placed in front of Anna. "You need only to complete this form to make it official." He moved to Anna's side, sat on the corner of the desk, and offered her a pen.

Anna knew without doubt he was caressing her throat and below with his eyes. She swallowed her repulsion for the hundredth time and took the pen from him. His fingers lightly grazed hers. She dared not look into his eyes for the impulse to deck him was very strong. But she did force a smile.

The first line required her name. She realized she needed to fabricate a fake surname. She hesitated slightly before impulsively lettering *Anna One* on the line. She listed Big Nosed Kitty's as her address, omitting her date of birth and a husband's name. She scratched her signature and shoved the paper toward Hopwood.

"You've left a few items blank, but in your case, I will allow it." The lewd smile returned. "I can now relieve you of that money."

Anna stood up, bringing her bust eye level with Hopwood. She saw a slight sheen of sweat form on his balding head as she slowly and provocatively pulled the money from between her breasts. She allowed him to gaze for a few seconds before gaining his attention by waving the bills in front of his eyes. "I believe this is what you need?"

Hopwood broke from his stare and stood up. "For the moment." He grasped her hand and slowly removed the money, his fingers lingering. "We are in a favorable position to help one another," He said and licked his lips.

"Are we?" Anna dared to move closer to him and held his gaze. She smelled his sweat and a hint of musky eau de cologne he'd probably dabbed on that morning.

Hopwood cleared his throat and swallowed hard. "Indeed. If you would allow, I could assist in increasing your earnings."

Anna purposely took a deep breath, which in turn lifted her bosom. "And how do you propose accomplishing that?" He is so weak, she thought, feeling the power she held over this little man blossom further.

"I. I." His eyes dropped once again to her chest. "These are so beautiful," he whispered.

Emboldened, Anna took his hand and singled out his index finger with which she traced a laureated line over the top of her breasts.

Hopwood closed his eyes and visibly trembled.

Anna dropped his hand abruptly, enjoying this emasculation. "You will be allowed more next time. But here are the rules: You will only touch these and there will be no sex. You will pay me double. Do I make myself clear?"

"Yes," Hopwood murmured hoarsely. "That's all I want."

"Very well." Anna stepped away from him and turned toward the door. "I will take my leave now."

"But when will you be back?" he said with urgent despair. His face had taken on the look of a desperate child, ugly as it was.

Anna stared at him, and at the same time calculated when she would indeed return. This man was putty in her hands at the moment. She needed him weak with desire so he would focus all his attention on her, ignoring any distracting noises.

"I will send word with Sarah. Make sure you treat her gently in the meantime. Do you understand?"

Hopwood nodded so fast she thought his head might fall off his neck. He walked past her on unsteady legs and unlocked the door.

"Until then." Anna twisted the door knob and made her exit.

Once out onto the street, she walked quickly back to Big Nosed Kitty's. She needed to talk to Betty. Things were moving much faster than she anticipated.

# Chapter Nineteen

"AND THAT'S ALL for today, children." Anna closed her daily planner and put her pencil down. "Remember to leave everything on your desks for tomorrow."

"When can we start taking our lettering books home?" Amelia, Edith's daughter, stood up from her chair. The six others paused, waiting for Anna's answer.

"I promise, soon. But for now, we have to keep this a secret school. Right now it would be dangerous to let your old teacher . . ."

"She wasn't a teacher," a girl named Flora interrupted, with mutterings of agreement from the others.

Anna put her finger to her lips. "As I was saying, if you want to keep this school alive, we must take care in keeping it secret." She took hold of the small sand timer, which resembled a framed hourglass and flipped it over. "Let's begin."

When the improvised school had opened, Anna had been worried that a group of children coming and going from behind the saloon would raise eyebrows and would be cause for unwanted investigation. One of the mothers, whose grandfather had been a sea captain, had produced the timer. The children took turns leaving in approximately five-minute intervals, never in the same order, and always silent. So far, no questions had been raised.

Anna moved around the room after the last student left. She busied herself by ruffling through each of their lettering books, taking note of who was making progress, and who might need additional help.

The women had done an impressionable job cleaning and setting the room up. They seemed to have descended onto the task with a vengeance, for there wasn't a speck of dirt or cobweb in sight. And somehow, three of the fathers had entered into the unlocked school and replaced various books with stacks of corrugated paper, usually used for starting fires. Pencils had been donated from within the homes. A few were casually lifted from the post office and the bank itself. Anna found the latter very amusing. Hopwood would be losing more than just a few pencils.

The sound of a purposed stomp on the hidden entrance above gained Anna's attention. After extinguishing the flames in two oil lamps, she took hold of the remaining third and climbed the stairs. When she reached the top, she knocked twice. The hatch complained on its hinges as it was lifted. Anna blinked against the brighter light of the saloon. A familiar hand grasped hers, and she felt a gentle tug.

"Thank you, Miles." She stepped carefully up onto the main floor, taking note not to trip on her dress. When she looked up, she broke into a huge smile. Betty and Emma stood waiting patiently behind Miles.

"Holy smokes, it sure is good to see you both." Anna handed the lantern to Miles and pulled both women into a hug.

"Betty tells me you've been busy. Grace would be shinning around corners trying to get here if she knew."

Anna chuckled. "That's a bottom fact." She looked past them and was relieved no one else had come into the saloon. "We better get upstairs before someone sees you."

"I agree," Betty said. She and Emma picked up and set their saddlebags onto their shoulders.

Once in Betty's room, the room still Anna occupied, they sat down on the beds.

"You're sure nobody saw you come into town?"

"We're positive. We left the horses tied in the woods behind Doc's. I was able to saunter in as usual," Betty replied. "I let Emma in through the back door where we get the deliveries"

"Good. All three horses are unbranded right?"

Betty and Emma exchanged a look.

"What's the matter?" Anna felt a rise of concern.

"We only brought two," Emma said.

"But, how will I . . . ?" Anna squeezed her eyes shut.

Betty took Anna's hand. "We thought you should stay here."

"You're joking. What will happen to me? Hopwood will surely raise an alarm." Anna's voice rose in pitch with every word.

"Listen." Betty clutched Anna's hand tighter and squished her fingers together, getting her attention. "Emma and I talked endlessly about it. We think that it would be safest for you to stay with Hopwood for a while after he discovers the money is gone. He would have to admit that there is no way you were able to rob him while you and he were . . . you know."

"And if you suddenly disappear, it would make you look guilty," Emma added. "You'd never be able to come back here."

"Oh, lordy. I sure hope you're right." Anna forced a watery smile and then grew her eyes wide. "We're doing this tonight?"

Emma nodded, and Betty grinned ruefully.

"I told him I would send word when I would visit next. I guess it'll be a surprise to him like it is to me." Anna shrugged.

"Good girl. Let's get you ready."

ANNA ARRIVED AT the bank before it closed. She made sure to draw the attention of the few people on the road with polite hellos and nods. At this point, many of them knew her as the secret teacher. When she entered the bank, Hopwood jumped up from the desk and quickly came around to meet her.

"Oh my dear, it's so lovely to see you. But it's not closing time yet."

"I realize that. But I have an urgent deposit." Anna indicated the roll of bills once again tucked into her cleavage. "I thought that this time *you* would like to make the withdrawal." She smiled and winked.

"Oh! Indeed, I would." He looked past her as a shadow passed by the door. "But it's too early." He reached inside his pants pocket and produced a key. "This opens the door in the back. I'll meet you in the rear room in a short while." He took her by the elbow and ushered her out, just as Agnes' husband came to the door. His eyes showed a moment of recognition, but he said nothing.

Anna quickly found herself outside the bank as the door closed behind her.

"Hello, Anna," Agnes called from the wagon, apparently waiting for her husband.

"Hello. How are things with you?" Anna stepped down and stood at the side of the horse to give him a gentle pat.

"I'm very well, thank you. And the family is extremely happy as we've finally gotten things in good order."

Anna knew Agnes referred to her daughter who was very intelligent. She could understand why the girl had been so foul because of the lack of instruction at the school. Quite simply, she loved to learn and excelled at all subjects, especially math.

"I'm very pleased to hear. If you will excuse me, I have to get back to work." Anna winked.

"Don't let me keep you. See you 'round."

Anna walked along the building fronts and stopped by an alley between the bank and the barbershop, which had already closed for the day. She ducked into the shadows when she was sure no one was looking and made her way to the back of the bank. Betty had told her about this entrance. Hopwood normally waited there for his "visitors." Anna was sure his excitement led to the lack of judgement in giving her the key. She unlocked the door and stepped in. Leaving the key in the lock, she closed the door behind her.

The room was small and barren except for a narrow mattress on the floor and a wooden box upon which sat a bottle of whiskey and two cups. The air was musty and smelled of mixed perfumes and spilled whiskey. The only light came from two tiny windows, spaced a foot apart up near the rafters.

The door to the interior of the bank opened suddenly. Hopwood stood in the doorway, clearly accessing her.

"I closed the bank as soon as I got rid of that feller," he panted. He loosened the bowtie from his neck and shrugged out of his suit coat. He tossed it carelessly onto the floor and stepped toward Anna. "About that withdrawal."

Anna tilted her head and smiled coyly. "Clarence, I would like to see the jars of gold again if you don't mind." She fanned herself with her hand. "It does tend to make me quite aware." *Oh dear heavens,* she thought.

Hopwood wore a mask of confusion until he seemed to suddenly understand what she meant. "Of course," he said with an exhale and touched the pocket where he held the key. He turned and walked with a fast-paced strut.

Anna glanced behind her as she left the room. The door had opened a crack. She followed him out to find Hopwood setting Lincoln to the side.

He missed inserting the key into the lock twice, fumbling with shaking hands. When at last he had opened both of the boxes, her turned to her with a wide grin and eyes that sparkled in triumph. His ruddy complexion shined with sweat.

Anna feigned excitement that was actually extreme nervousness. She shrugged her shoulders back and fanned herself. "Please, Clarence, take my money. You must do it now." She moved closer to him, pushing her chest forward.

Hopwood raised a shaky hand and reached up.

Anna quickly grabbed the back of his head and pushed it down onto her chest. "Oh, Clarence. Take it already. Take it with your lips." She pushed him harder and after a few moments, released him. She panted heavily, accentuating the movement of her bust.

Harwood looked at her with dreamy eyes. The wad of bills sat between his teeth. His heavy breathing whistled past it. "I would die a happy man within the clutches of your magnificent bosom," He managed to utter.

Anna grabbed the money and haphazardly tossed it over her shoulder. "Never mind the money. I must have you there again." She pushed Hopwood against the wall and held him by the shoulders. "You fit so nicely. Better than any man ever has." Would you like me to show you what I want?"

Hopwood nodded and licked his quivering lips. A trickle of sweat ran down his cheek.

She took his hands in her own. "Shall we take this into the other room, Clarence?" She didn't wait for an answer. She turned abruptly, and quite literally dragged him to the edge of the mattress. Two dark figures moved into her peripheral vision and prowled past and into the bank proper without a sound.

Shoving him hard, he fell backward onto the mattress. She knelt next to him and caressed the bottom of her bust. His eyes followed every movement of her hands. She lifted her dress and straddled his leg, allowing him to gaze longingly into her cleavage. "Clarence," She breathed. She collapsed onto him, his face fully engulfed by her breasts. At first he wiggled his face back and forth, clearly enjoying himself, nuzzling, licking, and searching for a nipple upon which to latch onto. When she felt him struggle to breathe, she lifted herself, allowing him to gasp once before dropping onto him again. Anna leaned forward, her weight on her elbows. She suddenly felt his hardness against her thigh. She fought the urge to dry heave, disgusted, as he humped her leg like a dog.

Anna groaned and wiggled her chest back and forth when Hopwood reached up to grasp either side of her. She lifted, let him breathe, and dropped. She did this for several minutes, feeling him grow tired, praying that Emma and Betty would hurry the heck up. When at last they appeared, and quietly slipped out the door, Anna sat up.

Hopwood suddenly lurched his hips upward as he exclaimed. He collapsed a few seconds later, clearly spent. He was a sweaty mess. Although he was thoroughly exhausted, he opened dreamy eyes and smiled. "You, my darling. You are beyond anything I've ever known."

Anna patted his cheek condescendingly. "As are you, Clarence." She stood up and straightened her brassiere and dress top. "I believe in our haste, we neglected to place my money in your strong boxes."

Hopwood sighed, clearly disappointed that his fun was over. He rose up on very unsteady legs, straightened the legs of his trousers, as they had ridden up past his calves. "Very well."

It took more than a few minutes to find the money that Anna had flung. The single oil lamp cast shadows everywhere, making it difficult to see anything. It was Hopwood who found it on the corner of his counting counter. He lifted it in triumph.

While Hopwood had searched, Anna glanced at the open boxes. She held her surprise in check when she saw nothing had changed. The jars of gold were still there. The stacks of cash looked undisturbed. *What happened? Had Betty and Emma lost their nerve and decided the plan was a failure? Or had she not given them enough time to go through with it?*

Anna reached out to the desk to steady herself. She looked around in confusion. Absolutely nothing was amiss. She cursed under her breath.

"Is there something wrong, my dear?" Hopwood was at her side instantly. He took her by the elbow and guided her to the armed bench.

"No, I believe I expended myself," she said, collapsing onto the indicated chair. Please lock my money away. I need to see it's safe with you."

Hopwood, more concerned with Anna than the neatness of the money, shoved the rolled bills between the jars, locked the boxes and returned to her side. "Is there anything I can do? May I suggest a glass of whiskey?"

Anna dropped her shoulders and let her hands lie lifeless and loose in her lap. "Thank you. That would be very kind."

Hopwood disappeared and returned quickly with a bottle in one hand and two cups pinched between his fingers. He poured a generous amount into each and handed one to Anna.

When Anna brought the cup to her lips she detected a hint of honey amongst the strong fumes. She dared a small sip and widened her eyes at the pleasantness of the taste. "This is very good."

"I have it sent post from Kentucky. It's very expensive, but I am able to purchase the things I enjoy."

"I have no doubt that you do. Might we add this to our evenings?" Anna was busily planning the next steps to take in the event that Emma and Betty would be willing to try again.

"Of course."

"I shall take my leave now, if you don't mind." Anna rose from her chair.

"Very well. I do hope you recover soon. I am already looking forward to your next visit. If you wouldn't mind leaving through the back door."

Anna hurried to the saloon, eager to learn what had happened. The way was dark but for the small amount of moonlight that escaped the cloud cover. She ducked through the back door of the cellar, carefully feeling her way by memory. She managed to avoid bumping into anything by creeping along the walls. When her shin met the first step of the stairs leading to the top floor of the saloon, she uttered a curse, but was relieved to have found them nonetheless. She pounded on the latch door, hoping Miles would hear her above a heated debate between some men already drinking at the bar. She pounded again and waited. The latch finally lifted above her, and a hand reached down to take hers. Miles helped her up and then walked close beside her until she reached the foot of the stairs leading to her room. When she opened the door to the bedroom, she was met with emptiness. She plopped down on the bed. It seemed that Betty and Emma had abandoned her in their haste, too frightened to allow her any explanation. She sighed. She was mentally and physically exhausted. Her ruse with Hopwood had sapped every ounce of energy her body had. She lay back on the bed and fell into a deep restless sleep.

When Anna opened her eyes the following morning, she squinted and blinked back the bright light coming through the window. Her head pounded in time with her heartbeat. She was sure the stress of the previous evening had more to do with it than the whiskey Hopwood had shared with her. She sat up in bed and put her feet on the floor, realizing she'd slept in her shoes as well. After pushing them off, she stood and took off the dress and Betty's brassier. Her stomach turned when she saw the suck marks on her breasts and streaks of dried saliva. She dampened a cloth with water from the wash basin and cleaned herself, then wiped the layers of makeup off her face. She looked in the mirror and although there were shadows under her eyes, her familiar face stared back at her. She ran a brush through her hair, changed into her own underwear, and pulled on a loose-fitting, yellow linen dress. She pushed aside the lingering questions in her mind and focused on her school tasks for the day. The aroma of coffee met her as she opened the door. She couldn't help but smile as she descended the stairs. Miles waited behind the bar. He'd already poured her coffee and was patiently waiting to have his own until she joined him.

"Good morning, Miss Anna. I heard you moving 'round up there and figured you be down quick smart." Miles lifted his coffee and slurped.

"Thank you, dear man. I am in much need of this today, although I'm not sure how quick nor smart I'm feeling this morning." Anna took a sip of the hot liquid, closed her eyes, and sighed. "This truly is the devil's libation."

Miles furrowed his brow and cocked his head. "I don't know that word, ma'am."

"Oh. It means a ceremonious drink. Quite simply, it is something my body must have in the morning. Are you familiar with the phrase, 'The devil made me do it?'"

Miles nodded. "I get it now." He looked away and cleared his throat, before meeting Anna's eyes. "I been thinking about somethin'. I sometimes hear the kids saying their lessons when it's quiet up here."

"Oh dear. That might be a problem."

Miles shook his head. "It ain't no problem. No body hears it but me. It's just that I never had a chance to get any learnin'. I can count money and bottles, but I can't read."

Anna finally understood what Miles was trying to ask. She decided to relieve him of the awkwardness. "I have an idea. What would you think of me teaching you to read? You normally have an hour or so between cleaning and getting ready for the evening. And it just so happens I have that time free before I go downstairs to the children."

Miles brightened. His moustache lifted high with his grin. "You'd do that for me?"

"Miles, I would do anything for you." Anna suddenly realized she had admitted the honest truth. She took his hand and squeezed. "You mean a lot to me. Of course, I will teach you to read. And anything else you'd like to know."

"If I'm being honest, I'd really like to know more about you, Miss Anna." He inhaled deeply, as if anchoring himself for rejection. He placed his free hand on top of their joined ones.

Anna smiled. "And so you shall."

A FEW HOURS LATER, loud voices and yelling gained Anna's attention. She'd been sitting at the bar, enjoying her third cup of coffee and reading as a diversion. She slid off the stool and met Miles at the saloon doors.

"What's going on?" She peered down the road.

"I ain't sure." Miles shoved one of the wings open and stepped out. Anna joined him, standing in front of him, acutely aware of the security his presence gave her.

"There's a bunch of people in front of the bank." Without a thought, Anna grabbed his hand. "Let's go see what the ruckus is all about."

An angry crowd had indeed formed in the street, shoving forward to gain access to the bank. Edith's husband stood in front of the door. Hopwood peered through the window. His eyes were wide with fright.

"He ain't got no real money!" Edith's husband yelled. "It's all fake. Fools gold, not colored gold. Stacks of blank paper instead of money. He done stole everything."

This sent a cry of anger amongst the crowd, and they renewed their efforts to gain access to the banker. Some raised clenched fists and others raised guns and pitchforks, cursing and yelling threats.

"Some unhappy people here."

Anna turned in surprise at the familiar voice. "Betty." She drew her into a hug. Then she did the same to Emma, who stood quietly next to her. Anna almost dismissed her as a stranger. She had her hair pulled into a bun and wore a plain dress. "Holy moly. I can't wait to hear what happened."

Suddenly two men dragged Hopwood through the door, each holding him by an arm. Hopwood struggled helplessly against the strength of the two larger men.

"I didn't do it! I tell you. I didn't steal anything." Hopwood caught sight of Anna in the crowd. He pointed and yelled, "It was her! That whore robbed the bank last night. She's the one that switched the money." His eyes grew impossibly wider, evidently having recognized Emma and Betty. "Wait! It was them three." He grappled and ruffled, finally managing to get an arm free. He pointed in Anna's direction, causing several people to cast eyes on their little group. "Them three took your money and gold. It was them. You gotta believe me."

"Don't be ridiculous, Hopwood. Betty was working with me last night," Miles yelled back.

"That's a load of crap, Hopwood," Millie protested. "My husband told me she got herself locked in the saloon cellar where she's been holding school for our children. He saw Miles rescue her."

Doc suddenly appeared next to Miles. "That's hogwash, Hopwood, and you know it. Emma was with me last night helping me treat a sick Indian boy."

"String him up," roared the crowd. "String him up."

The chant took on a life of its own. The townspeople surrounded Hopwood. They dragged him to the hanging tree by the sales paddock. Someone produced a rope.

Anna couldn't bare to watch. In a way, she felt sorry for Clarence. But he had brought all this onto himself. She took Emma's and Betty's hands. "Let's go. We don't need to see this."

Doc tipped his hat. "Ladies." He then strode off toward the direction of his house.

They walked in silence, not breaking it until they were safely in the privacy of the bedroom. Miles returned to cleaning the bar when they had entered the saloon.

Anna closed the door and faced Betty and Emma, who were sitting on the bed sporting wide grins. She shook her head in disbelief. "I didn't think you'd gone through with it. The money was still there after you'd left."

"It looked like the money was still there." Betty winked at her.

"I don't understand." Anna crossed her arms and leaned against the wardrobe. "I know what I saw."

"What you saw," Emma said, "were stacks of paper birch bark and jars of fools gold."

"Is that what you had in your saddlebags?" Anna chuckled. "Sure fooled me."

"It took me ages to strip the bark from the trees, flatten, it and then cut it to size. As for the gold, Grace has been collecting it from the river for years. I smashed a bunch of it up to make the dust." Emma reached into her long moccasin and produced a nugget. She handed it to Anna.

Anna fingered it in her hand. It was both metallic and yellowish, but not quite as bright as real gold. In fact, it was more a brassy dull color than she would expect from the real thing. But at first glance she understood why it would be mistaken for true gold. She rubbed it between her fingers, causing flakes of pyrite to fall to the floor. "I remember Grace shoving rocks into her saddlebags when we were fishing. I didn't think anything of it at the time."

A cheer floated in through the window. Anna sighed, knowing Hopwood's life had ended. The unwanted scene played out in her head. Hopwood would have sat on a horse, hands tied behind his back, while the people yelled at him. He would've been hoping for some last reprieve that wouldn't come while the noose was slid over his head and drawn tight. He would've sobbed for mercy or hurled curses, neither making the slightest difference. When the horse was pulled out from under him, he'd have kicked at nothing, tongue stuck out while he shit himself for the amusement of some no better than he. It was a thief's dance at the end of the rope.

"Miles and Doc stood up for you both. Were you really where they said you were?" Anna went to the window and closed it, cutting off the breeze. But she didn't wish to hear any more from the street.

"After we left the bank, we tied the saddlebags onto the horses and sent them home. They'll be there when we get back." Emma pulled her hair from the bun, releasing it with a shake of her head. "I had meant to come here with Betty to see you, but on the way past Doc's I saw a man who used to sometimes run a trapline with John. His wife is Shoshoni also. They were getting their son from their wagon. He'd been snake bit. I had to help them."

"And yes," Betty said. "I was in the back mashing potatoes. I didn't see you when you came in, but Miles told me you'd gone upstairs. By the time I had a chance to come up, you were sound asleep. I didn't want to disturb you."

"Holy smokes," Anna said with a wide smile. "We did it. Us three conquered Hopwood."

"The town is going to change some now." Betty stretched her arms behind her back. "I reckon there will be a constable appointed to protect the bank. When people trust it again, that is. And, well, after we get a new banker."

"I'm going to give that poor excuse of a teacher the boot," Anna said. "I'll move the children back to the school for their lessons."

Emma stood up. "I'm going to go back to the farm. John's friend is going to drop me off. Their son is well enough to go home. After I tend to a few things, I'm going to try and race the snow and be with my family. We'll be back in the spring."

Anna and Betty embraced Emma in a tight hug. "Them three did it," Betty muttered, and they all laughed.

# Epilogue

The townswomen quickly took matters into their own hands and escorted Hopwood's choice of teachers to the stagecoach that afternoon. It wasn't due to depart until the next day, but they left her there anyway. Led by Mile's sister, Millie, the group then moved all the supplies they'd stolen back to the school. The children resumed lessons there the next day. Their number grew from seven to thirteen overnight.

Anna married Miles four months later. He proposed after reading aloud to her, the Shakespeare play, *Romeo and Juliet*. She happily accepted. A year passed and she bore him a son, Murray, who went on to invent moustache wax.

Betty opened a formal cafe in the back of the saloon. The aromas of her cooking brought more customers into the saloon, which soon began opening for breakfast. The girls in her employment were given the choice to become waitresses or continue what they were doing. All but Sarah chose the cafe. She boarded a stagecoach to San Francisco and was never heard from again. Betty eventually met and moved in with a woman who showed up on horseback one day with pistols on her belt and a rifle in her hand. Some say she was a bush ranger on the run from Australia. They lived together until their deaths.

Emma became an assistant to Doc. With the influx of more natives and immigrants, she was able to bring new aspects to the old and new medicinal practices, especially after spending the winter working with Crow Old Man. Her visions continued to stop her in her tracks, most notably the one that foretold her bearing twins.

John's legs and pelvis healed, but he was never able to comfortably ride a horse again. The men of the town all agreed he was the most honest horse dealer they'd ever known and felt their money would be safe in his hands. John therefore became the town's banker and held that position until Millie's daughter took it over ten years later.

Grace attended school every day. In the morning, she sat aside her father on the wagon, with her horse tied to the back. After school she helped Anna grade papers before racing home to make the evening meal for her parents and Henry. She later attended the University of Idaho in Moscow, majoring in agriculture. She offered riding lessons to earn extra money.

Henry never attended school, content to have Grace tutor him in reading, writing, and arithmetic. With direction from John, he bred Appaloosa horses from pure Nez Perce Indian stock. He eventually crossed Longhorn and Angus cattle and supplied the major cities in the west with prime beef on the railway. He became very wealthy.

Fred Cooper, Edith's husband, was elected acting constable. He built a jail next to the bank with two cells. The first two men taken into custody were the troublemakers that were previously employed by the late Clarence Hopwood. Both were suspected of horse and cattle thievery.

Clarence Hopwood's widow made a miraculous recovery from the mysterious illness that kept her in seclusion for years. It soon became known that when Doc made his twice weekly house calls, he'd been tending her as his mistress, carrying on an affair behind Hopwood's back. The townspeople who knew Clarence's wife had always believed he was punching above his weight anyway. Doc and the happy widow were married two weeks after Hopwood's death.

The stolen money and gold were never found.

# Glossary of Terms

**natainappettsi**  dear husband
**kamangande**  love
**oos**  yes
**pistih**  big
**pehnaho**  hello
**babi**  brother
**bii**  mother
**baide**  daughter
**buhisea'-mea'**  May, budding moon
**nabusai**  dream
**doyaduku**  mountain lion
**tetteyannee**  friend
**pahah**  aunt

Originally from the United States, Laurie now calls the Northern Rivers of coastal New South Wales, Australia, home. She lives in a small town alongside the Clarence River with her three dogs, Maine Coon cat, and a cheeky Stockhorse named Harry.

As a member of a local wildlife rescue organization, she is active in preserving her town's population of endangered koalas, which often-times finds her face-to-face with sick and very cranky animals. Laurie also heads her region's Emergency Response Team, which conducts searches and performs triage for wildlife during emergencies such as bushfires and floods, as well as heat events, which adversely affect bats and flying foxes. Thankfully she's retired from the workforce.

In addition to the works published under Laurie Salzler, she has also co-authored two books under the pen name of Laurie Eichler.

www.ingramcontent.com/pod-product-compliance
Lightning Source LLC
Chambersburg PA
CBHW051918240626
47153CB00004B/1269